HOW TO JUGGLE
Ballads & Blades

JESS GALAXIE

jessgalaxie.com

Copyright © 2025 Jess Galaxie

All rights reserved.

The characters in this book are entirely fictional.
Any resemblance to actual persons living or dead is entirely coincidental.

ISBN 979-8-9889118-6-9 (eBook Edition)
ISBN 979-8-9889118-8-3 (Paperback Edition)

Cover Illustrator: Helena / @kremesarekrisp
Designer: Rachel Nugent
Sensitivity Reader: Emeric Davis

CONTENT WARNINGS

I care far more about your safety than your reading this book. Please take the time to consider whether you are in the right headspace to read *How to Juggle Ballads & Blades*.

Ableism,
Anxiety,
Bias Against Pregnant People,
Biphobia Mentions,
Blood Mentions,
Body Shaming,
Bullying,
Child Abuse Mentions,
Classism,
Clowns,
Deadnaming,
Diet Culture,
Disability Grief,
Disabling Event Mentions,
Disordered Eating Mentions,
Emotional Abuse Mentions,
Family Trauma,
Financial Hardship,

Frequent Intoxication,
Getting Kicked Out Trauma,
Homophobia,
Housing Insecurity,
Job Insecurity,
Low / No Contact,
Medical Malpractice Mentions,
Miscarriage Mentions (not main cast),
Neglect,
Objectification,
Pet Loss Mentions (not main cat),
Physical Abuse,
Pregnancy,
Religious Trauma,
Substance Use,
Taxidermy Mentions,
Vomiting.

DEDICATION

To all the silly little jesters
who haven't found their place just yet.

DEAR READERS

As many of you may know, the Bristol Renaissance Faire has taken place yearly in Kenosha, Wisconsin for over 50 years, and it is the one that I personally frequent each year during the humid Midwest summers. That is why I think it is important to state that Albion Renaissance Faire, while certainly inspired by Bristol, is completely fictional and is in no way intended to represent Bristol or any other faire.

I created the fictional Albion to act as a stand-in for the faires myself and many others love so dearly. There are a lot of reasons for this. Not wanting to defame a particular faire or community is the biggest one. Please continue to attend these faires, support the artisans who sell there, and as always, tip your performers!

Which leads me to my next important disclaimer before you begin this book. In my experience, the performers at Renaissance faires are dedicated, fun-loving people who just want everyone to have a good time. Therefore, I want to make it clear that while some acts or performers may bear resemblances to real ones you may meet at the faire, they are not intended to represent any real people.

That being said, there are vague references to some of my personal favorite shows, as well as several very famous performances, in both the main cast and background characters. These references are intended to be loving homages, and the characters in the book who perform these acts are not intended to represent or endorse the real performers. For example, the two characters you will meet who perform in an act called "Laundry Ladies" is a fun nod to the infamous "Washing Well Wenches", but these two characters are not based on any actors who perform as "Washing Well Wenches" in real life.

I also want to state that I have never worked as a Renaissance faire performer, and while I am part of the community, I may have gotten a few details incorrect or fictionalized certain aspects for the drama or humor of it. This is a silly little rom-com for silly little jesters, and I am just a silly little guy who did as much research as they could, so please keep that in mind.

Now that that's all out of the way, I hope you're ready for this romp. Hip, hip! Huzzah!

CHAPTER 1

Chicot stood in the blazing June sun, her hand just above her brow as she watched the group of pirates performing from backstage. She tipped her head back to drink her water, the hood of her unitard tugging awkwardly as she did. Her eyes were locked on the pirates moving about the stage. Their soft linen clothing made Chicot all the more aware of the tight spandex wrapping her entire body, sweat pooling in awkward places from lack of anywhere to go.

The Pirates Three: Big, Middle, and Wee were a mainstay show at the Albion Renaissance Faire and had been for about seven or eight years now. It showed in every lift and trick built into their performance; their movements were clean and quick, their acrobatics impressive, and even the basic stunts were stunning. They did just what they needed to for an untrained eye to see a spectacular show, while a trained eye would see a clever one. Chicot wasn't sure how she was going to live up to that sort of thing. She and Elijah were well practiced, but the pirates were on a level that came with experience that they lacked. It was a reminder that Chicot was still rather new to this, even if she and Elijah had started creating and testing their act over a year ago.

The sword fight on stage was coming to a climax; the smallest of the three pirates careened off a high ledge on the stage, hanging onto nothing but a rope as she exchanged swords with the largest. They pretended this was a surprise, shock coming over them as they turned their weapons against each other again, the third pirate getting in the middle of the fray and making a quip about everyone being on the same crew.

These rehearsals were chances for new performers, like Chicot, and nonperforming workers to get to know the shows so they could better recommend them to guests once the season started. She was currently failing at that assignment, and she didn't have any memories of this act to fall back on. *The Pirates Three* had become a mainstay shortly after Chicot had graduated high school, but the last time she'd visited Albion was in middle school. So, she had no familiarity with it like she did with some of the older shows, like *Sunnie the Spectacular* and *The Dirt Men*. As she took a sip from her water bottle, Chicot realized she had missed too much of the plot, but the pirates were now all agreeing to work together, which meant doing a precarious lift so the smallest among them could clamber her way up her friends to reach a flag hanging above the stage. Just as she got it, a small cheer rang through the crowd of crew members.

Brewhilda sat in the exact middle of the crowd, her pointy hat the only reason Chicot recognized her. Chicot still hadn't learned her real name, but she did know one important piece of information about her. The day before, official stage assignments revealed Chicot and Elijah were sharing the Castlerock Stage with the pirates, taking her time slots from previous seasons. Brewhilda had taken that to mean that Chicot and Elijah were now her mortal enemies. So, Chicot wasn't surprised to see her sitting there, arms crossed, head back, clapping for the pirates, and scowling. Chicot squeezed the leather handles of her juggling knives, running her thumb over the cool metal pommel.

"You nervous?" Elijah sounded eerily calm, with his lute in hand and a cowbell around his neck. He wore similarly colored clothes to Chicot's, only his were the same loose linen as the pirates'. Bright red, marigold, and light blue accents stood out nicely against his umber skin. They'd gone with a color palette that suited his complexion since Chicot's costume concealed her entirely for their performance. Now, as he grinned at her, all of his slightly crooked teeth showing, Chicot's shoulders gently relaxed.

"Always." Chicot set down her water bottle and adjusted her hood, the bells at each point on her hat jingling quietly. She looked down at her wrists, adjusting her cuffs and gloves before she gently nudged her ruffled collar in place. It was easier on her to wear it now, the unitard and bodice with billowy sleeves and brightly colored checkers running down her body. They'd adjusted it over the past several months and it fit Chicot perfectly now, and most importantly, she felt safe in it. Elijah chuckled, his voice warm and dark as he stuck out his pointy chin.

"I know," he said. "But don't worry so much. We'll be wonderful."

"I'll try." Chicot's shoulders drooped, and she sighed dramatically, Elijah rolling his eyes at her. She picked up her mask and secured it to the magnets around her face, her vision darkening as she adjusted it. Once she felt like she had it in the right spot, she had Elijah double-check it before slinging his lute strap over one shoulder and bracing himself against the wooden crate to push it onto the stage. Chicot followed, three blades in hand as she carried a small table for their props.

The Castlerock was located on the far side of the faire, near the large sand field used for the joust. Made of well-worn wood, it had a house-shaped structure at the back and several old trees coming up through the floor. Either side had a series of three platforms accessed by a ladder, all leading up to a treehouse-like balcony at the top, just below the lowest branches of an old oak tree. It also had a set of stairs at the back, separated by a curtain that Chicot had never seen when she'd just been a guest.

Their act only used the main portion of the stage, Elijah shoving the crate into position and slapping it briefly as he made a joke to the crowd full of other performers and workers. Chicot laid out the last of her juggling implements, in order of use, and turned to the crowd.

Brewhilda stared at her, the only person that Chicot could pick out. She knew that she had to have met some of the people there, but between her usual face blindness and her nerves, distinguishing anyone else was a losing battle. She had to use clothes or other distinguishing features, and right now, the only people besides Brewhilda she recognized were the three sitting next to her. They still wore their pirate costumes, which meant Chicot was able to confidently say they were *The Pirates Three*. As her gaze lingered on the pirates, Chicot found herself following the strong line of the middle one's shoulders. She hadn't noticed her before, and now that Chicot could see her clearly, she couldn't help but admire her physique.

She was happy no one could tell who had caught Chicot's eye; the doll-like mask she wore suddenly seemed completely worth it. Chicot shook her head slightly. She had to focus, to live up to this amazing opportunity they'd gotten. Her chest expanded, and she held her breath, counted to three, and then let it go. She just needed to do what she did best—be silly and make people laugh. She and Elijah had earned this spot at Albion fair and square over Brewhilda, and to them, the chance meant everything.

Elijah met Chicot's eyes briefly to confirm he was ready. Chicot straightened her back and set her hands on the box as Elijah began his intro to the crowd, a series of charismatic Shakespearean quips. Chicot listened closely as she hopped up onto the crate, quickly rolling onto her hands to do a handstand. Just as she did, Elijah hit his first mark at the front of the stage, turning a dramatic glare on Chicot, just as they'd practiced. She smiled to herself. Elijah had one hand holding the neck of his lute while his other rested on a popped hip, his mouth bent into an annoyed scowl with his jaw jutting toward her.

"And that's why we don't let her talk anymore!" Elijah grinned as he held up his hand towards Chicot. She responded with a dramatic head flick, feigning annoyance, not saying a word. The crowd laughed as Elijah recoiled and rolled his eyes, his movements exaggerated, theatrical.

This was how their show worked; it was the formula. Elijah did all the speaking and played the music, while Chicot took on the persona of the silent jester, begrudgingly performing the acrobatics with timed comedic sass. Something about it just seemed to make people laugh; their sibling-like antics made them relatable. The best thing about this? Chicot had no lines. All she needed to do was time her tricks right, do goofy dances when she was supposed to, and maybe pantomime. Which was how she'd found herself atop a crate at the Albion Renaissance Faire on their second largest stage, hip thrusting to a semi-raunchy pop song while her best friend rang a cowbell and encouraged the crowd to sing along.

"Wha—What are you *doing?*" Elijah clutched a string of imaginary pearls around his neck. "There are children here!"

Chicot set her hands on her hips, wiggling her shoulders and shaking her head as she put her lips on the mouthpiece inside her mask. When she did, she exhaled hard, causing a balloon she'd tucked into the hole in the mouth to expand. This part of the show worried her the most, since sometimes the balloon didn't inflate properly. This time, it did, quickly growing to the size of a baseball as Elijah rolled his eyes and sagged his shoulders.

"Don't throw a temper tantrum now." Elijah strolled across the stage, strumming a silly melody as the balloon became the size of a cantaloupe. "You heard me. Stop that!"

Plucking the balloon from the front of her mask, Chicot tied it off quickly, offering it to Elijah. He swept a bouncy curl from his forehead, shaking his head back and forth.

"Oh," he said, his voice now light with flattery. "It was for me? Thank you."

He reached up to take the balloon from Chicot, his hand nearly touching it when Chicot pulled a pushpin from her pocket and popped it. Elijah scrambled backwards with a shriek. The crowd laughed. Chicot threw her head back, her hand pressed to her belly as she mimicked laughter, the bells on her hat filling in for the noise she didn't make.

"Ugh!" Elijah dusted himself off and looked at the crowd with an incredible amount of disdain. "*Jesters.*"

There was another peal of laughter from the audience. Chicot quieted. She leaned forward with her arms crossed. Elijah jumped back into action. He strolled across the stage as he started to set up their next trick. The show went on like this, a half hour of contortion and songs and jokes and juggling and jingling, all ending when Chicot caught her blades while hopping off a balance board.

The small crowd was happy when they finished, both hooting and hollering as they clapped. Chicot's breathing started to even out. She wanted to bask in the noise of the crowd, the cheering and excitement, but Elijah was already grabbing their things. She waved, pretending to blow kisses from her mask, making sure to direct one toward Brewhilda before she started to help Elijah. They cleared the stage quickly, exiting through the small backstage area and onto the grass path leading to the jousting arena. They clasped hands, hidden by an old oak tree, and started to hop up and down excitedly. She quickly slipped off her mask. She was sweaty and breathless, but she was alive, and the crowd had laughed! They'd fucking laughed.

"Your mask worked perfectly!" Elijah set his hands on Chicot's shoulders. Chicot grinned.

"I know! I think we've finally fixed it." She bounced on the balls of her feet, letting nervous energy wash over her. Elijah made an indistinguishable noise of excitement in agreement.

"Yes! Shit, this is going to be such a good summer!" Elijah wrapped Chicot in a hug, her laughter growing louder and her anxiety melting away. "It's going to be great. We might even get the chance to make videos on a real stage." Chicot matched Elijah's grin, the two of them stepping side-by-side in perfect sync as they spoke.

Elijah whistled. "That's going to make us look real professional."

"Well, we are real professionals, right?" Chicot smirked as Elijah wiggled his eyebrows at the thought.

"We *are*, aren't we?" Elijah continued to pretend to be shocked as bubbles rose and burst in Chicot's chest. They had worked on this for over a year. Albion was one of the bigger faires in the country, and a dress rehearsal made the reality of it all hit at once. It had certainly relieved the sting of the rejection they'd gotten from the Pennsylvania Renaissance Faire at the time. In fact, Chicot had all but forgotten that they'd been rejected from the other faire now that they were getting settled at Albion. Although, a few months of constant rehearsing in whatever patch of grass they could find between kids' birthday gigs would do that to a person. It would make someone forget a lot of things.

"Let's get a drink tonight to celebrate." Elijah still had an arm around Chicot's shoulders, pulling her along as they walked around the back of the stage to join the crowd for the next act.

"Hell yeah!" Chicot clenched her fists in front of her, punching the air a few times as they walked. Brewhilda was no longer in sight when they came around the corner, so they sat behind *The Pirates Three*, who were talking amongst themselves. Chicot hoped they could be friends. She really wanted to make friends at Albion.

"Can we go to the Curd Castle?" Chicot unclipped her ruffled collar and started to undo the laces on the bodice she wore over her unitard, taking both off in favor of a large, dingy Ramones T-shirt. Her bodice was comfortable, but she preferred loose clothes that didn't touch her skin when not performing. Elijah snorted, unbuttoning his jerkin.

"What is your obsession with that place?" Elijah shook his head. Chicot pulled down her hood with a jingle. She shook out her sweaty hair, running her fingers through her fine brown tresses.

"Easy, they have the best fried cheese curds in a ten-mile radius," Chicot said. She pulled the few bobby pins from her hair that she'd used to keep her bangs from falling out of the hood. It was a nightmare if it wound up in her face while she was wearing her mask.

"Ah, yes, I forgot how deeply Wisconsinite you are." Elijah waved her off, rolling his eyes.

"Or I just have good taste?" Chicot nudged Elijah with her elbow. She ran a hand through her hair and tried to smooth it down. Now that she no longer lived at home, she could have it whatever length she liked without any unwanted comments. When she'd been able to cut her hair, she'd decided on a short, choppy pixie with bangs. Though, she was considering buzzing off the back for the summer, making her costume just a tiny bit cooler.

"Are you two talking about that place up the road from here with all the craft beer?" The smallest of the pirates had turned around. She was one of the performers who had been there for a long time, having been in a few different shows before they'd formed *The Pirates Three*. Chicot might have spent a lot of time looking at her social media when she'd first found it. She had looked at all the current performers' accounts when they'd gotten the news that they'd made it into Albion. She couldn't help herself.

"Yeah, want to come?" Elijah asked. "I would love some company in addition to the silly little jester."

He jutted a thumb toward her. Chicot moved his hand away from her face, shaking her head as a smile tugged at her lips. It wasn't like it was entirely untrue. She had come up with the silly little jester idea because she played it well.

"Yeah!" The smallest pirate swung her leg over the wooden bench, turning completely around to face them. She'd taken her hair down since she'd been on stage, the ends now gathering in loose waves around her shoulders with a dent under her ear from her hair tie. Her cheeks were round, eyes large and gray, but she was definitely older than she'd first appeared based on the fine lines that appeared near the corners of her lips and eyes when she smiled. Chicot took in as many details as possible to remember her. She was a ray of sunshine, and Chicot instantly liked her.

Chicot straightened her back, trying to put extra distance between them. The benches weren't exactly far apart, so when the pirate was facing them, it felt like she was in Chicot's lap.

"I'm Lyza, and this is Monty and Elvis." Lyza tapped her two costars, the medium and large pirate respectively, on their heads as she introduced them. Their stage names, Wee, Middle, and Big, made a lot of sense now that Chicot was close to them. Lyza was about six inches shorter than Monty, and Monty looked about six inches shorter than Elvis, making them a perfect trio, each with their own size and role.

"We've been wanting to talk to you since we're going to be sharing the stage. We can all go together." Lyza beamed, her grin so large, her face had to scrunch to accommodate it.

"We'll have to take an Uber. Umm ..." Elijah rubbed the back of his head. "Will we all fit in one?"

"I have a car. I can drive if you're both okay with that," Monty, the medium-sized pirate, offered. She hadn't fully turned around, but her gray eyes settled on Chicot like she wanted her to respond specifically. Monty had a striking round face, smooth beige skin, and sandy blonde hair, which was cropped just below her chin. She tilted her head, her eyes locked on Chicot.

"Yeah!" Chicot's voice was sharp, rising in pitch at the end of the word as if it cracked. She immediately wanted to simply disappear, clearing her throat. "I'm okay with it."

"Thank you, that would be great." Elijah leaned into Chicot's space. Chicot relaxed, letting Elijah smooth things over. She would need to thank him later. Still, Monty's eyes scanned over Chicot's face carefully before she turned her attention to Elijah, but Lyza beat her to respond.

"I'm sure we all want to clean up a little first." Lyza held up one finger as she spoke. "But maybe meet us at the entrance of the dog park an hour after the showcase?"

The "dog park" referred to the small village of campers and trailers that the performers lived in. Chicot and Elijah had been trying to ascertain exactly why it was called that, but no one quite had an answer for them.

"That works." Elijah nodded, so Chicot nodded too.

"Great!" Lyza turned back toward the stage just as the next act finished setting up for his performance. "See you there."

"Yeah, see you." Monty looked down her nose at Chicot. Chicot wasn't sure if it was because she was just so much taller than her or if it was purposeful. Regardless, it made Chicot nervous.

"Yeah," Chicot agreed, smiling again, and then turned her attention toward the performance. This act was a man who used a whip to cover pop songs. Chicot found herself impressed at his ability to do this on the spot, especially since she'd tried to crack a whip a few times in her life and had almost taken an eye out each time. And it hadn't always been her own she'd almost wrecked.

When the act finished, they all got up as a unit. Unintentionally, but it looked purposeful, which Chicot worried would draw attention. She'd caught people speaking in hushed voices and pointing at her and Elijah before. Chicot just hoped it was only because they were new, and not because they'd made a bad impression.

She put it out of mind. Even if people were skeptical of her and Elijah because they were new and had taken Brewhilda's spot, they would probably move on as Chicot and Elijah proved themselves. It was going to be a long summer, both as performers and community members, but they'd get comfortable soon enough.

CHAPTER 2

She stuck to Elijah's side as a form of security as they exited their camper. Since they'd left their hometown, he'd come to provide the same comfort her childhood stuffed animal or baby blanket would to her. He was the only person at the faire she could recognize instantly, regardless of what he was wearing or if he changed his hair. Her face blindness made meeting a whole bunch of new coworkers hard, but having Elijah with her made it a little easier. Also, he was weirdly good at indirectly saying someone's name so Chicot would know who they were. She was forever grateful to him for his service.

This was their first season, so their camper had been relegated to the very back of the dog park. Chicot had come to like being at the very back. It meant they got to enjoy walking past the glowing string lights and the warm brown lines on many of the beige, 90s RVs every time they wanted to leave. Even the dirt paths had been lined with pebbles over the years, following the curves of paths thousands of performers had walked. The sun had mostly set by the time they'd showered and changed, the workers preparing the faire for opening weekend had gone home, and now the performers relaxed in and around their trailers. If Chicot had learned anything in the week since she and Elijah had arrived, it was that all of the rumors about the performers being quick to sleep with their coworkers weren't really true. What was true was that they all drank together. Often. And in copious amounts.

Chicot especially liked the buzz of the dog park after working hours. Performers who were usually done up in heavy makeup and elaborate costumes now wore sweatpants while they sat in camp chairs and caught up with old friends they hadn't seen since last season. Chicot overheard stories of other faires, discussions of practice schedules, and congratulations on off-season accomplishments. She knew some of the excitement was just because they'd all just gotten there, but right now it felt like being at a holiday party. Lively conversations filled the air, mixing with the sound of crackling from smokey fires that were just being lit. People popped open cans of beer or soda while the smell of garlic and onions and meats wafted from RV kitchens or grills set up under sunshades. Chicot's stomach growled, as much excited for dinner as she was for sharing it with new friends.

Elijah nudged her as they walked by a group of people juggling hacky sacks who were dressed like clowns. Warmth bubbled up from her stomach as she smiled broadly at her partner. Being surrounded by faire folk, Chicot walked taller, her anxiety ebbing away as she remembered that many of the qualities she worried people would notice whenever they looked at her would be embraced by the people here. They would not pinch their faces or scrunch their noses and ask her what she was thinking. Her ripped jeans and the Nirvana T-shirt she'd cut into a crop top, the fact that she never carried a purse, her short hair, her piercings, her hobbies—no one in the here took a second glance at them, and if they did, it was usually followed by a smile or a compliment. It was easier to be herself here, and that made her love every rusty RV and dirt path in the little trailer park.

When they got to the front, Lyza, Elvis, and Monty were standing near a blue Subaru, waiting for them. Monty, her height helping Chicot recognize her, stood with her back against the car, wearing a soft, worn jean jacket that looked decades old with a plush rabbit charm sticking out of the pocket. Chicot quickly took in her outfit; she wore a loose jersey dress with lace frill along the hem, a soft, girly pink that matched the two flower clips holding some of her bangs out of her face. She looked like she'd stepped out of an old woman's guest bedroom, her broad shoulders and muscular figure hidden, daintiness that suited her taking over. It made Chicot's eyes linger on her; the cute clothes suited her. Chicot liked that Monty had such a distinct aesthetic, and the bunny charm was something she could spot easily against the denim jacket to help identify her if she were in a crowd. Her heart raced as she imagined Monty smiling at Chicot from a crowd and Chicot knowing immediately it was her. She wanted that.

Lyza was standing pressed up against Elvis's chest, a wide grin on her face as she teased him about something. She hugged him with his arms trapped against his sides, pinning him with no chance of escape. It was then Chicot remembered that Elvis and Lyza were married. She had seen the photos on Lyza's socials, and she remembered being captivated by the person she now realized must have been Monty standing at her side in a suit.

"Ah, Elijah, Chicot!" Lyza released Elvis, waving her hand wildly. Now that Chicot was able to really look at them, it was obvious that Lyza and Monty were sisters. Despite their difference in height and weight, Lyza had the same gray eyes and sandy blonde hair as Monty. Their warm, beige skin matched as well, their smiles equally crooked. Though, their faces were slightly different—Lyza's was more angular with an arched Roman nose, and Monty had a soft, rounded face with a straight nose. The family resemblance was there, especially in their eyes, and Chicot thought of her little brother and sister back at home. The neighbors always knew they were related just by looking at them. It was not a skill that Chicot usually had, which meant Monty and Lyza must really look alike.

Elvis, on the other hand, was a round man all over. His skin was deep brown with olive undertones. He had big brown eyes that squinted into smiles whenever he grinned, which showed as he waved at Chicot and Elijah.

"Hey." Chicot waved back as she approached. "Thanks for driving us."

"It's no trouble. Monty has to play driver since her car, Becky, is easier to take out than a whole camper." Lyza knocked on the car, introducing Becky. "If you ever need a ride somewhere, just ask her."

"C'mon, I'm hungry, Lyza. Just get in," Monty said. She narrowed her eyes at her sister as she opened the driver's side door, pulling her keys from her pocket. The bunny plush swung as Monty gripped her car key, revealing that it was a keychain.

Lyza remained chipper, unfazed, herding Chicot and Elijah into the back while Elvis took the passenger seat. Once inside, Chicot found herself in the middle, Elijah commenting that she was the shortest, so she got to be squished with her legs pressed into the center console. It wasn't comfortable, but she wasn't about to pass up a free ride.

"Don't worry, I'll sit in the middle on the way back," Lyza assured. "Or in Elvis's lap."

"No." Monty turned to look at Lyza, pointing. "You are not getting me another ticket."

Lyza laughed as Monty put the car in gear, Elvis joking about how he'd sit in the back with Lyza in his lap if that made a difference. According to Monty, it did not.

There were no other cars as Monty pulled out of what would become the faire's parking lot and impromptu changing room for patrons to switch into their faire garb. For now, it was just an empty field that surrounded the dog park, the grass cut short to prepare for the hundreds—perhaps thousands—of cars that would come in and out each weekend. Chicot wasn't sure exactly how big the faire would be this year, but she did know it was an old one and a good one to perform at.

Chicot smiled, listening to the din of the car as Monty, Lyza, and Elvis bickered like siblings. They reminded her of the way Chicot and Elijah acted. She unclenched her jaw and sank into the seat. Taking a deep breath, she grinned as Monty turned on her Spotify and "Kids" by PUP immediately started playing.

"I love this band." Chicot scooted forward and bent so she could lean on the center counsel of the car, shrinking her shoulders so she could fit between the front seats as she looked at Monty. "Is this your playlist?"

Monty twitched, raising her elbow slightly to glance at Chicot before she rested her hand on the gear shift as she drove. It gave Chicot a nice view of her biceps, the sight alone making her heartbeat kick up.

"Yeah." Monty pressed her lips into a tight line, her hands gripping the steering wheel.

"They're, umm," Chicot started. "They're my favorite."

"Cool," Monty quickly answered, not sparing her a glance. Chicot took the hint. She sat back against the seat, her hands clammy as she folded them in her lap. Chicot didn't want to annoy Monty, even if she could have talked about PUP for hours. She knew a lot about them, had listened to all their albums. Maybe Monty hadn't turned it on purposefully and she wasn't into the band.

"Don't worry about her." Lyza waved her hand at Monty dismissively. "She's been in a bad mood all day. She'll probably want to talk about music after she's had something to eat."

"Oh, I—" Chicot shook her head. "It's okay."

Chicot rubbed the side of her neck, glancing from Lyza to the windshield, catching Monty staring at her in the rearview mirror. A shiver slid across Chicot's stomach, and she turned back toward Lyza as she continued to chat about something. Monty must be one of Brewhilda's supporters—that was the only thing Chicot could think of. She would just have to push past it if she wanted to hang out with Lyza and Elvis, who were both being nice and welcoming. She could hear Elvis and Elijah frantically talking about tabletop RPGs, so she had a feeling Elijah would want to hang out with them again. Chicot just hoped she and Monty not getting along wouldn't turn into a whole thing.

She spared a glance in the mirror again. Monty was focused on the road, her fingers drumming on the steering wheel as she bobbed her head to the beat. Her hair moved around her face like whips, getting caught on her round cheeks and the creases at the edges of her eyes. Occasionally, a single strand or two would stick to her lips, drawing Chicot's attention to the rosy color.

Monty's eyes caught Chicot's in the mirror after just a few moments, so Chicot tried to look away casually, acting like she hadn't been staring. It was just … Monty was her type. She had known it since the first time Chicot had watched them rehearse, but now, seeing her out of costume and relaxed, it felt more obvious.

Chicot shouldn't be thinking about romance anyway. She had too many other problems to worry about.

Shaped like a medieval fortress with a blacktop parking lot mimicking a moat, The Curd Castle stood above them as they parked. The stone walls with tall turrets at each end stood as a reminder of just how strange the Midwest could be. Chicot waited patiently to get out of the car, and once she was out, she lost herself to the smell of fried food. Her stomach growling audibly, eliciting a laugh from Elvis, who was holding the door for her.

"I guess we'd better order right away." He closed the door behind Chicot. She rounded her shoulders, rubbing the back of her neck as she looked up at him.

"That might be necessary," Chicot agreed. Elvis tipped his head back and let out a single bark of laughter, following her and Elijah as they walked around the car. Monty was already halfway to the large double doors of The Curd Castle, while Lyza lingered in between, waiting for them to catch up.

Inside the restaurant, it was a typical Wisconsin dive bar with several levels of tables for diners, a large stage for live music, and a bar nearly as long as a camper trailer. Banquet chairs and folding tables were on floors covered in a thin, sickly green carpet. Ripped booths repaired with duct tape were the final touch. It was the sort of place Chicot's parents would have brought her to for a birthday dinner, and as they walked past a stuffed deer head on the wall, Chicot's whole body visibly relaxed.

Elvis, Lyza, and Monty slid into one side of a booth, and Elijah and Chicot took the other. Chicot was sitting directly across from Monty, her eyes drawn to a freckle on Monty's neck, just underneath her jaw. Chicot hadn't noticed it before, and as Monty slipped her fingers through her hair, tucking some behind her ear, Chicot couldn't help wondering about how she would react if it were kissed. She tore her eyes away, staring down at the table as she refocused her thoughts.

To his credit, Elvis immediately asked the server to put in two orders of fried cheese curds. A man of his word, which Chicot could appreciate. Lyza straightened up, folding her hands on the table as she launched into her speech.

"As you know, our acts will share the stage, which means we also share the storage areas behind them. We were hoping we could discuss organization of those areas before opening next weekend." Lyza nodded resolutely once she finished. Monty looked at her and pressed her lips together, brow furrowed.

"Why are you acting like you should be wearing a blazer and calling yourself a girl boss?" Monty asked. Elvis broke, cracking into a fit of giddy laughter that didn't stop even as Lyza turned to pout at him.

"Because this is important!" Lyza laid her palms flat, leaning toward Chicot and Elijah as she looked down at the musty bar. "I'm not doing another eight weeks of climbing over a cauldron to get our shit!"

"We don't use a cauldron in our act." Chicot blinked rapidly, trying to understand what was even happening. To her surprise, Monty snorted, a small smirk on her lips.

"All right, all right, calm down, Lyza." Monty looked between Chicot and Elijah. "Brewhilda was not fun to share with. We're hoping you won't mind splitting the storage area with tape and we each get a side."

"Oh." Chicot looked at Elijah, finding an equally surprised look on his face. They needed to talk about this later. Chicot had thought that everyone at the faire loved Brewhilda.

"Yes." Lyza sat bolt upright. "We just want to avoid any issues from the start."

"I think splitting it evenly is fair." Elijah shrugged, his palm pressed to his jaw. "Honestly, y'all could even take a slightly larger area since you have more equipment to store. Right, Chicot?"

Chicot looked between Elijah and Lyza. "Yeah, I think that would make sense."

"See, I told you it wouldn't be that big of an issue." Elvis brushed a disorganized cluster of his thick, coiled hair from his forehead. "And thanks, you two, but we think even is a good idea. Since you might need to change in there too, you'll need the space for that."

"I hadn't even considered that." Elijah pressed his knuckles to his lips as he gazed at the table. "Actually, I was kind of hoping we could ask you all for some advice and for any notes you may have on our show. We are really new."

"Wait." Monty shifted in her seat, setting one elbow down on the table and leaning toward them. "Is this your first faire *ever?*"

Chicot nodded, looking at Elijah as she picked up the wrapper from her straw and twisted it between her fingers.

"We're from Northern Wisconsin," Chicot explained.

"We didn't really know where to start, so we just auditioned for a bunch of faires."

"Well, shit." Elvis twitched when he let out a clipped laugh, the broad grin on his face making the edges of his handlebar mustache hit his round cheeks. "Good for you two. This is a premium faire. We'll help you."

"Yeah, honestly." Lyza's eyes glowed even in the low light of the bar as she spoke. "We were at this for about three years before we got into major faires like Albion."

"I think we just got lucky." Elijah bowed his head gracefully, always able to humbly take a compliment. "But thank you, we're really excited to be here."

"We are." Chicot's fingers still restlessly pulled at the straw wrapper. "So, anything you all can teach us, we would appreciate it a lot."

Monty slowly sat back in the booth, staring Chicot down. Chicot tried not to squirm as Monty opened and closed her mouth like she might say something. Not knowing what else to do, Chicot just smiled awkwardly, but that seemed to force Monty's decision to speak.

"Do you—" She paused as the server came over with two baskets of fried cheese curds, setting them in the center of the table.

"Oh, yay! Food." Lyza quickly started handing out plates. Monty dropped her head, and she didn't continue her question.

"What were you saying?" Chicot asked Monty softly as Lyza nudged a basket of cheese curds between them. Lyza looked over at Monty briefly but didn't seem to register that Monty had tried to ask a question. Monty just shook her head at Chicot.

"It wasn't important." Monty took the sauce cup from the basket, pouring some ranch onto her plate. Chicot just nodded. She knew she shouldn't press it. If she wanted to have a good eight weeks at the Albion Renaissance Faire, she probably shouldn't pry. Even if Chicot sort of wanted to. After all, Monty maybe didn't hate her over the Brewhilda situation, but that left Chicot wondering why she acted so standoffish.

But Elijah and Elvis had started a very boisterous conversation about local beer, arguing over whether Spotted Cow or another New Glarus was the best. As Chicot listened to them, she shivered in the AC and thought about all the interactions she'd had with Monty so far. Trying to spot something that she'd done wrong in hopes of finding anything she could apologize for. Chicot came up short, and she didn't want to apologize unnecessarily since that had always made her mother angry. Although Chicot couldn't determine if Monty would react the same, it felt risky.

"Ay, Chicot, you listening to us?" Elijah snapped his fingers in front of her face. Chicot perked up.

"Shit, sorry, no." She shook her head, putting a cheese curd in her mouth on instinct. "What did you say?"

"I was asking how you did the balloon in the mask trick? Like, how'd you rig that up?" Lyza's elbows were on the table, her hands around her beer as she played with the foam on the rim rather than drank it. Chicot, remembering hers, reached out and pulled the pint closer.

"Oh!" Chicot always sat taller when she talked about it, zeroing in on Lyza and Elvis, who looked invested. "So, there's a hole in the mask's front with a mouthpiece behind it. The balloon is blue, but when it's not inflated, it's dark enough that you can't see it through the hole. It sits between the mask and the mouthpiece with a rubber band around the neck to create a seal, but it's weak enough that I can just pull the balloon off the mouthpiece."

"How'd you come up with that?" Lyza's eyes, wide with wonder, fixed on Chicot, her face alight with wonder. Chicot shrugged.

She rubbed the back of her head, trying to think of the days they'd spent writing the show to see if she remembered exactly how she had come up with it.

"It was sort of based on some puppeteering tricks that the Jim Henson company uses," Chicot said, "and it evolved from there."

"That's so cool." Elvis brushed a coil from his face. "I wouldn't have thought to look into puppet stuff for that."

Chicot's cheeks tingled as she popped another cheese curd in her mouth. "Thank you. I'm pretty proud of it."

"You should be," Monty said as she brought a beer glass to her lips. Chicot's head snapped in her direction, her stomach flipping as she looked at Monty. Her eyes, wide and glowing, met Monty's as a jolt of excitement ran down Chicot's back. Monty turned slightly to the side, facing Lyza, but her eyes didn't leave Chicot.

Elvis caught Chicot's attention, asking her about their props. Apparently, he handled all the props for *The Pirates Three: Big, Middle, and Wee*. It meant they had a good deal to talk about because outside of Elijah's lute, she handled all the blades and balls and balloons they used in the show. Though, they had fewer props since Chicot was still nervous to do certain acrobatics on stage. It was one thing to juggle some knives or torches; it was another to do it while riding a unicycle.

"If you two want," Elvis said after a while. "Y'all could come with us to the gym sometime for rehearsal. I'm sure Lyza and Monty can teach you more about the unicycle."

"You both know how to ride one?" Chicot turned to them. They both confirmed, Lyza grinning.

"Our parents were acrobats too." Lyza leaned against Monty's side. "We've been doing this stuff since we were kids. Monty here was almost in Cirque du Soleil, but she turned it down."

Monty rolled her eyes. "That was a long time ago."

"Yeah, but it's still cool!" Lyza threw her hands up and rolled her eyes. "Anyway, I was in circus school when I met Elvis, and the two of us started working at faires shortly after that."

"Why didn't you do Cirque?" Elijah furrowed his brow. Monty leaned toward him, her eyes catching the low, reddish light above them. Chicot watched Monty's lips shift to one side, her nose scrunching as she did it.

"I was dating a guy at the time, and I didn't want to travel and be away from him that much," Monty explained. "Plus, we had worked on this show, he was supposed to be in it, but we broke up before we debuted the act. Since then, it's always been the three of us."

"Yep." Lyza's chest jutted out as she proudly and she said, "Big, Middle, and Wee."

She tapped Elvis, Monty, and then herself on the head as she said each stage name. Chicot thought that was cute, watching Monty look fondly at her older sister. It was private, small, and something that Chicot could admire. It reminded her of how her sister, Juni, always looked at her. Like Chicot had the coolest ideas and did the coolest things. A thought which made her own smile fade slightly as it crossed her mind.

"What about the two of you?" Elvis had one elbow on the table, swishing the beer in his glass in circles. "How'd you get into this?"

"We ran off and joined the circus," Elijah said wistfully, putting both of his hands under his chin, tilting his head to one side. "Well, the Renaissance faire."

"We were also adults working at a gas station when your mom let us have the RV to start traveling. We didn't *really* run away," Chicot added. Elijah snorted, agreeing with her quickly. Chicot's mother had wanted her to stay and continue paying rent for the room she'd shared with her little sister. In a way, Chicot ran, but Elijah certainly didn't.

"You're self-taught!?" Lyza slapped her hands down on the edge of the table. It shook Chicot, clanging the silverware together, causing Lyza to grimace.

"Sort of," Chicot piped up. "I've done competitive dance since I was little, and my teacher liked to give me acrobatics routines. I was a cheerleader in high school too."

"And the juggling?" Lyza asked.

Chicot stuck her thumb in Elijah's direction. "He taught me."

Elvis looked at Elijah, his jaw slack. "And where'd you learn to play the lute?"

"My mom is a music teacher." Elijah shrugged his shoulders, smiling. "She had all sorts of weird instruments. I know how to play the lute, the lyre, the marimba, the pan flute, the regular flute, and the guitar."

"You two really are impressive." Monty laughed, her lashes fluttering as her brows went up nearly to her hairline. Chicot watched her coral lips for a moment, entranced as Monty's delighted laugh washed over her. Oh yeah, Chicot was in trouble.

"Thanks," Elijah said. "It's been nice getting to do something creative. There wasn't much creativity working at a gas station."

"The only one in town," Chicot mumbled. Elijah nodded quickly.

"Yeah, I'm familiar with that life." Lyza shook her head, her eyes wide. "Never easy, especially during a night shift."

"Where do you two plan on practicing here?" Elvis stopped spinning the beer in his glass around.

"Behind our RV." Chicot rubbed the back of her head. "We've removed most of the rocks and sticks already, so it's pretty easy to work there."

Lyza and Monty's jaws dropped open, the two of them exchanging a look. Elvis brought his glass toward his lips, pausing halfway to glance at Chicot and Elijah.

"Well, we pay for a time slot at a local gymnastics gym. Would you be down to share?" Elvis asked. "The place is big enough for both our acts."

"Oh, well, we wouldn't want to——"

Elijah cut her off with a sharp noise. He leaned in front of Chicot, nodding with exaggerated bobs of his head.

"Yes! We would really appreciate that!" Elijah looked toward Elvis. "How much would that cost us?"

"We already have the slot, so you don't have to pay us for now." Elvis shrugged.

"It's a gymnastics gym for children, though." Monty pursed her lips.

"There are rarely kids there when we're there." Lyza waved off Monty's comment. "It's not like it's open gym time or something. It's private."

Elvis scratched his beard, waiting for their response. He looked like he was trying to feign casualness that Chicot thought was maybe to keep from scaring her and Elijah off.

When she turned to Elijah, he had almost completely faced her in the booth, nodding his head as subtly as he could, which wasn't all that subtle. Chicot snorted, rolling her eyes at him.

"Okay." Chicot smiled at Elvis in particular. "We'd really appreciate the help since we're still starting out. And we have some … things to take care of."

"Things?" Monty looked at Chicot.

"She means expenses. You know, operating costs." Elijah said quickly.

Monty looked between them, her eyes narrowed and her lips parting like she might speak. Lyza, unable to contain herself, shot across the table to grab their hands in a firm grip, nearly launching Chicot from the booth with her enthusiasm before Monty could react.

"It's a deal then," Lyza chirped, a grin growing on her face. Elvis encouraged them to raise their glasses in a toast to their agreement.

"To new friends!" Elvis shouted, catching some stares from other guests. Chicot barely noticed as she held her glass up to clink with everyone else's, Lyza's drink sloshing onto the table. Even Monty, who rolled her eyes, met their glasses and smiled.

CHAPTER 3

Their most important "expense" stared at Chicot from Elijah's bed, looking up at her with bright yellow eyes, her tail swishing back and forth. She hunched her shoulders, and her ruffled black fur hung around her face like the mane of a mighty lion. The one major difference between Duchess and the king of the jungle, however, was about 388 pounds. That didn't mean that Duchess wouldn't cover Chicot with scratches in an attempt to play while she passed the cat on her way into her hammock. That had been their cute nightly play routine since they'd moved into the RV together, but right now, Chicot just wanted to sleep.

"Duchess, please," Chicot pleaded. She'd had just enough alcohol after a long day in tight-ass spandex, baking in the sun, to feel like she'd run a marathon. Playtime usually resulted in Chicot running up and down the length of their small camper a few times. That was not going to happen now. She'd slammed into the bathroom door as Elijah emerged from the shower just a few nights ago. Chicot would like to avoid repeating that if she could. With only a week until opening day, she didn't want to risk hurting herself or her partner.

Chicot set a foot on Elijah's bed to get to her hammock hanging above, and Duchess immediately lunged for it, trying to grab her calf and pull it in for a bite to the shin. Chicot pulled her leg away before Dutchess could sink her claws into it, but Chicot knew she would just do it again. "Okay, okay."

She reached slowly for the small shelf above their sink and grabbed a ribbon toy, waving it. Duchess's eyes turned black, her pupils fully dilating as her head moved from side to side, following the end of it. Chicot grinned, wiggling the ribbon, and waited for Duchess to pounce. This was a song and dance they did often, and unfortunately it largely happened when Chicot wanted to go to bed. Not that she really minded; it was horribly cute every time.

When Duchess finally grabbed it, chomping down hard and gnashing her teeth as she tried to get it off her tongue, Chicot pulled a treat from the jar. She tossed it onto the floor, causing Duchess to chase it and run onto Elijah's bed. Duchess realized her mistake as Chicot clambered her way into her hammock.

"Haha, I win!" Chicot pointed down at the small cat. Loud, annoyed meows came from Dutchess as she decided whether to jump into the hammock with Chicot.

"You are speaking to a cat." Elijah was pulling a shower cap off his head, standing next to their tiny bathroom in his pajamas, which were a compromise after Chicot had seen his junk one too many times after his boxers had moved in his sleep. Now he was required to wear pajama shorts, and Chicot had to wear a T-shirt because he didn't want to keep seeing her boobs after she fell out of the hammock in a tank top. They were still working on living together full-time.

"She started it!" Chicot raised her hand, shaking her fist at Duchess in mock contempt. Duchess voiced her complaints to Elijah instead, running up to him and screaming like a toddler who'd had a toy taken from her.

"She's just a baby!" Elijah laughed as he stepped around Duchess, her fur moving in beautiful waves like the dress of a rococo aristo-crat. She was Chicot's royal lady, who she'd refused to part with even when she'd left her parents' home.

"She is nine years old! And she tried to bite me," Chicot chided. Elijah didn't pursue the argument further. He stretched out on the bed, which was too small for him, and the mattress gave a soft thud. He angled his body to fit, his feet safely on the mattress, as Duchess gracefully jumped up, heading to the corner, a safe distance from Chicot's swaying hammock. It had fallen in the middle of the night once and, thankfully, had not hurt Duchess, but it had scared her off sleeping under it for the rest of her life.

"What do you want tonight?" Elijah asked. Chicot peeked over the edge of the hammock, looking down at him. He had his phone in his hand, the screen adding a strange blue color to his shiny skin. His cheeks glowed like polished mirrors from a sleep mask of some kind he had put on.

"Can you play the Sherlock Holmes book?" Chicot asked. "But a couple chapters back, I fell asleep."

Elijah just grunted a confirmation. Their little family had fallen into this routine since Chicot had dropped her phone and shattered it on the pavement of the last campground they'd stayed at. They'd only been there because Elijah had found them some work at a circus-themed birthday party for a five-year-old. Said five-year-old had been a know-it-all and had called out that Chicot was not a circus clown, but in fact a court jester. It had been embarrassing to have their whole gag given away by a child, but then to also break her phone that same day? Cursed. Chicot made Elijah play audiobooks from his phone for her now—explaining it had been his fault—until she got a new one. Elijah didn't seem to mind, even if it meant he couldn't watch YouTube videos at night.

"We need to see if we can finally scrape together enough to get you a new phone," Elijah said. Chicot sighed, gently pulling the edge of her hammock around her face, feeling the vinyl rub her cheeks.

"Yeah, I know." They had used Chicot's phone fund twice in the last month, clearing it out entirely. There'd only been fifty dollars in it the second time they dipped into it. She sighed, leaning back into her hammock and looking at the ceiling.

"Not 'cause this bothers me." Elijah's voice was calm. "But because you should be able to talk to people again and get their numbers. I mean, seems like Monty might want it."

"You mean Lyza?" Chicot asked. He was right, it would be good for her to make some friends, but what had really hurt about finally putting her old phone out of its misery had been that she couldn't talk to her siblings. They'd saved the SIM card though, so there was still hope.

"Well, Lyza too." Elijah shifted. Chicot could hear him move, and in the quiet of the camper, Duchess purred. He must have been petting her.

"Wait, what gave you the impression Monty would want my number?" Chicot poked her entire head over the side of the hammock to make sure Elijah could see her frown.

"I don't know. You two are like, the same age and both seem a little ..." He quirked his lips at Chicot. "Fruity."

"Says the biggest fruit to come off the tree." Chicot rolled her eyes and fell back into her hammock. She had hoped that he would tell her she'd been misinterpreting the looks that Monty had been giving Chicot all night, but that was obviously too much to expect. Monty seemed cool, and Chicot wanted to know that Monty maybe didn't hate her for being some kind of invisible rival to Brewhilda. Some performers had acted strangely toward them after the announcement of stage assignments. Only Brewhilda had been openly hostile, but Chicot couldn't tell if simple awkwardness had caused the strained atmosphere with some folks or if anger fueled it. She struggled to read subtle social cues, which made every interaction so much more challenging.

Elijah's laughter caught up with Chicot, shaking her mood. She felt Elijah reach up with one long leg, nudging her and gently rocking her side to side.

"You're right." Elijah's voice bounced in the same way it did when he was on stage, as if he were ready to sing at any moment. "But she is your type?"

"Just like the guy at the bangers stall is yours?" Chicot asked. She had noticed that Elijah, who typically did not like bratwurst, had suddenly been frequenting the stall for lunch. Elijah choked, his foot stopping her hammock.

"I have no idea what you're talking about."

"Aw, come on." Chicot rolled onto her back. "It'd be good for you to have a little fling. Don't worry, the choking guy bailing on you after you saved him was a fluke."

"God." Elijah groaned. "*Don't* bring up Allan. Please and thank you."

"All right. Turn on the book though. We have to be up early for safety training."

"Yeah, yeah." Elijah rolled, the sound of the bed creaking under him louder than the slight squeak of Chicot's rocking hammock.

The soothing voice of the narrator began. *The Hound of the Baskervilles* was taking them the longest to get through. Because they both adored it, they kept going back to listen to the parts they'd missed while dozing off, rather than imagining them.

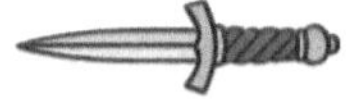

They quickly put on practice clothes when they woke, but the morning was for a long meeting about signals that performers and stall workers could use to ask for help. Chicot sat on a hard wooden bench, trying to memorize signs for "get me away from this person" and "I need a medic" while Elijah took notes on his phone. It didn't take long for her mind to wander. With so many people sitting at the Castlerock Stage, it was easier to see why someone would be mad they'd been bumped from this spot. The seating easily fit more than a hundred people, which meant Castlerock was the biggest stage at the faire.

The days went on like that. Important meetings in the morning, then lunch, then time to practice on stage. This meant Elijah and Chicot got to watch the pirates several times before opening week-end, which was good because Chicot had been far too nervous to pay attention during the showcase. *The Pirates Three: Big, Middle, and Wee* act was simple, and even though Chicot had to watch it over and over, it made her laugh almost every time.

"God, they're good." Elijah adjusted his shoulder strap, his lute in his lap as they sat waiting for their turn.

"I know. I wish we didn't have to follow them all the time," Chicot said. Elijah hummed softly, tapping on the body of his lute, and looked at Chicot, his eyes intense.

"I'm kind of glad we do." Elijah looked toward the stage again, his fingers still tapping rapidly as he bobbed his leg. "It'll push us to do better. Maybe enough to get into more than one faire next year."

Chicot was glad Elijah was already looking ahead. While her focus was on Albion right now, they were trying to start a career doing this. Which meant more faires were in their future.

"Good point." Chicot nodded. "But focus on opening weekend for now."

"I know, don't worry." He flashed a sharp-toothed smile at her, nudging her with his shoulder. "We're going to do great here."

"We are. We're professionals, after all." Chicot straightened her back, puffing out her chest as Elijah snorted, poking her ribs, so she deflated with a laugh. Chicot looked back at the stage, losing herself in the show again.

The pirates were doing their second to last lift, where they weren't tall enough to grab the flag from where it was hanging. Elvis was lying on his back on a wooden box, legs straight in the air as he set his hands on Monty's shoulders while she positioned herself. She settled her hip creases on Elvis's feet, her head between his legs as she spread her legs in a "V" shape. Once in place, Lyza stood on top of Monty's thighs, reaching for the flag, still unable to grab it due to her height.

"We're not tall enough!" Lyza made sure her voice was clear for everyone to hear, including Chicot and Elijah in the back.

"I told you I should be on top!" Elvis dropped his hands from where he was holding Monty, making it clear she didn't *actually* need his support. He flailed his arms dramatically, but his balanced and controlled movements didn't knock the three of them over.

"Use your sword! Use all three if you have to, you goose," Monty said.

"Oh, right!" Lyza pulled a short juggling blade from her belt, using it to reach for the flag. When she still couldn't touch it, she gasped. "Wait, let me try one more thing!"

She pulled the other two blades from her belt and juggled them, trying to knock her prize off the rope that way. One blade always barely grazed the material, but it was never enough to knock it down. Lyza finished by stepping off Monty's thighs. To the untrained eye, it looked like she fell, but in reality, she was in control the whole time, her foot landing right next to Elvis's head.

"Oh, good heavens!" Elvis shrieked in a posh British accent. She lost her ability to keep a straight face every time he did this. Elijah tuned his lute as he listened to the performance they'd now heard in full twice before.

As *The Pirates Three* started their next acrobatic attempt to retrieve the flag, Chicot looked up at the trees, listening to their fake bickering and Elijah strumming quietly. White, fluffy clouds drifted above the trees as Chicot took in the canopy, the rustle of leaves barely audible over the performance. Her hair fluttered in the cool breeze, making the heat infinitely more bearable as the sun rose high above their heads, and the whole faire started to smell like warm wood.

When Lyza finally succeeded, Chicot and Elijah both clapped. Even though this was just practice, and the pirates usually left before Chicot and Elijah began, it felt wrong not to.

Unlike the previous days, when Chicot applauded, Monty's eyes caught hers. Chicot couldn't really make out her facial expression, so she just offered her a small smile. Monty promptly looked away when Chicot did this, turning to help Elvis remove the crate from the stage.

"Oooo." Elijah pitched up his voice. "She's looking at you."

"Fuck off." Chicot gently nudged him with her elbow as she stood, brushing off the back of her leggings. "Come on, we have practice." She promptly walked away from Elijah, toward the back of the stage so they could get their props. He followed close at her heels, still snickering and playing a wedding march on his lute, to Chicot's horror.

CHAPTER 4

Opening weekend at Albion Renaissance Faire meant that the cast were moving around the dog park as soon as the sun was over the horizon. Those getting into heavy makeup or with early shows were already getting breakfast. Meanwhile, Duchess snoozed peacefully on Elijah's bed as Chicot and Elijah ate cereal standing in their tiny kitchen.

Chicot's hair stood at odd angles, and Elijah lamented how she could simply tuck it into her hood so it wouldn't be seen while he had to carefully sculpt his. She wasn't even planning on doing more than brushing hers.

Elijah's hair was currently in a protective style, separated into thick twists that looked like celosia flowers to Chicot. His preferred do required him to take all the twists out and form his hair into a collection of bouncy curls that sat like a crown on top of his head. Perfectly shaving the sides of his head, he could add fun shapes in his undercut. Right now, he had a stripe that traveled from his temple down the side of his head and a star above his ear that he'd let Chicot add. Chicot thought it was rather befitting of him. He *was* a star.

After about ten minutes of bemoaning caring for his hair, Elijah went to actually start it with his coffee in hand. Chicot left him to his devices, only telling him when to close the door so she could start squeezing herself into her costume. The base layers fit well, but they were meant to be tight. They formed a sort of second skin for Chicot, protecting her from some of the scratchier elements of her costume. Once she had the bodysuit on, she told Elijah he could open the door again and situated her collar as Duchess picked her head up to look at her. The sound of the bells always got her attention, but she was too lazy in the mornings to attack them.

"Do you need help with your laces?" Elijah stepped out of the bathroom, his hair now a perfect collection of coils on the top of his head.

"Yes, please," Chicot chirped. Elijah just nodded, pulling on his shirt.

He helped Chicot fasten the snaps at the back of her ruffled collar. After that, she pulled on a bodice that had billowy sleeves, buttoning it up before finally tugging on her gloves. It had so many more layers than the workout clothes she'd been practicing in earlier that week, and she briefly wondered if she'd made a mistake when designing this outfit. But she hadn't overheated in any of the dress rehearsals in the past few days, so she felt confident she would be fine. Her heart was only racing because her anxiety was acting up. Once she had it all on and was looking in the small mirror to line up her hood so the points were straight and to tuck in the last bits of hair, she knew any discomfort would be worth it.

She looked like a true court jester, in her slim pants with red and marigold stripes on one leg, while the other had checkers in the same colors, the bells on her hood jingling. Chicot smoothed down her bodice, making final adjustments to her shiny blue belt with a moon-shaped buckle. Her pointy shoes squeaked as she hopped on her toes, spinning as she stepped out of the bathroom, looking at Elijah.

"What do you think?" She did a ball change, pretending to tap dance. Elijah laughed.

"You look amazing." He set a hand on his hip. His outfit was simpler, but he still had the flair of a real bard. His shirt was open enough to bare his smooth chest, which he had painstakingly waxed even though Chicot kept reminding him he probably didn't need it. Over his shirt, he wore an open vest, a belt over it to keep it from flapping. A short cape was held onto one of his shoulders by a thick leather strap, which matched his belt.

They wore coordinating colors, but Elijah's outfit had flashier materials. The flamboyant blue jacquard and light red damask accented his simple vest and pantaloons to make him look more bard-worthy.

"So do you." Chicot bounced on her toes again, the pointy ends of her shoes wiggling. Each jangle of the bells made her want to move, so she struggled to stay still as Elijah took her hands.

"First Albion," Elijah said, "then every ren faire in the country!"

"Well, not *every* faire." Chicot laughed. "Some of them happen at the same time."

"But we'll get *into* every faire." Elijah beamed, reaching for his bag and slinging it over his shoulder. "We'll have our pick of the litter, the jester and the bard."

He threw his hand out dramatically, his voice taking on the quality of an excited announcer for the joust. Their ruckus caused Duchess to slip under the bed with her ears back, annoyed at having her sleep disturbed.

Elijah handed Chicot her bag with her mask and props for when they were wandering around the faire. Chicot gave Duchess's sleepy head a smooch too, just for good measure. Then, they stepped out into the dog park, walking toward the Albion Renaissance Faire, *their* faire.

Chicot didn't make it two steps into the grounds before someone had linked arms with her. She startled slightly, giving herself a few moments to recognize who this person was.

"Good morning!" Lyza's voice was loud. She held a travel coffee mug in her other hand, and she moved like she'd already downed four of them. She already wore her unitard, the stirrup legs tucked into heavy boots, but she'd yet to tie any of the accompanying pirate paraphernalia on top of it. Chicot smiled politely, excited for the day but not ready to interact with anyone outside of Elijah. Especially since she hadn't fully realized it was Lyza until she'd started talking.

Two small braids ran along the crown of her head, meeting at a ponytail in the back of her head, her bangs gelled at the front to keep them in place. She looked so different without the lazy bun or French braid Chicot had gotten used to her wearing.

"Morning." Chicot curled in on herself, her shoulders pulling in and her head angling away from Lyza so she didn't hit her with the points of her hood. Lyza didn't seem affected by the one-word response or the attempt to move away; instead, she squeezed Chicot's bicep lightly to pull her closer and lowered her voice.

"May I discuss something important with you?" Lyza asked. Chicot blinked, turning to look for Elijah in hopes he might save her, but the traitor was already flirting with the sausage stand guy, who was carrying several plastic racks full of sausage buns as Elijah serenaded him with his lute.

"Of course." Chicot shifted on her feet, trying to put at least some distance between her and Lyza. She let Chicot go, waving for her to follow.

Lyza led Chicot toward the main office, stopping them near the gazebo and standing directly in front of Chicot. Lyza placed her hands on Chicot's shoulders briefly before stepping to stand next to her. She gestured to tell Chicot to straighten up, as she did the same.

Chicot complied but followed Lyza with her eyes, as if that would clarify what the hell she was doing. Lyza had been nice so far, if a bit forward, so Chicot didn't sense any ill-intentions in her odd behavior. Once Lyza finished inspecting Chicot, the pirate mumbled to herself and stepped in front of Chicot again.

Chicot glanced over her shoulder to see if Elijah had seen them walking this way. She couldn't find him. He was lost in a sea of people hurrying about, trying to prepare for the first day of the season.

"So—" Lyza pointed toward Chicot with her travel coffee mug. "We need a favor, and we were thinking it might be mutually beneficial to ask you."

Chicot tilted her head, a chorus of bells jangling in her ears. Normally, that was a fun and festive sound, but now it put her further on edge. Lyza smoothed the front of her bodice, her big, gray eyes on Chicot's as she took a deep breath.

"The thing is, I might need someone to take my place in our show for a little while." Lyza glanced over her shoulder, looking toward the main office doors as people slipped in and out. Chicot's eyes bulged—she couldn't help it. *The Pirates Three* had been a staple of the Albion Renaissance Faire for the better part of a decade. It almost didn't feel like the faire without them. Lyza made herself smaller at Chicot's reaction.

"I wouldn't be considering this if it wasn't serious," Lyza rubbed the side of her neck. "But I don't want to put Monty and Elvis out of work, you know?"

"Oh, okay." Chicot set her hand on her hip, leaning to one side as she wiggled her toes inside of her shoe. She didn't understand what Lyza was getting at or why she was telling Chicot any of this, and then it hit Chicot.

"So, we were wondering …"

"If I could take your spot in the show?" Chicot asked. Lyza nodded quickly, putting up her free hand.

"I *know* it's a big ask, but it's only if I get told I need to stop performing, and you would get my cut of the tips and money," Lyza added quickly. Chicot paused, standing still for a moment as she looked Lyza over again.

"So, I'd be like … an understudy?" Chicot squinted. "I'd only fill in if you need me to?"

"Yes." Lyza said quickly.

If Chicot was more of an understudy, that would at least give her more time to learn Lyza's part in the show, and this would be additional experience she could list on auditions. It might help Chicot and Elijah get spots at other faires next year. If she could only half-ass both shows, that would look terrible, but she believed she could manage two performances, especially since the acrobatics in *The Pirates Three* were intended to be impressive, but not overly complex. Either way, she needed to talk to Elijah about it first.

"Why though? Why me?" Chicot asked.

"Well, about a month ago, I got some news." Lyza's lips trembled and she sighed. "We hadn't figured out what we were going to do, but we were talking the other day and Elvis pointed out that you and I are about the same size …"

Chicot furrowed her brow, about to ask what news Lyza had gotten, when her mouth went dry. Lyza was absently resting her palm on her navel. "Oh my god." Chicot shook her head quickly. "I can't take money from you. I'll do it, but I—"

"No, no." Lyza waved at Chicot quickly and pressed a finger to her lips. "Listen, okay? Elvis will be able to make enough, and we'll figure it out. This was just … unexpected."

Chicot rubbed her head and then stopped so she didn't mess up her hood, instead moving to grip one of the points, toying with the bell at the end.

"No, Lyza, I'm willing to help you. I mean, I have to talk to Elijah, but …" Chicot didn't know what to do, so she took Lyza's free hand in hers, trying to offer some comfort to her. Lyza pressed her lips together as she looked at Chicot again, her chin low and her eyes filling with tears. Chicot felt a knot in her stomach. She didn't know what she would do if Lyza started crying.

"Okay, I wouldn't feel comfortable with you doing it for free, and I want you to know what the money's going to look like when you talk to Elijah." Lyza squeezed Chicot's hand and then let it go, wiping at her eyes briefly. "What if I keep the money the faire pays us, and you keep what would be my share of the tips?"

Chicot shuffled her feet. She wanted to go back to being excited about her first day at the faire instead of thinking about the kid that Lyza and Elvis were going to have to support. There wasn't a good answer and as she looked up at Lyza's set jaw and stiff back, she knew there was no arguing. At least she could use the money to justify her choice to Elijah. Though, knowing him, he also probably would have tried to refuse.

"Yeah, okay. One sec." Chicot turned, looking around for Elijah in the crowd again. This time she spotted him, his eyes catching Chicot's, and he immediately started toward them without Chicot even waving for him.

"Thank you for this." Lyza said it before Elijah was within earshot, reaching out to squeeze Chicot's shoulder. Chicot smiled at her.

"What's going on?" Elijah shifted his lute to his back as he approached them.

"Sorry for borrowing her suddenly. I was asking Chicot a favor on behalf of my group," Lyza explained. Elijah started telling her it was okay, but he stopped the moment he looked at Chicot. Apparently, the look on her face was too grave, so she tried to force herself to smile. She just didn't want him to be mad when he realized she'd basically agreed to this already without consulting him.

Elijah's jaw wiggled at the corners as he gritted his teeth. "Chicot."

"I'll give you both a minute." Lyza quickly walked around the side of the gazebo to give them some privacy.

"Lyza asked me to be an understudy for her in their show, and I sort of already agreed to it. I mean, we haven't told the directors or anything, so I could still back out." Chicot dipped her chin, trying not to make direct eye contact with Elijah as she made nonsensical gestures with her hands, as if it would help explain her line of thinking. "But I don't think I should. I mean, I only did it because—"

She cut herself off, looking at Lyza on the other side of the gazebo. Was it really her place to tell Elijah that Lyza was pregnant? She didn't know what she was allowed to say.

"Because?" Elijah pushed his head forward, crossing his arms. Chicot groaned.

"I'm sorry. I should have asked you." Chicot rubbed her knuckles together. "It's Lyza. Well, you see, she needs help."

Elijah's eyes darted back to Lyza, his arms uncrossing. He sighed and waved to get Lyza's attention, and she quickly joined them.

"What's going on exactly?" Elijah asked. "Chicot seems afraid to tell me."

"Oh, I should have said you could, sorry." Lyza rubbed her arm awkwardly. "I'm pregnant."

"That's why." Chicot's nerves were fraying as she tried to stand still. She wanted to do something for Lyza, take action—but there wasn't much to take action about. Not an hour before the faire gates opened at least.

"You're pregnant?" Elijah's jaw fell open. Lyza now had his rapt attention. She nodded, a grimace washing over her face.

"Miracle of life over here!" Lyza pointed at herself as her face settled into something muted and scared. Elijah collected himself.

"Well, guess it can't be helped." Elijah shrugged. Chicot whipped her head up from where she'd been looking at her feet, bells jingling as her eyes brightened.

"It's really a beneficial situation for us all," Chicot blurted. "She keeps her pay from the faire, and I get a third of the tips, so we'll have a little more money to play with if we get an audition. Maybe I can even get a new phone."

"With our luck," Elijah teased, "we'll do a bunch more shows and still not get to replace your damn phone."

Honestly, he was right. They didn't have much luck when it came to her stupid phone.

Lyza looked like a stiff breeze might knock her over. Chicot couldn't fault her for being terrified by an unplanned pregnancy. She wanted to make sure that Lyza was taken care of.

"Hey." Elijah stepped closer to them, lowering his voice. "Lyza, it's okay. C'mon, we'll find Elvis."

Lyza shook her head. "No, we still have to talk to the directors."

Elijah looked at Chicot over Lyza's head as he gave her a side hug. "Okay, we'll all go together, then we'll find Elvis."

"Thank you." Lyza leaned into Elijah's chest, letting him squeeze her. She turned to Chicot, about to hug her too, but stopped when she realized she'd crush Chicot's collar. Instead, she took Chicot's hand. "I still have to confirm the timeline with a doctor, but let's give the director a heads-up."

Lyza led her and Elijah into the main office. Chicot glanced back at her partner, who was holding the door, and gave him a nod. They were probably thinking the same thing: Elijah's parents hadn't planned for him either. But Elijah had turned out great.

The three went to the Castlerock Stage together after a short discussion with the directors, and there was Elvis, Monty helping him with stilts. Chicot's eyes swam over Monty, her heart suddenly pounding in her chest. She hadn't even thought of it when they'd talked, but being Lyza's understudy meant working with Monty for the rest of the summer. In fact, it meant an entire summer of Monty lifting Chicot, catching her, juggling blades with her, and even sword fighting with her. Chicot swallowed.

Lyza immediately folded into Elvis's arms. Monty frowned as she watched her sister for a moment, then her eyes slowly dragged over to Elijah and finally to Chicot. Chicot waved politely, trying to smile like everything was normal, but it wasn't. Chicot had clearly just agreed to a summer of being in Monty's strong arms without giving it a second thought. It seemed to confuse Monty more than anything, as she looked askance at Chicot before she turned back at Lyza.

"You okay?" Monty asked, stopping her adjustment of the stilts. Lyza turned without leaving Elvis's arms, nodding at her sister.

"I'm good," Lyza said, giving her a thumbs-up. Nodding, Monty walked past Chicot to reach the backstage door, meeting Chicot's eyes.

"We can talk later then." Monty only pulled her eyes away from Chicot to look at Lyza. "You probably shouldn't get on stilts today." Lyza sighed, agreeing with her as Monty stepped into the small green room they all shared.

Chicot's shoulders relaxed as Monty disappeared behind the door. At least this would help them get auditions. Something Chicot would be telling herself daily for the rest of the season. She followed Monty. For now, she needed to get her promotional flag and put her mask on. Once she did that, she could focus on their primary task, which was getting people to watch her and Elijah's show. That was where her priorities needed to be for the rest of the day; she could panic about working with Monty after the faire closed.

CHAPTER 5

Chicot fastened her mask to her face as Elijah adjusted the strap of the flag belt so it sat properly on her hips. She needed to attract people to their show, and opening ceremony was only an hour away. Monty was currently backstage with Elijah and Chicot, casually getting the rest of her pirate outfit over her unitard. Chicot felt the biting at the back of her throat, the urge to ask Monty a million questions about why she'd agreed to this. Surely, they'd talked about it at great length before Lyza had asked Chicot, so it left Chicot wondering why Monty had acted so surly toward Chicot if she was willing to work with her? Why pick her? Why not literally anyone else? There were other acrobats working the faire. They could have made a show with just Elvis and Monty, so why did they instead ask Chicot to fill in? Lyza or Elvis must have suggested it, but that didn't explain Monty's agreement, since they wouldn't have asked Chicot without her approval.

Elijah patted her on the back. "Okay, all set. It's not too tight, right?"

That pulled her from her thoughts, and she shook her head as her bells jangled loudly. Monty, distracted from the sash she was tying around her waist, looked up at Chicot and snickered.

"That must do some serious damage to your stealth," Monty said. The joke surprised Chicot, and she let out a deep laugh, making her jingle even more. Monty smiled back, shaking her head as she looked Chicot over again.

"Only when it comes to humans. Cats seem to think she's a toy until she moves. Then she becomes the ultimate prey." Elijah picked up his lute, lifting his chin, plucking out the infamous *Jaws* theme with Monty's laughter joining in and making Chicot's breath hitch.

"Anyway, break a leg out there today, you two." Monty picked up her stilts, opening the backstage door again. "I have a feeling you will be the talk of the faire shortly."

"Thank you." Chicot folded her arms and watched as Monty left. Elijah shook his head slowly, setting his hands on his hips as he sighed.

"This is so weird," Elijah said. Chicot turned to look up at him, the mesh making it seem like she was looking at him through a fence, thin black lines cut through her field of vision.

"I know. Since we haven't talked about it as a group yet, I feel like I ... I don't know, like maybe I did the wrong thing?" Chicot groaned, looking up at their props lined up along the wall. She had not considered Monty at all because she'd been too focused on Lyza, who'd looked like she might cry.

"You didn't do the wrong thing." Elijah's forehead creased as he looked up at the ceiling. "I mean, what else could we do? Not like we could say no."

Chicot sighed. "You're right. As soon as I figured out what was going on, I felt like I should say yes."

"Yeah, because you wanted to do the right thing." Elijah leaned on the wall, taking a deep breath. "Okay, come on. We have a show to get people to watch and audiences to entertain."

Chicot nodded more vigorously, causing her bells to become a cacophony of tiny metal beads banging on thin metal plates. She followed him with flag in hand, tucking the end into the belt once they were in the blazing sun. It was bordering on sweltering and it wasn't even 10 a.m. yet. Chicot put the heat out of mind as best she could, carrying her heavy flag to the entry gates where they'd be ready to beckon people toward their show as they filtered into the faire grounds. Their flag hung like a medieval banner from the cross bar at the top of her flagpole. It matched her costume, a bright marigold with bold red lettering that read: *The Jester & Bard: Forever at Odds* above a carefully painted silhouette of a jester's head with the pointy hat on. Underneath, it listed the times of their performances, with *Castlerock Stage* written at the bottom. Chicot shifted her flag to face outward as she adjusted the belt bag she used for anything she may need while walking around the faire.

Ticket takers were readying themselves at the doors, and Elijah split off to work a separate area with his lute. They did this to cover more ground. The more people that saw one of them advertising their show, the more they could draw to their stage for performances.

Albion was a series of twisting and turning dirt walkways with large, old trees scattered throughout. Where there weren't trees, there were stages painted to look like castles, shops adorned with brightly-colored wooden signs beckoning patrons with promises of trinkets, and stalls selling foods that filled the air with smoke, cinnamon, and fried batter. Peppered throughout there were work-shops where glass blowers and blacksmiths gave demonstrations, some even offering to let the guests try their hand at the craft. Of course, there were also bars with punny names that boasted the Queen's finest ale, mead, and cocktails. Performers tucked them-selves among the trees or near the wishing well across from the main entrance. Workers moved about shop buildings full of flower crowns, held wooden racks with hot pretzels hanging from each peg, and sold art from small carts placed in shaded spots. Above it all, a dragon head with red lights in its mouth mounted on a Tudor-style turret was attached to the gates, welcoming patrons with fake smoke and a glowing tongue.

On Elijah's side of the path, Elvis and Monty stood on their stilts, chatting as they took small steps so they wouldn't fall over. Chicot watched Monty in particular, her broad shoulders and muscular arms at her sides as she balanced, a pair of loose, draped pants cov-ering the metal structures that held her aloft. She wet her lips, the thought of Monty's strong arms around her waist or her hand on the small of Chicot's back causing the hair on her neck to stand. She shook her head, bells ringing loudly as she did.

Chicot thankfully didn't have time to spiral about having to work with Monty. The trumpets sounded, and the gates swung open. Sounds of joy and huzzahs swelled from the herd of people making their way in. It was a welcome distraction.

Performers dressed as fae creatures danced between the patrons, kicking up dust and handing out printed schedules and maps. People in elaborate costumes, their bodices tight and their belts slung around their hips, wandered into the faire, trumpets from the opening ceremonies still playing. Even in the heat, there were people in full skirts and petticoats, others in real metal armor, their chainmail clinking as they walked.

Chicot placed herself beneath one of the many old oak trees, waving at kids and dancing jigs as she gestured silently toward her flag. People in a range of fantasy and realistic Renaissance costumes passed her—some with flowing satin and silk skirts, others in pirate attire complete with tricorn hats. Some waved and others smiled as they strode past her, farther into the faire that was already filled with the scent of cooked turkey legs and sweet funnel cake.

Three little girls ran by Chicot in knight costumes, their leader yelling about finding treasure as their father chased after them, his Cubs T-shirt already soaked with sweat. There were cosplayers, their brightly colored wigs shining in the morning sun and their hand-sewn outfits bobbing and weaving through the crowd. Chicot spotted a worker carrying a tall stick heavy with soft pretzels covered in pure white salt, hocking the tasty treats along with cups of mustard or cheese.

Performers mingled as people rushed inside, most in unitards while others had on baggy, dirty outfits for the shows that required them to roll in the mud. Others had flags like the one Chicot carried, including Lyza, who opted not to wear stilts to promote their show like Monty and Elvis.

Lyza waved at passersby, laughing as she joked with a man dressed in a jester's costume, not unlike Chicot's own, as if nothing troubled her at all. Chicot realized she needed to do the same, so she took a deep breath and focused on miming for people who walked past her. It was part of her character and an eye-catching tactic to get asses in seats. Gestures and dances often got her point across, despite people still sometimes trying to speak with her directly. It was only a problem when someone asked for directions to the bathroom and she couldn't actually tell them. She hoped her frantic pointing was enough, and luckily the woman laughed as she walked away, thankfully heading in the right direction.

Working the crowd became second nature as she threw her concerns from the morning to the winds; each spin she did and note on her slide whistle making it easier to forget. She made room for other performers, bowed deep to the Queen as she passed with her entourage, and posed for photos. Girls in hats that looked like mushrooms grinned at her as she did magic tricks, and she joined them to do little dances, making yarn pom-poms appear and disappear before leaving one with them.

She felt at ease, like she was in the dog park, with people enjoying her costume or laughing when she did a trick. People wanted to see her; they liked her showmanship, and that left Chicot ready to do flips down the aisles of shops. She sadly had to control herself, and she surged with happiness and relief. This was going to work.

Chicot eventually started making her way back to the stage, whizzing past patrons with turkey legs and parents with strollers. She forced herself to slow down after she bopped a man on the head with her flag while weaving under the water booth's large wooden mermaid sign and the long line for the coffee shop. Chicot pantomimed a frantic apology as the man laughed and assured her she'd only hit him with the material, not the pole. There was more of a learning curve to carrying the banners than she'd realized.

More importantly, she had thirty minutes before she and Elijah were supposed to be on, which meant *The Pirates Three* had fifteen left in their act. She didn't stop to watch them—too focused on getting the flag belt off and her mask ready. Elijah was already there when she arrived, plucking her bag of balloons from the shelf and offering them to her. He gave her a thumbs-up, and as Chicot prepared for their first show of the year, she felt a lightness within her body, allowing her to breathe easier. She had Elijah there with her, and as she helped him arrange the jewelry on his fake elf ears, everything felt fluttery. This was the right thing for them to be doing, the place where they belonged.

CHAPTER 6

Opening weekend became a blur of jigs, bells, and popped balloons. Each of their eight shows went off without a hitch, Chicot's mask not giving them a lick of trouble. On Saturday night, they hung out with other performers at the dog park, Lyza bringing them from RV to RV, introducing them to people they hadn't met yet, helping Chicot and Elijah meld into the faire community. She also used Chicot and Elijah to pawn off any alcoholic drinks she couldn't refuse from fellow performers as they chatted.

Chicot didn't push any deeper conversations about being an understudy, leaving it alone and simply making firm plans for her and Elijah to join them at the gym the next time they went. She worried about what working with Monty would look like, and she didn't want to overstep any boundaries.

Luckily, when Chicot interacted with Monty, it wasn't hostile. That eased Chicot's mind each time it happened. Monty was still surly sometimes, sure, but she wasn't impolite— which was all Chicot needed to deal with filling in for Lyza. Monty had even gone out of her way to drop off a printed script for Chicot at her RV, the pages carefully placed in a binder so she wouldn't immediately lose them all.

On Sunday evening, they all piled into a car together to go to the nearest dive bar, a place called The Final Frontier, a haven for giant nerds. By the time Chicot was pressed up against the bar, the foreboding feeling of meeting them at the gym to train on Monday had subsided.

It seemed like the entire faire wound up there, unlike Saturday when many had abstained so they wouldn't be hungover Sunday morning. At least, the smart ones had. Chicot and Elijah had both been hungover that morning. Nothing a shower and a bottle of water hadn't fixed, though.

As she took her drink and tipped the bartender, Chicot felt a presence behind her. A tall one. At first, she assumed it was Elijah, so she simply tipped her head back and looked straight up into an unfamiliar but cute face. She drew away from the warm body quickly, her beer sloshing as she spun, a few drops escaping the can. Chicot's eyes dragged over muscular biceps, following a well-defined collarbone until Chicot spotted the plush rabbit charm on a carabiner clipped on the narrow strap of her dress. Monty.

"Sorry." Chicot wiped the few drops of beer off her hand with the bottom of her baggy T-shirt. She looked at Monty's blue cotton dress, which clung to her chest in a heart shape. Her soft blonde bob formed a halo around her head, a clip with a strawberry on it holding her bangs back as she eyed Chicot. It didn't seem like Chicot's beer had gotten on Monty's pretty dress, thankfully.

"You're good." Monty tilted her head, her lip twisting up to one side as she looked down at Chicot, setting a hand on her shoulder to still her. Chicot didn't think she was off balance, but Monty's warm touch wasn't unwelcome either. She still had not sorted out how she was going to handle Monty holding her ass while doing acrobatics in the show. Something told Chicot she was going to have to get real normal about how hot Monty was soon.

"… you okay there?" Monty's voice brought Chicot out of her thoughts. She hadn't realized how long she'd paused.

"Yes! Sorry, I just have a lot on my mind." She couldn't tell her that "a lot" was mostly code for Monty's hands. Monty nodded in response, leaning over to say something to the bartender before she looked down at Chicot again. She rubbed her brow, squinting.

"Okay," Monty said. "It's weird to see you and not hear a bunch of jingling."

Chicot's voice rose in pitch unintentionally, and she giggled, "Oh, yeah. I know."

Part of her had wanted to crawl under the bar the moment the giggle had come out of her. Monty seemed unfazed, just smiling as she set cash down on the bar and grabbed her beer.

"I guess it's just as strange for you, huh?" Monty continued as she turned back toward the crowd. She said nothing further, just walked back over to Elvis and Lyza. Chicot's face burned, her ears hot as she walked back over to Elijah, who had the sausage stand guy in a booth with him. Chicot really needed to learn his name.

When she sat down, it was the sausage guy who snorted, smiling at Chicot. "What's up with that face?"

Chicot covered her ears as she rested her elbows on the table, her lips pressed against the beer can. Elijah just laughed.

"Ah, leave her be." Elijah nudged him. "She looks like she may have had a run-in with someone hot and now she's overheating."

Chicot balled up a napkin and threw it at Elijah. She smiled, because it wasn't like he was wrong; she just didn't want to say that it had been Monty.

Eventually, she found out that the sausage guy's name was Ken; and he was sober, so he was driving them back to the dog park. Apparently, he lived nearby in Albion rather than at the faire grounds themselves. Chicot had learned that wasn't uncommon for the food vendors; most of them were locals who worked seasonally and then did something else. For Ken, that was working at a restaurant up north during snowmobile season.

When they got back to their trailer, Elijah showered first, coming out with his fake elf ears in hand because he'd still been wearing them. His ears would have been sticky if he'd taken them off earlier, so he'd elected to just be an elf at the bar. Chicot showered after him, getting the sweat from the day and the bar off her before she lazily rinsed her hair.

As she stood under the cool water with her head pressed against the wall of the tiny bathroom, she let her mind drift. She couldn't help thinking about all the tricks she had to learn to take Lyza's spot, her mind revisiting how Monty and Elvis tossed her around. It didn't take long before her focus narrowed in on Monty's hands again, and she had to shake her head hard to make her thoughts come back to the real world. She turned off the water. She needed to get out of the only real private place she had in the RV. She didn't want to be tempted to let her mind drift anywhere inappropriate. Monty didn't seem to even like her that much, so Chicot shouldn't be thinking about how nice her hands would feel.

Duchess awaited her when she stepped out, ready for her to play their little game of guard cat and tired human who just wanted to sleep. Chicot just threw a treat across the RV for her. It always landed somewhere difficult to get when Chicot was drunk because her aim got worse.

Soon, the three of them settled in to sleep while Elijah's phone played the last few chapters of *The Hound of the Baskervilles* and Duchess purred softly on Chicot's chest.

It was tough to wake up after two days of drinking, particularly with Chicot's cat snuggling her, but the day off made things a little better. They started slowly, stretching with Duchess and getting into comfortable clothes. Lyza asked them to meet at noon, so they had some time to wake up before they went, eating breakfast while standing in the kitchen as usual. Elijah then grabbed them each a water bottle before they left to meet Monty, Elvis, and Lyza.

When they got to the car, it was already started, Monty in the driver's seat with Lyza waving at them from the passenger side. Elvis squished into the back with them, so Chicot was shoved in the middle, forcing her to make eye contact with Monty every now and again in the rearview mirror. Something about it tortured her, Chicot keeping her eyes on her hands after the third time it happened, her mind drifting to similar thoughts as the ones she'd had in the shower. She breathed deeply, disguising it as lack of sleep or a hangover.

Once they parked, Elijah nudged Chicot, speaking under his breath as they followed the other three inside. "You good?"

"Yeah." Chicot took a deep breath.

Elijah nodded back at her, and then they stepped into a real gymnastics gym. Even if it smelled like sweaty feet, Chicot's excitement didn't wane. As she looked at the boxy, white room, Chicot's steps became light enough that she was almost hopping.

"We really have this whole place to ourselves?" Chicot asked and Elvis confirmed they had it to themselves. There was a large spring floor in the middle and mats stacked in various places. On the far wall, uneven bars hung over a foam pit, a vault horse in one corner that looked unused, and so many trampolines.

Chicot moved faster to set down her water bottle and bag, making a beeline for one of the trampolines. Before she could do that, though, Lyza said something to Monty that resulted in Monty's brow furrowing.

"I didn't realize we'd need to start right away," Monty said. Her eyes quickly moved from Lyza's face to Chicot. Chicot stopped mid-step, her eyes darting between Lyza and Monty before she smiled awkwardly.

"If she might take my place, she has to know my part." Lyza set her hands on her hips. "We need to start teaching it to her now."

Chicot felt her stomach do a backflip, a knot quickly forming. Monty lowered her voice as she turned back to Lyza. Not enough that Chicot couldn't hear her.

"Okay!" Monty threw her hands up. "But I thought it would be just for closing weekend, not more than half the season."

"I don't know what's going to happen, so we have to be ready," Lyza said. "Which means starting now. We probably should have started last week."

Monty's mouth fell open, but she took a deep breath rather than responding immediately. Seizing the opportunity, Chicot quickly stepped away from the foyer, retreating toward Elijah, who was on the spring floor already. She didn't need to be part of this sister fight. Elvis seemed to have the same plan, trying to follow Chicot, but Monty and Lyza both called him out for it.

Chicot's hair prickled. She knew she was being talked about, but something in Monty's tone and question caught Chicot off guard. Chicot had expected Monty to be boorish or awkward about working with Chicot, of course, but as Monty's face fell as they discussed Lyza missing more than a weekend or two, it seemed like Monty was more upset at the prospect of Lyza not being in the show than Chicot being in it. Which was probably a good thing because Monty being sad about her sister not being around was easier for Chicot to deal with.

"Do you really think Lyza might miss more than half the season?" Elijah crossed his arms, his lips pressed into a hard line.

"I'm not sure. She said she found out a month ago, but I don't know how far along she is." Chicot ran a hand through her hair, frowning as she watched Monty and Lyza quietly bicker. Elvis stood at their side awkwardly, trying to gently coax them into not being annoyed with each other.

"Chicot, can you come here please?" Monty waved for Chicot to join them. Chicot looked to Elijah for help, her mouth hanging open, but he just held an open palm out toward Monty as if Chicot should go. So she complied, her hands growing clammy as she walked over to join them.

"Yes?" Chicot folded her hands in front of her, standing like a twelve-year-old boy ready to get yelled at by a teacher.

"Do you think you can do sixteen shows a weekend for more than three weeks if it comes to that?" Monty set a hand on her hip. Chicot blinked.

"Well, I used to work sixty-hour weeks at the gas station," Chicot said. "So I think I can handle it."

Monty looked Chicot over briefly, then turned back to Lyza. "Okay, but we have to have a backup plan if she can't keep up."

"What's going on?" Chicot asked. Elijah was now at her back, looking over her head.

"Monty's worried Chicot can't handle the extra shows." Lyza crossed her arms. "But she can."

"She *thinks* she can." Monty rolled her eyes. "Can you learn this in two weeks if we need you that soon?"

"All the lines and choreography? Yeah." That was the one part about this she was sure of. It was no different than learning a routine for dance.

Monty sighed. "Okay, we'll start now just to be safe, but we're assuming Lyza will be in the show for the majority of the season. And we might need to make changes to the jokes."

"Why? She can just pretend to be your sister," Elvis asked. Monty wrinkled her nose, shaking her head.

"Nope, weird. Absolutely not." She paused and quickly added, "No offense."

"None taken?" Chicot rubbed the back of her head, furrowing her brow. "I don't think."

"I can help you rework jokes if needed," Elijah offered. Lyza quickly asked for Elijah's opinion on the ones about Middle and Wee being sisters. They settled on some of the mats nearby, Elijah digging Chicot's script from her bag to write notes as he and Lyza batted ideas around.

Elvis then went to his bag, getting out three stage combat swords and handed one to both Monty and Chicot. Apparently, the fight choreography worried him the most, which made sense to Chicot. The swords might not be sharp, but they would hurt if you got hit.

Chicot looked longingly at a trampoline before she followed Monty and Elvis to the mat where they could practice stage combat. Luckily, Chicot could absolutely handle choreography, and that was all fighting on stage was.

It didn't take long for Elvis to have the three of them working on blocking. Even if they didn't have all the lines settled yet, they needed to start because Lyza's doctor could tell her she needed to stop performing at her next appointment. If that was the case, they'd only have a short time to sort this out.

Chicot gave it her best. She offered options for fight scenes, tumbled away from certain "blows" she received in an exaggerated, goofy way that made Elvis laugh. Each time, she turned to Monty quickly, hoping to see her laughing too. Monty barely even smiled through most of it, her brow wrinkled and her eyes darting to Lyza whenever she had a moment. Somehow, this was a relief to Chicot. She might not be making Monty laugh, but it wasn't because she wasn't funny. It was because Monty was worried about her sister. That, Chicot could handle.

What she could not handle was Elvis pointing at her and Monty, directing Monty to pick Chicot up. Before Chicot could abscond, Monty got her hands around her middle, lifting her with ease. Chicot's cheeks burned, her eyes on the floor mats.

"Jeez you weigh, like, nothing." Monty set her back on her feet easily, her eyes going wide when she saw Chicot's face. "You okay? You're pretty red."

"Fine! I'm fine." Chicot waved her hands, trying to tell herself as much as she was telling Monty and Elvis. But the feeling of Monty's hands on her waist *lingered*. They were large and soft, her fingers thick at the bases and tapering to nearly squared-off ends. Being held by Monty's strong hands, Chicot could already tell, was going to become one of her favorite parts of this whole situation.

"Okay ..." Monty watched Chicot as Elvis finished marking the size of the stage on the floor with painter's tape. "You know, if this bothers you—"

"What?" Chicot looked up at Monty, her head shaking slightly. "No, no. I'm excited actually."

She grinned at Monty, maybe wider than she really should. Chicot had never been good at contorting her face into the right shape to get her feelings across to other people. It was why Elijah had suggested her jester outfit include a mask, and it had quickly become her entire identity. It was easier to get across to people that she was just a silly little guy when she had painted expression and some bells on her head.

Monty pressed her lips together for a moment and sighed. She looked Chicot in the face again with her lips parted like she might speak before she narrowed her eyes toward her sister, who was still writing lines with Elijah.

Chicot's chest expanded with the sudden desire to make sure Monty knew she was really in this. She wanted to be friends with her, Elvis, and Lyza, and this was what friends did, didn't they? They helped each other. They were each other's village. Or something like that. Chicot had really only had Elijah up until now, but adding more people sounded good to her. She wanted that. So, Chicot might not fully understand all the intricacies of what was going on with Lyza being pregnant, but she knew she wanted to help. Her dad had always said that was enough.

She straightened herself up and nudged Monty with her elbow, hair standing on-end as her arm slid against Monty's soft skin. "You guys will be okay, and I want to help. Don't worry about me."

Monty's eyes returned to Chicot slowly, her lips pinched into a frown and her head tilted. Her fingers were on her ear, nervously rubbing it as she started to answer.

"No, I mean, well …"

Chicot shimmied her shoulders, mimicking something she did on stage with Elijah, just being goofy. She didn't want Monty's face to look so tight, but she didn't really know the words she needed to say to help her relax. Either way, she managed to catch Monty's attention, one of her brows arching cutely as she tilted her head. Her frown dissipated as her mouth opened in a confused "O" shape. She looked like a fish. A cute fish, like one of those fake ones everyone in Wisconsin had in their cabins in the early aughts that sang and wiggled. Chicot liked it.

"Plus, I'm an easier lift," Chicot said. She wasn't sure how true that really was, but she was going to run with it. "This summer'll probably be easier on your back. That's good, right?"

A single, high laugh came out of Monty and her lips turned up. It was small, and there was still a worried wrinkle in her forehead, but she did laugh. It grew louder when Chicot wiggled her shoulders again and made a joke about this being better for her knees too. Monty swatted at Chicot's arm gently, shaking her head.

"Yeah, yeah, okay." Monty rubbed her cheeks. "I'll stop being so worried."

"Good." Chicot hopped in front of Monty. "Oh, actually. Have you ever been a cheerleader?"

"Umm, no." Monty looked down at herself, and Chicot could tell in a moment she was thinking what many girls had thought before. Monty then confirmed it by saying, "I wouldn't have fit into the uniforms. But Elvis and Lyza were."

"Well, they made me wear the mascot costume in my senior year because I cut my hair short and couldn't put a bow in it anymore," Chicot confessed. This elicited another laugh from Monty, and Chicot beamed. Chicot wanted to bathe in Monty's infectious laughter.

"But," Chicot continued, "before that, I was a flyer. We might be able to speed up the acrobatics if we insert some cheerleading moves. If Elvis knows some, we can teach you."

"That's a good idea actually." Monty smiled. She genuinely smiled for the first time since they'd gotten to the gym. "Let's talk to him."

Chicot bounced, doing a ball change and a dance flourish as she turned to walk toward Elvis, Monty jogging to keep up with her. Once they had him on board, they started to discuss what they could cut and replace with easy but impressive cheerleading or acrobatic lifts. Once they'd decided on their plan, Monty, Elvis, and Lyza sat down to continue working on the script, sending Chicot away so she'd have time to practice with Elijah. They had the gym for another forty-five minutes, so they could only run the show once at that point.

Before they could start, Chicot clapped her hands together, dropping to her knees as she pouted at Elijah. "Can I jump on the trampoline for one minute?"

Elijah groaned, his eyes lidded and his brows raised as he pinched his lips into a line. He agreed though, gesturing with an open palm toward the trampoline.

"Go ahead," Elijah said. Chicot jumped to her feet, thanking him quickly as she ripped her socks off. She ran to the trampoline, carefully examining it before she climbed up. It had been so long since she'd gotten to tumble with this much bounce under her. She started easy with cartwheels going down the length and then bounced back like an excited kid doing flips. Once she'd done that, she stayed in the middle, getting as high as she could so she could do a solid 360, landing on her feet and falling back onto her butt.

When her minute was up, she tore herself away, receiving applause from Lyza, Elvis, Elijah, and even Monty. Chicot panted, climbing off and rejoining the group.

"So, you never went to circus school?" Lyza asked. Chicot shook her head, picking up her water bottle.

"I did gymnastics, dance, and then I was a cheerleader." Chicot sat with the group as Elijah was still trying to figure out how to Velcro the foam box they were using in place of their crate to the floor so it wouldn't move too much.

"You should consider it in the offseason." Lyza gestured at herself, Elvis, and Monty. "We all take classes when we're not going faire to faire. Makes sure we keep up our skills."

Chicot thought of the jar they had for her new phone. They'd pulled everything out of it twice—once to put a new tire on the RV and again to pay for Duchess's regular yearly checkup, which had snuck up on them. She sighed softly, looking at the ceiling as she answered.

"Hopefully we can set some aside for it," Chicot said. Lyza suggested a circus school in Idaho that was cheap. However, the mention of it resulted in Elvis, Monty, and Lyza arguing about whether the price was worth it considering how cold their winters were. Chicot let out a shallow sigh, listening as the three of them began to bicker. She liked how it sounded, siblings arguing with each other. It made her miss debating with her brother and sister about what to watch on TV. They'd never been mean to each other—they'd just had different tastes being that they were so different in age. Of course, her mother had always had to ruin it by yelling at them to stop fighting and taking the remote from them. Even when they weren't fighting in the first place. Nothing could convince Chicot to return to her mother's house.

She didn't have to linger on those thoughts for long, thankfully. Elijah called to her, and she turned to join him. They ran their show straight through with the same ease as always. Then they double-checked all their blocking on the tape version of the stage before they finished.

The five of them cleaned up quickly, another group coming in as they were leaving. It was the two older swordsmen who did a fun comedy show where they cracked jokes at each other's expense and then fought over it. Chicot was fairly certain the name of it was something along the lines of *Gert & Salvio: The Swordsmen*, which they'd been doing for nearly twenty years at Albion. And there was good reason for it. Chicot had seen their act once as a young teen when her dad had brought her and her siblings, and she remembered laughing so hard she'd dropped her ice cream. Even if their acrobatics were simpler now, their jokes were unmatched. The swordsmen were followed by a short woman holding a unicycle that Chicot didn't recognize. She had beautiful mahogany curls that touched her shoulders. Chicot was fairly certain the woman was another acrobat, doing both the unicycling and contortion for her show. As they left the gym, the woman smiled brightly at them and waved, chipper as she hopped toward the area she was using to practice.

Chicot waved back, which earned her an even more excited wave. When they got to the car and piled in, she was earnestly feeling good about everything. They stopped at a Staples to have their scripts printed for the new version of *The Pirates Three: Big, Middle, and Wee*. She wasn't even worried about being on stage without a mask.

CHAPTER 7

Monty turned up at their RV later in the evening to give Chicot a finalized version of the script. Her fingers twisted in her long, flowy skirt, a simple white T-shirt on top as she handed Chicot the binder, offering her a small smile. Monty always wore such sweet-looking clothing, and now Chicot could smell the waft of an oak moss and black current perfume she wore.

"Lyza's next appointment is on Thursday," Monty said. "We'll know for sure if or when she has to leave then."

Chicot nodded. "I'll make sure I'm ready. Are you okay?"

"I'll be fine." Monty rubbed the back of her hand with her thumb. Chicot pressed her lips together, unsure what to even say. She'd be devastated if Elijah was going to be out of their show very suddenly. In fact, she couldn't even imagine it or how she'd feel. Chicot's lips pursed. She didn't know if there was anything she could say to make her feel better, but Chicot didn't have the chance anyway, because Monty turned to start walking away.

"Anyway, if you need to run lines, just text me or Elvis," Monty called.

"Okay, we might have to practice in the field too," Chicot said. Monty looked at Chicot over her shoulder.

"Yeah, we can do that too." Monty then linked her hands behind her back as she went back to her place.

Chicot sighed, setting down the script and picking up Duchess as she made her way toward the bed. Elijah was sitting on it, spread out like it was a couch, his phone in one hand as he watched YouTube videos.

"I have bad news," Elijah paused his video. Chicot frowned, bouncing Duchess in her arms like one would a baby.

"What's the news?"

"We didn't get into Canterbury Festival in Colorado." Elijah sighed and let his phone drop flat onto the bed.

"Fuck." Chicot pressed her face into Duchess's fluffy chest, ignoring her as she pressed a paw against Chicot's temple. She didn't want to think about getting another rejection, or the many places that simply wouldn't respond to their application, so she buried her face in her cat even though she sort of smelled like tuna. Once Duchess started to squirm, Chicot let her go, gently putting her on the bed. Duchess immediately turned around for ear scratches.

"Want me to help run lines?" Elijah pointed towards the script Chicot had brought in.

"Yeah," Chicot said. "I need to try my absolute best. And it will be a good distraction."

Elijah nodded, putting his phone aside so he could pick up the script. Chicot settled on the bed next to him, at first reading her lines and then looking at the ceiling as she tried to remember them without looking. Eventually, Chicot stood up, needing the book less so she started to play with Duchess as Elijah said Elvis's or Monty's lines to her, and she would respond with her own.

She only had a week before they had to finalize the blocking. Luckily, they could meet often, and Lyza was always there with them, an umbrella to shield her from the sun as she held the script and gave them notes. Monty even warmed up to everything as the week went on, meeting with Chicot and Elijah at their RV to run lines on Thursday while Lyza and Elvis were at the doctor. They sat in camp chairs under their measly, old sunshade, drinking lemonade and having Elijah fill in for Elvis's part.

In the afternoon sun, things were easier. Monty laughed at Elijah and Chicot's antics between reads and joked about her skirt getting in the way of her trying to practice certain movements. She was soft, Chicot noticed, and her demeanor was quiet. However, when Monty did speak, it was usually happy and gentle, even when she was correcting Chicot or giving her notes. Her critiques were careful, constructive, and kind. It made Chicot's chest feel like it was made of wax, slowly melting in the early July sun as Monty helped Chicot remember blocking or where to tuck her sword so she wouldn't hit Monty or Elvis accidentally. Elijah seemed to notice it, too, notably making himself absent to make more lemonade. Then he'd come back and they'd force him to play Elvis's part again.

Without Elvis, practice was casual, and even if they needed to get serious, this was important too. Chicot's entire being relaxed, and so did Monty's, the two of them exchanging jokes over Elijah's head or at his expense. Sometimes, something self-deprecating would slip through, and Monty would assure Chicot it wasn't true.

They were still outside their RV when Elvis and Lyza returned from the doctor, the early evening sun just starting to dip low in the sky. It wasn't dusk yet, and it wouldn't be for a few more hours. Lyza's eyes were red around the rims as they approached, a smile cracking on her face the moment Chicot raised her hand to wave at them. Monty stood up, going to meet them, but Lyza waved for her to stay where she was, her and Elvis joining the group even though they were out of chairs. They still managed to be in the shade, and that was what was most important.

"Good news, the baby is great." Lyza laughed softly, tears coming to her eyes as she said it. "I'm 9 weeks along, but the doctor is worried about the strain from the acrobatics. He said I should probably stop after this weekend and focus on aerobic exercise."

"Here, sit, have some lemonade." Elijah stood, and Chicot immediately started to help him coax Lyza into his seat. Before Elijah could get the pitcher and pour Lyza her own glass, Monty simply handed Lyza hers. Lyza took a large swig, her face scrunching.

"Thank you." Lyza was actively crying now, wiping tears from her face. "You all are so sweet."

Elvis sighed softly. "Really, thank you all. This would be much harder without you three being so supportive."

"It's okay," Monty said. "We just have to be ready for Chicot to take your spot by next week, right? Which we've been preparing for from the start, just in case."

Monty looked at Chicot, who promptly nodded in agreement.

"And I'll be ready, I promise." Chicot leaned toward Lyza slightly, still holding her lemonade in one hand as Elijah and Elvis stood over the three of them.

Lyza hiccupped, another sob rocking her shoulders. Monty grasped at the air with one hand, as though she could find a way to grab the words she wanted out of thin air. They all blinked at her, Chicot pressing her lips together because she wasn't sure how to react.

"Sorry!" Lyza trembled, crying and laughing simultaneously somehow. "I'm just so lucky to have you all."

"God, you had me worried." Monty nudged Lyza gently. Elvis then swept them all into a big group hug, much to both Monty's and Chicot's dismay.

"Okay, okay." Monty dragged herself away. "We only have another week. Let's get back to practicing."

Elvis and Chicot agreed, and all five of them walked out to the field to find a place where they could run the show again. Chicot chewed on her nails as they did, her mind wandering until they had finished clearing away any rocks or sticks that could potentially hurt them.

The second weekend of the faire was a blur for Chicot, her focus during the day on her show with Elijah and getting patrons to come see it, while her nights were consumed by *The Pirates Three* and managing to play Wee by next weekend. They dedicated their entire two hours of gym time to it, which meant Chicot and Elijah had to find another time to practice. Elijah seemed unbothered, but Chicot still asked him probably thirty times if he was really okay with it. By the time Friday came, Chicot was feeling better, but she still had that strange feeling that the first show would be messy somehow. Every time it came to mind, Chicot would repeat to herself that the audience probably wouldn't notice even if it was.

Luckily, *The Pirates Three* went on before her and Elijah, so Chicot would have some time between shows. This meant all her costume pieces were now stored in the backstage area, which Monty and Lyza had helped her organize. Monty had even found an old clothing rack in their RV that they stuck in one corner so Chicot could hang her costume on it properly, rather than using the pegs that were already there that could damage her costume over time.

She learned quickly that she should have been more worried about being on stage without a mask on. The first time she got up there alongside Elvis and Monty, Chicot nearly puked. She spent the entire show narrowly making her lines and marks, and the nerves never really shook off. Chicot still managed to do all the acrobatics correctly, her hand easily reaching the flag hoisted on the rope above the stage at the end. People cheered when she grabbed it, her smile getting wider as she stepped down from the lift, Monty and Elvis popping up beside her, their arms raised before they each grabbed one of Chicot's hands. The three of them bowed together, people excitedly approaching the front of the stage to fill their tip baskets as Elvis reminded them to tip their performers.

Chicot spoke with kids who handed off their parents' money and thanked her for the show. None of the adults seemed to have noticed anything amiss, which made Chicot think that maybe things were going worse in her head than in reality.

Her thoughts were confirmed when they got backstage, and Monty and Elvis clapped Chicot on the back and congratulated her. They both told her how well she'd done, and she looked for wavers in their grins or sneers in their words, but she didn't find any. Monty especially made a point to stop her and tell her that she would only improve, which made the whole thing feel even more genuine. Chicot hadn't been perfect, but they hadn't been hoping for that.

It eased her mind, and her show with Elijah went off without a hitch. Their second shows went even better, the pirates really coming together as Chicot reminded herself that she was trying to be present, not perfect.

After her second show with Elijah, there was time on the schedule for them to all eat, and then they were released into the faire to advertise. Lyza took over when walking around with a sign with the times that *The Pirates Three: Big, Middle, and Wee* were on stage, while Chicot carried her own for *The Bard & Jester: Forever at Odds.*

She kept her mask on as she walked through the crowded avenues along the food stalls. Men stood shirtless in the summer heat, basketball shorts and baseball caps on as they held beers or fruity themed drinks. People in costume milled about—fairies and armored men, people wearing leather masks that looked like animals, and even some people in full fur suits, heat be damned. Chicot could barely handle a plastic mask, let alone a furry one, but she had to respect their dedication to their vibe.

People asked her for pictures, took photos of her sign, and when she put it down, she made balloon animals for kids and did jigs with people in dirndls. Fully covered and getting to follow someone meandering through the faire as she walked on her hands just to see their surprise and hear their delighted giggles when they turned around had become a favorite of hers. Someone offered her a flower, a few people tried to give her trinkets, but she turned them down with a few gestures about not having pockets even though she had a belt bag. It was full of balloons anyway.

When she returned to the break area in the center of the faire, Chicot was bouncing with every step. The large, old trees formed an extra barrier from the sun, and on all sides, the tall backs of stages or shops blocked them in. It was like a forest clearing in the chaos, with picnic tables set out for performers and workers to sit at. She didn't see Elijah or any of the pirates, but she was mostly there for water, so she just slipped her mask off and headed to the far side, where there were several large cooler jugs of ice water set out for them. Each was bright orange, and Chicot could see where they once had a brand name on them, but they were long gone by now. She unscrewed the top of her water bottle, waiting in line behind a few other performers.

"God, and what is going on with the pirates?" The voice cut clear across the break zone. A group sat around a picnic table near the water, their salads and sandwiches spread out in front of them. At the center was who Chicot was fairly certain was Brewhilda, her pointy hat giving her away. She wasn't the one talking, though. It was the woman next to her; the one who played the music for Brewhilda's show. Chicot only recognized her because she wore a headband with a mini witch's hat on her head. She had her eyes on a crowd that looked riveted by whatever gossip she had.

"To replace someone in a tried-and-true act with someone so green." The woman shook her head slightly. "And those cheerleading moves they're using? What are they trying to do? Make the pirate show appeal more to the normies?"

The group laughed, and Chicot tried not to turn her gaze toward them. It wasn't worth it, like the girls on the cheerleading squad who had thought she'd gotten on because the coach pitied her or the football players who would jeer at her whenever she'd rejected them, calling her a lesbian like it was an insult. Chicot didn't need to rise to this. She was better than this. Chicot knew that for certain.

"I doubt they're trying to appeal to anyone specific. They're still doing a pirate show. They can't be following the trends." Brewhilda's voice was slick and cool. "If I had to guess, they replaced Lyza because she's done something stupid, like get pregnant."

This caused a series of gasps, and Chicot finally broke, glancing over her shoulder at them. There was a wave of whispers, all of them leaning toward each other, asking questions, each of them trying to confirm if anyone had any evidence of whether or not Lyza was really out of the show because she was pregnant. As they did this, Brewhilda's lip curled, her bright blue eyes moving from the group to Chicot. Chicot put her water bottle under the spigot, pressing the button and watching it fill, training her face so that it was blank, like she hadn't heard anything.

"Shame on you." The voice was sharp and low in tone, coming from Ken the sausage stand man of all people, the bedazzled sausage on the front of his tunic sparkling slightly. He sat at the picnic table next to Brewhilda's group, his face twisted in disgust and his brow furrowed low over his eyes. "You shouldn't be gossiping about things like someone being pregnant."

Chicot met Ken's eyes, a knot forming in her stomach. She should have said something. They were her friends. Pretending to be above all of this didn't really help. She knew that. But Ken was there. She was no longer alone. If only she had something good to say. She stepped away from the water cooler, moving toward towards Ken's table because that felt safer than approaching Brewhilda's.

"Damn, even the sausage stand guy has better morals than all of you," Chicot said. Ken's eyes bulged as she said it, and for a moment, Chicot felt her heart hammering in her ears. The group surrounding Brewhilda clammed up as Brewhilda's nostrils flared, her elbows going out wide as she slammed her hands on the table. It made Chicot jump, but she continued walking towards Ken.

"If she can't perform, their show should be cut and replaced with the next available," Brewhilda snapped. "That's what other faires do. That's why we're talking about it."

Ken's eyes went from Brewhilda to Chicot, wide and brown, his lips pressed into a tight "O". Chicot's stomach turned, a shiver running down her back, and she said the only thing she could think of. She couldn't be too mouthy, as she didn't know what kind of connections at other faires Brewhilda had. If she wasn't careful, this could ruin everything for her and Elijah.

"That isn't very punk rock of you." It sounded so goddamn stupid as it came out of her mouth. "Favoring cutthroat competition between performers and tearing down other women."

There, that sounded better. She wasn't sure it entirely made sense, but she knew one thing: Brewhilda used a medieval punk sound in all of her shows, and even if Chicot wasn't usually one to call out posers, if Brewhilda used that—which even Chicot had to admit was pretty fun—she should at least adhere to some of the morals and politics associated. After all, Brewhilda ran around talking about how much she liked punk music, but it wasn't very punk to shit talk other women down for getting pregnant or doing better than her.

Chicot was pretty sure she said the right thing when Ken smiled at her. He then turned to Brewhilda, his brows nearly in his hairline, goading her into saying anything further. Brewhilda ground her teeth so hard, Chicot swore she could hear it. She then hissed about needing to make her next show and stood up. Chicot took that as her chance to stop next to Ken's table, her fingers trembling as she tried not to completely panic. If Brewhilda didn't hate her already, she certainly did now, and even if Chicot felt righteous air fill her lungs and puff up her chest, she was still afraid of the consequences of what she'd just done. But *The Pirates Three* had to have more sway than Brewhilda. They could probably help if Brewhilda tried to add her to some sort of blacklist.

After she finished her water, she pulled her mask from her belt. Before she could get it on, Ken was at her side, his reddish-brown skin shiny from the layer of sweat none of them could escape and his full lips turned up.

"That was, and I don't say this often, *amazing*." Ken patted her on the back. "Good job."

Chicot curled in on herself, her lips quivering. She was safe. No one could see them at this point. "It didn't sound stupid?"

"Eh, a little." Ken shrugged. "But you were *right* and she couldn't refute that."

"Thanks." Chicot smiled, "Uh, Ken, right?"

Ken nodded. "That's me."

"Is she always like that?" Chicot asked. Ken laughed, shrugging his shoulders.

"I don't know, but she doesn't tip when she gets food from any of the vendors here, so take that as you will." Ken smiled, his cheeks round and soft and his eyes a pretty, almost perfect oval shape. Wide by the bridge of his nose and tapered at the ends with long eyelashes. She could see when Elijah liked him so much. He was handsome with a soft jawline and chubby cheeks that exuded happiness. Chicot couldn't help but grin back at him, nodding.

"Noted," Chicot said. "And thanks for the help."

"No problem." Ken winked. "Always happy to be the sausage stand guy with good morals."

Chicot laughed, falling forward slightly. "Not a bad thing to be."

"Not at all," Ken said. "Have a good rest of your day, okay? Stay hydrated."

"You too." Chicot smiled. Ken then paused, sheepishly adjusting his sparkly tunic.

"Oh, uh, and do you and Elijah maybe want to come to a party next Sunday night?" he asked. "I was hoping Elijah would go. It might be better if you ask him about it."

"I think it would go fine if you asked him," Chicot said. This seemed to shock but also excite Ken. "But I'll let him know. Who else will be there? Mostly food vendors or … ?"

"I invited a lot of the performers too." Ken waved at the table where Brewhilda and crew had been sitting. "Not them."

Chicot tapped her toe on the ground. "Monty, Lyza, and Elvis?"

"Yeah." Ken confirmed. "And there's a pool. Monty said she's excited to swim. I can send you the address if you're interested."

"Oh good." Chicot wasn't even sure why he called out Monty specifically, but she did think Monty would be cute in a swimsuit. Her mind also brought her directly to thoughts of seeing Monty's very … *nice* chest on display. Chicot wanted to see her cleavage again. She should probably try to learn some shame before next weekend.

"So, you and Elijah will be there?" Ken asked.

"I'm sure we will. Text the address to Elijah though. I don't have a phone." Chicot smiled, and Ken excitedly confirmed, telling her how good that was and how he was excited. He then realized he was five minutes over on his break and literally ran away from her. She just put her mask back on and headed for the stage.

CHAPTER 8

There was renewed vigor backstage as Chicot got her pirate outfit on. For some reason, Monty and Elvis were singing some nursery rhyme and high-fiving each other a lot. Chicot didn't question it. She simply absorbed the energy in the room as she pulled on her gear and tied a bandana around her hair.

Monty took a step toward Chicot after she finished with the bandana. "Here, this will look better."

She slipped her fingers into Chicot's hair, tugging on it gently so she could pull parts out of the bandana. Chicot couldn't really tell what this accomplished, only that Monty's fingers felt nice and Ken's comment about swimming was ringing in her ears. When she finished, Monty held up a mirror, and Elvis whistled.

Whatever Monty had done, it meant Chicot's hair, which had been bullied by her jester hood, now hung in an artful mess around her face. It made her look boyish in a good way, androgynous and young and ready to strike out on the open sea. This was exactly what Wee had become for their version of the show.

"Wow," Chicot said. "You're good at this."

Monty pursed her lips. "I've just had short hair for a long time. I know what works."

Then, they stepped on stage together, bantering as they set up, much like they would with Lyza. This time, after Elvis made his usual short jokes about Chicot, he added:

"And the poor thing can't even do her own hair!" He gestured at Monty. "Our resident tough lady pirate had to do it. That's Middle, if you didn't know!"

Monty threw her head back and laughed, the crowd roaring in agreement. Chicot responded like she would in the jester costume, because she wasn't so great at spoken improv yet, and shook her head, letting her hair flop around. The crowd seemed to like this too, and after the show went off well, the three of them laughed with Lyza—who had been waiting for them backstage—about it. She was often there between shows, sitting on the crate and swinging her legs as they all talked.

"For some reason, I thought you were about to call me 'our resident lesbian' on stage," Monty said. Elvis snorted, throwing his head back as another chortle came out of him. Chicot grinned at the noise, pulling up her jester hood and looking at the small mirror they'd hung on the wall to straighten the points.

"I know better than that!" Elvis looked at Monty and grinned. Chicot could see them in the mirror.

"I know, but once it was in my head, it took me a second to realize you said lady pirate." Monty slipped her bandana off since she had to change for the final show of the day, where they used lit torches for their juggling, rather than daggers. It was a requirement that whatever she wore be fire retardant, which to Chicot seemed fair. She then waited for Elijah, who would probably turn up shortly. He'd decided to continue to promote for them until *The Pirates Three* were finished, since Chicot couldn't.

"Well, we could call you our resident bisexual disaster on stage if you'd like." Lyza gently kicked the crate she was sitting on with her heel. "It would be accurate."

"No, thank you!" Monty threw her hands up in the air, laughing as she looked at Chicot. "Can you believe these two?"

Monty was doing this more often now, including Chicot in their bickering. It seemed to be a subtle way of saying they had actually become friends. Chicot shrugged though.

"Seems about right for siblings." Chicot hopped on one foot as she put her jester shoes back on.

"See, Chicot agrees." Monty smirked at Lyza, nudging her as Lyza stuck her tongue out at Monty. Chicot shook her head, tying the laces on the backs of her shoes as they continued to bicker.

"Chicot!" Elijah burst through the door, causing them all to jump, Chicot in particular because she'd been standing closest to it.

"What?" Chicot drew her arms in close, like she was about to get yelled at by her mom. Elijah closed the door behind him, then reached out for Chicot, setting his hands on her cheeks.

"What did you say to Brewhilda?" Elijah asked. Chicot scrunched up her face, waving him off so she didn't have to have this conversation in front of Lyza. She didn't need to know the hurtful things that Brewhilda said.

"Nothing really," Chicot started. They all stared at her now, Monty in particular looking between Chicot and Elijah. Lyza bit her lip, worrying it as her large eyes darted over Chicot.

"Well, she's reporting it to the director, so it's not *nothin'*." Elijah put his hands on his hips, letting Chicot pull away from him. She pressed her lips into a hard line, glancing once toward Lyza, trying to signal to Elijah that it was *about her*.

"Ken can tell you the details," Chicot added. "But it was really nothing that serious. I don't think the director will be mad."

"He probably won't," Lyza said quickly. "Brewhilda makes at least one complaint like that a season."

Elijah sighed, looking at Lyza and then at Chicot again. It seemed like he'd noticed the way that Chicot had looked at her, so maybe he'd drop it. He patted her on the shoulder, the small wooden space suddenly feeling so much tighter as everyone stared at her.

"I believe you," Elijah said. "But try not to get us into any trouble, yeah?"

"I won't." Chicot bowed her head. "Promise."

Elijah settled down as Elvis and Lyza started to placate him further with other stories of Brewhilda telling the director about this or that. Monty stood in the corner, her arms crossed as she watched Chicot, eyes narrowed. Luckily, there wasn't really time for her to stop Chicot before she had to be on stage with Elijah. The two of them had their crate and table in hand before Elvis even had his stilts fully ready, so Chicot narrowly escaped whatever conversation Monty wanted to have.

After they'd finished their show, Elijah left her backstage to get the details of what happened with Brewhilda from Ken. She was still organizing their props when Monty slipped through the back door, standing in front of it once it was closed.

"Okay, so what did Brewhilda say?" Monty asked. Chicot held her ruffled jester collar in front of her like a shield. When she didn't answer, Monty tapped her foot impatiently and told her to spit it out, so Chicot sighed.

"She said something nasty about Lyza." Chicot made quotation marks with her hands. "Something like, 'she probably did something stupid, like getting pregnant.' Which, I know Lyza is pregnant, but it's not like Lyza's openly telling people that yet, and Brewhilda was being mean."

Monty's throat bobbed and she set her jaw, looking down her nose at Chicot. "And what did you say?"

"Well, Ken from the sausage stand called them out for gossiping about someone being pregnant first." Chicot rubbed the back of her head, then stopped herself for fear of pulling her hood down accidentally. "Then I called them out for having worse morals than the sausage stand guy."

Monty's lip quirked up at the side, but her jaw was still firmly set. Chicot could even see her muscles flexing under her skin.

"Was that all?" Monty asked.

"Pretty much." For some reason, Chicot wasn't afraid. Monty ground her teeth, her shoulders squared. But Chicot hadn't attracted her ire. That anger was directed elsewhere. *Which, reasonable,* Chicot thought. Brewhilda had said something pretty fucked up.

"Okay." Monty released her fists, wiggling her fingers for a moment before she looked at Chicot. "Sorry, thank you for telling me."

"Of course." Chicot shrugged. "It was nothing, but Monty? Don't do anything stupid."

Monty froze. After a moment, she shook her head, raising her open palms at Chicot.

"I'm not going to," Monty said. "I just needed to know."

Chicot nodded and finished getting her belt flag on. She stepped out into the faire again, her mask on and her bag full of tricks. She stayed fairly close to the stage in the afternoons, not wanting to stray too far since she had a shorter break between shows.

When she returned, Monty was already backstage, carefully setting her stilts between two studs on the wall so they wouldn't fall over. Chicot just started to change, the two of them getting ready for their next show in a comfortable silence. Soon after, Elvis appeared in the doorway, the three of them quickly finding their rhythm again, and they didn't lose it the rest of the weekend. The shows flew by, and Chicot fully got things down and polished out the last of the rough edges at practice the next week. The summer started moving much faster, maybe faster than Chicot wanted it to.

CHAPTER 9

It was over a hundred degrees, and as such, most of the dog park were hiding in their air conditioning. It was Tuesday, so it wasn't like anyone had to work, and those who took the chance to film content or practice had left and come back already. Her and Elijah had finished *The Hound of the Baskervilles* halfway through the day, leaving them with even less to do than normal. Chicot played with Duchess until the cat grew bored and refused to chase anything, and Elijah tuned his lute over and over until he couldn't anymore.

Finally, once the sun had been down for a while, they started to hear people outside. Some lit fires, sitting around them in small groups and chatting as they drank cans of beer or from red Solo cups. Chicot herself had been sipping a very fake margarita during dinner that Elijah had made with a mix and some awful tequila they'd had lying around. It had been the last of their bad alcohol at least. If they wanted any more this week, they'd have to drink the good stuff.

Chicot stepped out of the cool RV interior to find the soupy air still angry and assaulting anyone standing in it for too long. She picked up the bug spray they kept on a small ledge under the attached sunshade of their RV and sprayed herself down, the caustic smell making her cough and debate whether getting bitten was maybe worth it.

"Hey, little jester friend!" The voice rose from a few RVs away, a small group of older performers sitting around a fire pit that was putting out more smoke than fire. It probably kept the mosquitos away, which was for the best. "Come here a moment!"

Chicot's eyes wandered over the group in the dim glow of the string lights until she realized where the voice was coming from. Her fingertips began to tingle as she pointed at herself, slowly walking toward the performers, who grinned brightly at her. In the dark, it was hard for her to tell who was calling her over, and the thought of getting one of their names wrong or mixing them up with someone else made her skin crawl worse than the bug spray. She could feel every bit of fabric she was wearing as she was approaching, a layer of sweat forming on her skin that wasn't just due to the heat.

"Yes, you!" the one who'd called to her confirmed, waving for Chicot to join them. She only realized who was speaking to her once she got closer. The red bandana around Sunnie's head seemed, thankfully for her, to be a universal constant. He wore it in all his shows, and really all the time. Even when Chicot had seen Sunnie perform when she'd been a kid, he'd had a similar bandana wrapped around his head. The ladies were harder for Chicot, none of them wearing anything particularly identifiable right off the bat.

Sunnie gestured to a red camp chair. Chicot sat and fidgeted with the hem of her shirt. They were not likely about to lecture her about the fact that her and Elijah took Brewhilda's spot. And Chicot was certain when Sunnie started to introduce everyone.

Two of the women were in the infamous *Laundry Ladies* show, which had a lot of crowd work in it, and an equally infamous older woman whose performance involved poetry and tea. She'd been at Albion for decades, and there weren't many people as old as her performing either. Regardless, they were all so open to Chicot, waving excitedly as Sunnie introduced them, all of them with drinks in hand as Sunnie offered Chicot a cold can of beer.

"Umm, thank you." Chicot offered Sunnie a polite smile, unsure what to do with herself. She wasn't sure she had ever seen Sunnie this closely before. In fact, she had only ever seen him off stage in passing. But she'd been enamored ever since.

He still wore his hair roughly the same, with long bangs in his face that he used the bandana to keep in check. Sunnie grinned back at her, his smile splitting his rich terracotta skin and making his round cheeks more pronounced. He had large, dark brown eyes and black hair with edges of gray here and there, sections slowly turning with age. His voice had a nice tenor, though it was strange to hear him talk since he didn't speak at all during his shows. He whistled and pantomimed, but still spoke to the audience more effectively than anyone who used words.

Chicot wanted to be just like him. She'd practiced pantomime alone in her room for hours when she'd been a kid. She'd used it to make the other cheerleaders laugh, and she did it whenever they were at children's birthday parties. It only occurred to her right then and there that she'd managed to really "make it," as they said. She was now doing an act where she didn't say a word on stage at the Albion Renaissance Faire. When had she celebrated that? She should do something special.

"Of course, Chicot." Sunnie sipped his drink. "We just wanted to speak with you since you and Elijah are so new."

Chicot hadn't expected him to know her name. She couldn't help but grin genuinely as he said it, a glow starting to come from her chest, making her sit straighter.

"Yes, and you two are *so* funny!" one of the Laundry Ladies added. The other agreed.

"It's always exciting when the new hires are so talented," Sunnie said. "And of course, us clowns have to stick together."

He nudged Chicot's arm gently, and it rocked her as if she were an unsecured fence post. Sheepish, Chicot held her can of beer with both hands. The layer of nervous sweat on her was dissipating, in favor of a soft, bright sense of security she hadn't felt in a long time. Goose bumps rose on her arms, her eyes glancing over the other performers surrounding her. This felt good.

"Thank you," Chicot said. "That means a lot to me."

The four older performers all shared a rosy look.

"You should be really proud," the older woman encouraged. It was so strange to see her without her hat full of trinkets on.

"What made you start?" the second of the Laundry Ladies asked.

"Oh, well." Chicot rubbed the side of her neck, looking down at her feet. None of them commented on her fidgeting, which settled Chicot. "Sunnie, actually. I saw you when I was a kid and just decided this was for me."

Sunnie flipped his hair back, his chin high as he said, "You have good taste."

The first of the Laundry Ladies swatted his arm gently, a laugh coming out of her. Sunnie laughed just as much, and for a moment, Chicot pictured her and Elijah like this. Older, happy, still in the faire circuit. It sounded good. They just needed to get into more faires.

"Also," Sunnie started. "I'm curious how you wound up in *The Pirates Three*."

"Well …" Chicot wasn't sure what she could say about Lyza's pregnancy, as she wasn't telling people widely yet. Squinting, Chicot tried to think of a way to put it. "Well, Lyza couldn't perform and they needed help. So, when they asked me, it just seemed like the right thing to do."

That felt diplomatic enough, however, the looks the four much older performers exchanged after she'd said it made her shiver with nerves. The fire let off a good amount of light, so she could see them all clearly, but their expressions were hard for her to read now. As the buzzing of AC units filled her ears, she feared she'd said too much or too little, or maybe she'd said the wrong thing entirely. Her grip on her beer tightened, the can crunching quietly.

"So, you've got the most important part of being a performer down already then." Sunnie slapped her on the back, patting her quickly as she shook. The second Laundry Lady told him to be gentler with Chicot, but they were all grinning now. Chicot couldn't tell what about.

"Huh?" She was still vibrating from where Sunnie had hit her. Sunnie threw his head back and laughed, nudging her again.

"Community," Sunnie said. He held his arms out, gesturing at the many RVs and trailers surrounding them. "We're here to help each other."

"Oh." Chicot felt that small sparkle come back to her. Her fingers felt tingly, so she tightened her grip on her can, sitting up straighter as she smiled. "Well, that just seems obvious, right?"

"Not to everyone," the older woman answered. Her eyes flickered to an RV, but Chicot couldn't tell exactly which one. Chicot bit her lip, thinking of the way Brewhilda had spoken about Lyza. She was the type that these four didn't like. Though, that made Chicot wonder why people had seemed so standoffish to her and Elijah at first. Maybe they hadn't been. Maybe Chicot had just been anxious, or maybe they'd been. Funny, the thought that a bunch of people who earned their living on stage in front of strangers could be so afraid of each other.

"Listen, you've got a great show and a good sense for the people to hang out with." Sunnie set a warm hand on her shoulder. "You can relax. You're doing good things."

Chicot's shoulders went slack, her head turning to truly face Sunnie. "Thanks, Sunnie. I just hope we can keep getting spots at faires."

Sunnie looked at the three women sitting around the fire with him. "Maybe I can help you? With your pantomiming. We are both silent clowns, after all."

"Really?" Chicot perked up. The chance to work with Sunnie sounded amazing. It was the kind of dream even her brain couldn't come up with.

"Yes! I love teaching people who are dedicated, and you obviously are," he said. "We can start next week. I'll find a time that works for us to practice in the field. Before the sun is high, of course."

Chicot nodded quickly. She was fairly certain she would be free, and if she wasn't, she'd make herself free. Chicot happily bobbed her head and listened to the four of them talk a while longer. They all told her to make sure to tell Elijah how good he was for them and how excited they were to have them at the faire. Then, Chicot left to go about her actual reason for being outside.

She followed the pebble-lined path out of the dog park and slowly made her way through the massive open field of grass it sat in. There was a fence that ran around the entirety of Albion, protecting the grounds from anyone who might try to sneak in, during the day or otherwise. Chicot walked along it, just looking to get her fidgety cabin fever out. They didn't have a car, so it wasn't like they could go to a gym or store like many of the others did during the day to occupy themselves. This meant her options for outside time were blazing sun, which would assuredly result in a burn, or cool moonlight, which meant mosquitos. Chicot would take the mosquito bites any day, and with enough DEET lotion, she really didn't get that many.

Dark, puffy clouds hung in small clusters, blocking out the stars and moon, but it was hard to see the stars anyway. Even though they were in a large field, the neighborhood and highways around them provided enough light pollution to make them hard to see. When she rounded the corner of the faire grounds and could no longer see the dog park, she did a couple of cartwheels in the soft grass along the fence. Once she'd done that, she ran a few tumbles, just exercising her usual muscles. If Lyza had seen her doing this, she would have told her not to do it in the grass where there might be rocks. She was already such a mom to anyone younger than her. Lyza and Elvis were going to make good parents.

Chicot stood from a back handspring and sighed. She let herself imagine what it would be like to have someone like Lyza as a parent. Chicot would be loved and doted on. They probably wouldn't have a lot of money, but Chicot's family never really did anyway, and she probably would have never been given an ultimatum about her bisexuality. She was fairly certain this would have been the superior family situation for her. People who didn't think she was weird for wanting to learn contortion or act like a mime. A mother who didn't find out she'd just broken up with her first girlfriend from community college and threatened to kick her out instead of comforting her.

She picked her way through the taller grass along the tree line on the north side of the faire grounds, looking for frogs that had escaped the large pond inside the faire so she could nudge them back inside. There weren't many out as far as she could tell. They had probably retreated on instinct into deeper waters to stay cool during the day and therefore had not made their it all the way out of the fence that day. So, with no frogs to rescue, Chicot hummed to herself and thought about home. It was ill-advised thing, but she did it anyway. At least her mind was mostly on the duck pond, where she'd picked up frogs as a kid. She touched the tall prairie grass that had been planted there, as she was fairly certain it wasn't native to Wisconsin, and hummed "Puzzle Pieces" by LEMON BOY to herself.

"Evening." Elvis's voice was smooth and even, a Tupperware container under his arm. He was coming from the other direction, on a walk of his own, but now he settled on a bench under some trees. As Elvis moved and adjusted, a small lantern hooked to his belt blinked at Chicot, surrounding him in a firelight-like glow. He smiled at her, waving for Chicot to join him. She smiled back, her humming ending as she approached.

"Evening." Chicot walked over to meet him. "What are you doing out here?"

"Just"—Elvis glanced toward the fence that surrounded the faire and lowered his voice—"enjoying some gardening. Would you care to join?"

Pot, Chicot filled in quickly. She shook her head, sitting.

"Nah," she said. "But I'll keep you company."

Elvis nodded, his Tupperware now open as he pulled out a grinder. He made quick work of packing the bowl, and soon they were surrounded by the sweet and acrid smell of marijuana. Normally, Chicot would have been interested, but with how hot it had been, she didn't want to add cotton mouth to her list of issues.

"You know." Elvis blew smoke out slowly. "We have a spot at the Pennsylvania Renaissance Faire after this."

"You do?" Chicot's head turned quickly. Elvis's smile was broad, and for a moment Chicot couldn't help but wonder if he'd had braces, as his nearly perfectly straight teeth glinted in the lantern light.

"Yep." Elvis pressed his lips together. "Not sure what we're going to do yet. We want to talk with you and Elijah about it once we have a plan."

Chicot didn't need to hear it. Her mind immediately filled in the blank. If Lyza couldn't perform, they probably couldn't take the slot. The show likely wouldn't work right without a third, so they were really stuck.

"We submitted a video to Pennsylvania but never heard back." Chicot looked out at the field, pulling her legs up to wrap her arms around her knees. "I don't think we got in."

"It's a tough one." Elvis sighed. "It took us a few years to get a spot."

"I'm worried getting into Albion was a novelty already. You don't have to make it worse." Chicot grimaced, no actual malice directed at Elvis as he took a long drag from his pipe. He shook his head as he blew the smoke out, being careful not to blow it directly at Chicot.

"It's not," Elvis shifted the lighter in his fingers, fidgeting with it. "You two are good. Really good."

Chicot sighed. "Everyone keeps saying that, but that hasn't gotten us another callback."

"But you have gotten a job, and now you have a reference." Elvis let his hand rest against his thigh, pipe still carefully cradled in it. Chicot sighed again, more dramatically this time in hopes she wouldn't have to communicate to Elvis that she didn't want to talk about this anymore. He seemed to take the hint, not saying anything more for a while.

"How are you feeling?" Chicot broke the silence. "About everything?"

"Ungodly terrified about being a dad." Elvis picked up his pipe again, pausing with it near his lips to ready his lighter. "And ungodly relieved that you came to our rescue."

"I didn't really." Chicot watched as he pressed the pipe to his lips. She could see Elvis side-eyeing her in the light of the flame, and for a moment, one brow rose high while the other formed a ridge over his left eye. His barrel chested, stocky form smoking a pipe and smiling as he did made Chicot pictured him like Pippin or Merry from *The Lord of The Rings*. Maybe a bit cliche, but in his T-shirt and basketball shorts, it just sort of suited him. If she'd looked down and seen he had large, hairy feet, she wouldn't have been surprised at all.

"Okay, maybe I did," Chicot conceded. "But you don't have to fall at my feet. I hope you all know that."

Elvis lowered his pipe again.

"You know, I think Monty likes you quite a lot." Smoke escaped his lips as he spoke.

Chicot felt a whole new rush of energy go through her, her back straightening and her fingers drumming on the seat of the bench. She looked at her feet, biting her lip as she was caught between giddy and something unmistakably terrifying. Monty, Elvis, and Lyza might be moving on to Pennsylvania after this, and Chicot only knew that she wanted nothing more than to do the same. However, the only concrete plans she had were to stay with Elijah in the RV and a dentist appointment she'd scheduled for right after the season at Albion was over, so she could get it out of the way before they moved on. She leaned forward, nearly folding herself in half. Her posture always devolved into something shrimp-like, as Elijah called it, while she was thinking of her future plans.

"Really? I thought she was putting up with me for Lyza's sake," Chicot admitted. A bark of laughter came out of Elvis as he sat back and looked at Chicot.

"She definitely isn't just putting up with you." Elvis shook his head. "Is that why you haven't been answering her texts?"

Chicot flinched back slightly, looking at him over her shoulder. Her fingers gripped the wood on either side of her knees, her cheek pressed against her shoulder as she stared at Elvis, trying to search his face for any signs that he was being disingenuous or sarcastic. Even in the dark, she could see the gentle purse of his lips and curious tilt of his head.

"What?" Chicot asked.

Elvis's brow wrinkled and he opened his mouth. Then, after a moment, he closed it. Then it opened again, and Chicot grew impatient.

"Elvis, I haven't had a working phone since May." Chicot gripped the seat of the bench harder. If Monty had been texting Elijah and he had not been relaying those messages to Chicot, well ... She wasn't sure what she would do about that. It didn't seem like Elijah at all, and even the thought of a betrayal like that made her skin sting.

"Ohhh." Elvis's speech was slowing down, a drawl coming out that wasn't usually there. It sounded Northern, like Minnesota or Canada.

"She has Elijah's number, right?" Chicot asked. This had to be some kind of genuine mistake and not something Elijah was doing intentionally. That wasn't like him.

"No, I think she's been texting you?" Elvis didn't really sound sure of himself. Chicot sighed softly, rubbing her temple.

"That's not possible since I don't have a number." Chicot stood up, setting a hand on her hip as she looked down at Elvis. Well, as down as she could. Even when he was sitting and she was standing, she didn't really have much height advantage.

"But she said you, not Elijah." Elvis pressed his lips together and shrugged. "Maybe I misunderstood. You should ask her."

That would be the adult and logical thing to do. But Chicot was still nervous. She didn't know what she wanted with Monty, and while she wanted to clear up any accidental insult her supposed nonresponse had caused, she also didn't want to string Monty along. Of course, Chicot hadn't been outright flirting with Monty. She had been playful and at times complimentary, but that didn't mean … Well, she didn't know what it didn't mean, and that was exactly the problem. Chicot needed to be sure before anything went further with Monty, but she also needed to know if Elijah was intentionally blocking her from speaking with her.

"Thanks, Elvis," Chicot said. "Umm, maybe don't mention this conversation to her until I can talk to Elijah?"

Elvis held up his palms. "I'm already meddling more than I meant to. I'll keep my mouth shut."

A chuckle broke out of Chicot's lips, running her hands through her hair. If it was a release of stress or frustration, she wasn't sure. Regardless, it came out of her, and it caused Elvis to grimace.

"I am sorry." Elvis rubbed the back of his head. "I usually try not to fuck with things like this."

Chicot drooped. "It's okay."

She wasn't mad at Elvis, just confused and a little hurt, and none of those things were Elvis's fault. Chicot could understand why Elijah might have wanted Chicot to stay unattached, especially from other performers. But still, this was low if it was true.

"I'll see you around?" Elvis asked.

"Yeah, see you. And thanks again, Elvis." Chicot started to walk back around the faire grounds, waving at him as she went. He waved back, his hand loose and fingers not fully open. He was relaxed, which was nice to see.

When Chicot got back to the RV, she had lost all nerve about asking Elijah directly what was going on with the texts and if it had been some sort of misunderstanding. It didn't help that when she walked in, Elijah was snoring loudly, and therefore Chicot had a good out for not bothering him. The next morning, however, she knew she had to spit it out. Mostly because Elijah immediately noticed something was weird with her, staring at her expectantly while they stood in their kitchen, eating their cereal.

"Okay." His voice was low, cracking slightly at the edges since this was the first time he'd spoken since waking. "What's going on, CoCo?"

He rarely called her that. Usually, it was only when he was genuinely worried about her. Like the time she'd had an allergic reaction to the laundry detergent they'd bought at Dollar Tree and had broken out in hives, only to then refuse to go to the ER. She'd been fine and had just needed some Allegra. Chicot stood by that choice. It had saved them thousands of dollars, and she'd only suffered for about twenty-four hours.

"Have you been …" Chicot wasn't sure how to ask, sighing as she set her cereal bowl on the counter. She didn't want to accuse him of anything, but she didn't see any other way. "Has an unknown number been texting you and saying it's for me?"

Elijah's nose scrunched, his spoon halfway to his mouth as he paused. "What? No, I don't think so."

He pulled out his phone immediately, looking at his text logs and then any that had been sorted into spam. Elijah shrugged, showing Chicot the messages.

"Why?" he asked. Chicot took his phone, looking the messages over slowly. This unfortunately meant she caught the tail end of whatever sexting was happening between Elijah and Ken, but the relief was worth the mild disgust. The tension even released from her shoulders. They'd been practically against her ears since Elvis had first mentioned this the night before.

"Nothing, I think Monty just has the wrong phone number." Chicot handed back his phone, rubbing her head. "Elvis said something about me not responding to her texts."

"Weird." Elijah picked his spoon back up, shoveling more Cheerios into his mouth. "But yeah, probably has the wrong number."

He shrugged, chewing on his breakfast as Chicot picked hers back up. She needed to eat.

Chicot nodded. "Anyway, now that we've cleared that up—"

"Why do you say that like it was more of a problem than you were letting on?" Elijah asked. Chicot ignored it.

"Guess who has a pantomime lesson with Sunnie next week?" Chicot set her hands on her hips, straightening her back, chin up, and beaming. Elijah perked up.

"Wait, like, Sunnie as in *Sunnie the Spectacular?*" Elijah asked. Chicot grinned, trying not to spill her cereal as she did.

"He caught me before I went on my walk last night," Chicot said, "and wound up offering."

"That's amazing, Chicot!" Elijah lowered his empty bowl, dropping his spoon in it, his big brown eyes wide with excitement. "I actually have something cool to share with you too."

"I know!" Chicot nearly squealed, but she managed to contain it. Instead, she hopped. "What's your show and tell?"

Elijah laughed, throwing his head back as he nudged her shoulder and he set his dishes in the sink. "Randy and May invited me to help with some new music for their Dungeons & Dragons themed show they're working on."

Randy and May both had their own individual performances, but also did a show together that involved rolling a large d20 and improvising music based on crowd input. Lyza had introduced them to Chicot and Elijah on opening day, and Elijah had been practicing with them on and off ever since.

"Really? That's great, Elijah." Chicot set her bowl in the sink and took both his hands in hers, the two of them shaking each other for a minute.

"Yeah!" Elijah nodded vigorously. "Now, we just have to get another audition."

"And we will," Chicot said, but her chest tightened with it. They'd already missed out on Pennsylvania and Georgia, and even Michigan. She knew she couldn't linger on it, but it crept up into the back of her throat no matter what she did.

"And we will." Elijah clutched Chicot's hands, his fingers trembling slightly. Neither of them acknowledged it because it felt like if they did, it would make their fears a reality. Elijah's mother would probably tell them to pray in the genuine way that a good Christian would. She'd told them she'd prayed for them to get the spot at Albion and had been so excited for them when they'd landed it that Chicot had a hard time feeling off put by the statement. It was different than when her mother had said that. Probably because whenever her mother had done it, it had been to change something about Chicot, not in hopes God would somehow help her succeed at something.

Either way, as she and Elijah continued to share their excitement about their new projects and lessons, Chicot couldn't help but think about their next audition. The faires that didn't already have a lineup of performers were rapidly approaching auditions, and if they didn't get one, Chicot didn't know what that meant for them. Maybe they needed someone to write a letter of recommendation? She didn't even know if faires did that, but Elvis had said they now had a reference. She wondered if he'd meant from *The Pirates Three* or the directors at Albion. Chicot would have to ask Elvis, so she put that on her list. They couldn't sustain themselves just on birthday parties either. They didn't pay well, nor were they consistent enough to support them. She couldn't go back to the gas station, even if it was only for the off season, so they'd have to do something.

CHAPTER 10

Chicot stood in the unforgiving, early evening sun with a tote bag containing her swimsuit and extra sunscreen just in case with Elijah next to her suffering equally. They already smelled of artificial coconut, and it was only going to get worse. She shuffled her feet in the grass, wondering why she'd bothered to shower after their last show when the sun just continued to be in the sky and make her sweat well into the evening. There were still cars in the lot, but it was clearing out for the day, the faire closing about an hour after their last show. Of course, to get all of the people out of the faire and then out of the parking took a lot much longer than that. Luckily, that was not the responsibility of the performers.

"July should be illegal," Chicot said. Elijah nodded, groaning softly as he started to wax poetic about how he loved the warmth of the sun, but it came at a cost he wasn't sure he could pay.

"Maybe I should incorporate that into the show." He tilted his head, chewing on the inside of his cheeks, which made the dimples on either side of his mouth more pronounced. Chicot just rolled her eyes, tempted to ask if he meant skin damage.

"I'm not sure when the sun is blazing down on you that you want to be reminded about it," Chicot mused.

Elijah snorted. "Good point.".

Ken pulled up in a chic electric sedan with the AC blasting not long after. Chicot threw herself into the back seat, lying out as if it would allow her body to cool off faster. Both Elijah and Ken chuckled in response.

"Sorry I'm late," Ken said. "Traffic getting to the liquor store was worse than I thought."

"It's no problem." Elijah waved his hand dismissively. Chicot, though, wanted to grumble that this only happened because Elijah had insisted on sprucing up in their RV between their last show and the party, rather than going with Ken to the store and changing at the house. He had offered, so she didn't see why they hadn't. She kept her mouth shut. Chicot didn't need to embarrass Elijah. Not yet at least.

"Still, I probably should have just told you to ride with Monty," Ken said. "They're already at the house and in the pool."

Chicot perked up, her eyes finding Ken's in the rearview mirror. She immediately looked literally anywhere else, folding her arms over her chest. He didn't need to tell her like that. It felt like he was implying something.

"Eh, no biggie." Elijah seemed unaware of what was happening with Chicot and Ken. "We'll ride with them next time."

Ken looked straight ahead again. "Well, my parents are going to the cabin again for the entire month of August, so I'll have the house to myself. I can have another party."

Chicot wrinkled her brow. She hadn't realized Ken lived with his parents. It wasn't all that uncommon among the local workers. It just always surprised her when anyone over twenty wasn't out on their own. But not everyone's mom had kicked them out at eighteen and had to have their dad convince her to let them back into the house. Chicot tried to remember that.

"Where's their cabin again?" Elijah asked.

"Up in the U.P.," Ken said. He glanced at Elijah as he pulled onto the highway. "They're up there kayaking."

"Huh." Chicot's lips curled into a smile. "So you've got the house to yourself?"

"Yeah, it's nice to feel independent since I still live at home at twenty-four. Even if it's just for a little while." Ken made eye contact with Chicot in the rearview mirror, his long lashes fluttering as he flashed a grin at her. "Oh! I meant to tell you both that I bought an ice cream cake for tonight."

"I also heard there was a keg of Spotted Cow," Elijah said. Ken shrugged.

"Yeah, that was Martina's doing. You know, the sausage stand girl." Ken smiled fondly. "She said it is not a proper party without more alcohol than we could ever consume."

"How many people will even be there?" Chicot asked.

"Not nearly enough to warrant a keg," he scoffed. Chicot and Elijah both laughed.

When they pulled into the small, log-cabin style house, Chicot had to wonder what Ken's parents' cabin looked like because frankly this looked like a cabin to her. The blacktop drive had heat rolling off it as she stepped out of the car, a small yard next to them displaying well-manicured grass with a tall evergreen tree in the center of it. Chicot rubbed the back of her neck, trying to keep the first wave of evening mosquitos off it as she followed Ken and Elijah to the front door. There were already a few cars parked around the area, but Chicot mostly took note of Monty's.

The house itself was a 70s build A-frame with an addition on it. Chicot had grown up around these houses, their reddish-brown paint standing out among the tall green trees that seemed to consume Northern Wisconsin. There weren't as many around Ken's family home as there had been in Chicot and Elijah's hometown, but the effect was mostly the same. Stepping through the front door led them directly into a small living room, a fireplace at one end and the entrance to the kitchen on the other, just as every house like this that Chicot had ever been in. The only difference was to the right, where there was normally only a set of stairs, a closed door stood with a sign taped to it which read in bold letters: "Master Suite, Do Not Enter." She looked at the photos of Ken and his parents on the walls as she followed him through the living room toward the back of the house. The kitchen opened to a large den that led out to a covered porch and pool deck, people already milling about or helping to set out food and drinks.

Chicot smiled as they stepped onto the porch, quickly losing track of Elijah and Ken as they were called over to a group of other food stand workers who were trying to tap the keg in the corner. Lyza immediately called through the screens to Chicot, sitting on the worn wooden deck built around the aboveground swimming pool.

"Go change! The water's nice." She grinned, and next to her, Elvis lounged on a lawn chair, his dark skin shining like smooth stones in the sun.

"Okay, I'll be out!" Chicot called. She asked the nearest person where the bathroom was, turning quickly once she'd been directed.

As she spun, she nearly ran into someone. They caught Chicot's shoulders, a familiar strawberry hair clip catching Chicot's attention, then her sandy blonde bob confirming who it was. Monty's hands were firm, stopping Chicot from tripping as she stumbled back. Chicot almost wished Monty had let her fall because then she wouldn't have been slack-mouthed staring at Monty's chest for any period of time. Instead, Monty kept her on her feet, and Chicot was left shamelessly looking down at her boobs and getting an eyeful of Monty's bare thighs. Chicot picked her eyes up, trying not to think about how soft Monty's skin was. Monty was damp, holding a canned margarita, and had on a bikini with frilly straps, a deep V at the front pressing her breasts into an immaculate chasm that Chicot sort of wanted to dive into. Underneath, there was a thick band that held them up, a cute pink-and-white checkered pattern that looked like a picnic blanket over the whole thing, including the bottoms, which were high waisted, her tummy creating a soft hill in the center of them before smoothing back down.

"Sorry!" Chicot held up her palms, trying to pretend like she hadn't just been ogling Monty. Then, she realized that it maybe best to just lean into it. Even if her face felt like it was hotter than the surface of the sun, she added, "Your suit is really cute."

Monty, to Chicot's surprise, lost the dimple that formed in her cheek whenever she was annoyed and frowned in a cute, slanted way as she blushed. People moved around them, slipping past as Chicot stared up at Monty. They were currently in the middle of the main walkway between the door to the backyard and the kitchen, but no one paid them any mind, getting their drinks and chatting as they enjoyed the party. Monty curled a hand around the top of the can she was holding, moving closer to Chicot to let someone behind her have more space to pass as she glanced down at herself.

"Oh, thank you." Monty's shoulders pulled in slightly. She glanced over her shoulder, taking a small step back once she knew she had room. "I was a little worried it was too frilly for me."

Chicot's mouth fell open as she took in this more nervous side of Monty. She had never seen her like this. Chicot took a step back, looking Monty up and down briefly, not really caring that they might be in the way of other people.

"Nope, not too frilly at all." Chicot only just realized there were also some frills on the edges of the bottoms, sliding over Monty's thighs. For a moment, she couldn't stop herself from imagining getting to slip her fingers under there. She had to remind herself they were at a party with people around, so she shouldn't let her mind wander too far. "And it really suits you."

Monty's cheeks shined as she smiled, her hips twisting from side to side to make the ruffles flutter, and then she giggled. It startled Chicot. When they were at the faire, Monty always presented herself as the strong, silent type, standing behind Lyza with a stone face while Lyza and Elvis grinned. Now, Chicot wanted to make Monty giggle as much as she could. It was maybe not the smartest thing to do when they were supposed to be working together and neither of them knew exactly where they were going after their season at Albion was finished, but Chicot wanted it anyway.

"Thanks, Chicot." Monty rolled back on her heels, feet bare as she played with a ruffle on her swimsuit. "Um, do you want a margarita? I can get you one while you change."

Chicot nodded quickly. She didn't care that she didn't really like tequila or that lime juice often gave her heartburn. She just wanted to keep talking to Monty. Chicot knew she should be careful, that Monty might have feelings for her and Chicot didn't know if she was going to get to be with Monty like this for more than a summer. Still, if she could at least make Monty laugh like she just had, that would make Chicot very happy.

"That sounds great." Chicot carefully stepped around Monty. "I'll be out quick."

Chicot slipped herself into the bathroom, catching a glimpse of Monty as she closed the door behind her. Monty held her can to her lips, her eyebrows squished together and lips parted. She turned away before Chicot saw anything more, so Chicot just closed the bathroom door, locking it. As she pulled her swimsuit out of her tote bag, Chicot pressed her lips together, the look on Monty's face stuck in her head.

The thought was gone once she got changed. She was suddenly hyperconscious of the width of her hips and her, to be frank, lack of breasts. To top it all off, she'd let Elijah convince her that the sports bra she'd brought looked fine as a bathing suit top, but now that she had it on, she felt almost prudish in it. Even with her board shorts on, which barely touched her mid-thigh, she felt like she was trying to hide something. But she wasn't. She just liked to have pockets. She suddenly regretted all of her life decisions that had led her to believe this was good enough to be seen in. Sure, it would have been fine for a day at the lake, but a party with other adults and drinking?

She felt like a child as she stepped out of the bathroom, her tote with her cargo pants and black cami under her arm, wondering if she should turn tail and run to put them back on. But Monty was standing outside the door, her lips curved up on one side as Chicot stepped out and a second canned margarita in hand.

"That suit is very you," Monty said. "It's nice."

Chicot looked down at her board shorts, which she was fairly certain came from Walmart while she'd still been in high school, and her years-old, black sports bra that had gray leopard print on it. The shorts were a light green color, and honestly now that she was looking at them again, it was a good color for Chicot. She played with the ends of her damp hair, smiling shyly.

"Thank you." She reached out to take the other can Monty offered, and they were off. It only occurred to Chicot that she maybe should have brought up the thing about not having a phone while they'd still been by the bathroom. They'd been mostly alone, and now as Chicot followed Monty out to the deck, she realized she might not get another moment to clear things up, and she'd like to do it sooner rather than later.

Chicot quickly counted about ten people outside, either sitting on the deck that ran along the long side of the pool or in the water. Nearly everyone had a drink in hand, not all of them alcoholic, but they held them out of the water or set them on the side of the pool. There were people Chicot had seen inside in the water now too, some with just their legs in and others hanging onto inflatable animals or pool noodles as they floated. The pool itself was large—an oval shape that took up a good portion of the yard—allowing people to congregate in small groups and share the space easily.

Lyza was in an inner tube that looked like a donut, while Elvis remained on the deck, basking in the sun. Monty stepped directly into the pool, so Chicot simply followed, both of them still holding their drinks. Chicot had to hold hers much higher since the water came up to nearly her chin. She promptly found a noodle to keep her at least somewhat dry. When Lyza saw her, she snorted and yelled for Elvis to throw them another inner tube.

"Fellow shorties gotta help each other out," Lyza said. Chicot just chuckled, happy to have something to float in while they all enjoyed the cool water.

Monty settled herself against the side of the pool, smiling as they listened to Lyza chatter about faire gossip. It was already half past six, but being July, the sun was still high and warm. Eventually, they were joined by more people, many of them food stall workers who were local to the area. Chicot learned quickly that more people would be coming to the party now that the faire had fully closed. The food stalls worked in two shifts, morning and afternoon, which Chicot hadn't been aware of since she was always so busy with performances and she usually ate PB&J sandwiches for lunch rather than buying one. They also asked questions about Elijah after politely making small talk for an appropriate amount of time before trying to pry information out of Chicot.

"Well, you know—" Chicot shrugged. "We decided after we spent summer being birthday clowns that we'd rather spend our time at ren faires, where there were fewer children."

She knew they'd believe it, though she hoped Lyza didn't give her away since she knew the truth. It wasn't entirely untrue either, but they hadn't been clowns. They didn't really want to have to constantly explain that they'd been Circle K employees before Elijah's mom gave them the RV and gotten their first audition at Albion. This was more whimsical.

"Wait, I thought you worked at a gas station?" Lyza asked as the food stall workers wandered off. Chicot shook her head slightly, smiling.

"Yes, but don't tell them that." Chicot winked at Lyza and she laughed.

Elijah came by at some point to make sure that Chicot was okay. They had floated to the far side of the pool, and he was standing in the grass, complaining that his legs were being bitten by bugs the whole time. He still agreed to bring them more drinks, and so Monty and Chicot got a second round.

It was all exceedingly normal for a while. Chicot drank, then took a shot with Lyza—though Lyza was drinking tonic water with lime—and made jokes about body shots. When Chicot was comfortably buzzed, the party felt like a dream. She had spent most of her teenage years and early twenties bumming around odd places like graveyards or parking lots with Elijah, and the short time she'd gone to community college, she hadn't made many friends. This felt like what she should have been doing as a teen. Especially when Ken ran out onto the deck and yelled:

"Chicken tournament!" He then unceremoniously hopped into the pool, splashing most of the people who were floating.

Chicot was just enough drinks in to find this endearing rather than annoying, as people started to grab partners or move out of the way. She didn't expect Lyza to grab her, pulling her toward Monty. Playing chicken meant sitting on Monty's shoulders, which also meant a lot of Monty touching Chicot and Chicot trying not to think about Monty's nice hands or skin.

"These two are a team!" Lyza yelled and gestured at the two of them wildly.

"Wait—" Monty started, but before she could say much more, Ken had Elijah add them to the list.

Lyza had already paddled away, absconding from the pool to be with Elvis. He reached up a big hand, pulling her down onto the lawn chair with him as she laughed.

"Guess we're a team?" Chicot looked up at Monty, still holding her inner tube, which looked like a watermelon. Monty just sighed, setting her drink down on the deck.

"Yeah, you good with that?" Monty asked. Chicot took a small step closer to Monty.

"Course, I know you can hold me."

This made Monty's smile waver slightly, her lips parting, but she didn't say anything. She seemed to do this to Chicot a couple times a day now. Chicot was starting to think that maybe she had a much better filter than anyone she'd ever met. She also sort of hoped that Monty felt comfortable telling her things.

She didn't have much time to think about it because they were soon being called into the center of the pool to face off against Martina, the sausage stand lady, and Brad, who worked in one of the leather shops at the faire. Chicot only knew who they were because Elijah announced their names loudly for the group. Martina was already on Brad's shoulders, grinning as she wiggled her fingers in anticipation at Chicot, the two of them shouting corny trash talk as the crowd laughed. Chicot tried to think of a rebuttal, but nothing good came to mind, and then Monty was swimming between her legs so Chicot could get on her shoulders, and she was promptly distracted.

Monty's strong hands wrapped around her calves, holding onto her tightly. "You better win up there."

Chicot laughed. "Uh, I'll try?"

Ken had procured a whistle from somewhere, standing between Monty and Chicot and their opponents with his hand up. He quickly explained that they were not to claw each other with their nails and that the first to fall from their partner's shoulders into the water lost. Once Ken confirmed that both Chicot and Martina understood, he waited until they both seemed ready and blew the whistle.

Chicot yelped as Monty took three quick steps forward, but she managed to lock hands with Martina. Martina grinned, trying to push Chicot back, her arms strong, but Brad hadn't gotten close enough yet, so she was leaning forward. She didn't have the core strength behind her, so Chicot tried to take advantage of that, twisting their arms to push Martina to the side, hoping that putting her off balance would be enough to bring her down.

They struggled for a few seconds before Monty let go of Chicot with one hand, just nudging Brad's shoulder. It caused him to let go of Martina, and with no counterweight holding her down, Martina promptly squeaked and plummeted into the water.

"Hell yeah, Chicot! Go, Monty!" Lyza was yelling from the deck next to Elvis, who had his fingers in his mouth to whistle next to her.

Chicot threw her hands in the air, whooping in response to Lyza before she looked down at Monty between her legs. Monty was grinning, and between the drinks and excitement, Chicot had half a mind to lean down and kiss her. She didn't. She realized quickly she shouldn't do that, and Monty let her go so she could fall back into the water. When she came up, Monty was grabbing her hand and leading her back to the side of the pool, so they were out of the way of the next match.

They cheered for Elijah and Ken, hollering as the turkey drumstick stand worker and the cheesecake on a stick girl fell into the pool together. The two came up laughing and swam up next to Chicot and Monty. Chicot high-fived them both, downing another margarita quickly as they watched another match between four boys that Chicot didn't know. She thought they might work in one of the kitchens, but Chicot hadn't seen them before. The group that won were both sort of buff and looked like they might have cared more about football than the ren faire. At least until they opened their mouths. Then they were shouting Dungeons & Dragons jokes, and Chicot had a feeling these two probably wouldn't have been hostile if Chicot said she didn't like sports.

The two D&D bros went up against Elijah and Ken next. Chicot wolf-whistled for Elijah, cheering as Ken struggled with the boy on top and Elijah batted at the guy holding him up. It was short, especially once Elijah got close enough to hook his foot under their base's leg. The two tumbled into the water with their arms flailing about, laughing all the way down.

That meant the last match was Elijah and Ken versus Monty and Chicot. Chicot grinned, smiling at Monty as they swam toward the middle.

"Watch out for him trying to trip you," Chicot cautioned. Monty swam under Chicot's legs again. Lyza cheered from the deck, Elvis whistling behind her.

"We're not going to go easy on you just because we're friends," Elijah warned. Monty snorted.

"We don't need you to," she quipped. This made Elijah grin, and now the whole party was cheering at them, raucous and loud. Chicot wondered if the neighbors were bothered. The lot was big, but not that big.

She focused on Ken and Elijah, her arms up as one of the D&D bros took the whistle. When it blew, Monty moved in quickly again, Chicot grabbing onto Ken while Elijah tried hooking Monty's leg. Chicot was able to force Ken back, using all her weight to push him as she tried to give Monty the chance to deal with Elijah's attempts to trip her.

"Shit, you're stronger than you look." Ken ground his teeth together, getting the upper hand and pushing Chicot back. She managed to hold on, twisting slightly on Monty's shoulders.

"I walk on my hands a lot." Chicot tried to shove Ken away, but he grabbed her wrist, yanking her forward. She yelped, trying to right herself, but she spun like a top around Monty's head. Honestly, all Chicot could think about was how she hoped she hadn't hurt her and also how her crotch was now basically in Monty's face.

As Chicot tried to get back into position, Elijah must have hooked Monty's leg finally, pulling it out from under her so they both tumbled toward the water. Monty managed to catch Chicot, her arms around her middle as Chicot grabbed onto Monty's shoulders and wrapped her legs around her waist. It took her a moment to realize what she'd done, now holding onto Monty like she was a koala clinging to a tree.

"You good?" Chicot looked down at Monty. Their faces were so close, Monty's lips were parted and her round eyes were big and blinking, then she laughed. Chicot wanted to kiss her so badly, but the crowd of people cheering for Ken and Elijah stopped her.

"Yeah, are you?" Monty let Chicot go, Chicot's feet touching the bottom of the pool so only her head was showing. Chicot was laughing now too, a hand wiping some of the water away from her eyes.

"Yes." Chicot grinned. "Guess we couldn't beat the party host. Might have been rude if we did."

Monty nudged her with her elbow. "The game was rigged in his favor."

They both laughed, getting out of the pool as a second chicken tournament started, since someone had shown up with pizzas. Lyza had gotten them both plates since she was dry, handing them off as Monty sat on the lawn chair next to her, and Elvis and Chicot sat in succession like it was a bench. They cheered for Elijah and Ken as they played another round, this time losing to the D&D bros.

Everyone laughed and drank, and at some point, Ken got an ice cream cake out that was far too frozen still to cut.

Chicot drank; in fact, too much. She was stumbling and shaking her head as she changed back into her dry clothes in the small, wet bathroom she'd been in earlier. When she wandered back into the screened-in porch sometime later, Monty was holding a slice of ice cream cake for her.

"You're an angel," Chicot said. The cake had been too small, the pieces going quickly with all the people there, but Chicot couldn't stay in her damp swimsuit a second longer, so she'd given up to change. Monty had seemingly realized how much of a struggle that had been for her.

"No problem, I only got one though," Monty relayed. Chicot shook her head.

"We can share." She wobbled on her feet as she followed Monty back out to the yard, sitting on the lawn chair on the deck again. Elvis and Lyza had disappeared at some point, Chicot wasn't sure where, but she was happy to be mostly alone with Monty, trading a plastic spoon back and forth as they ate. Though, there was a group of boys in the yard now loudly playing a game called rock, paper, wizard, and while Chicot couldn't tell how it differed from rock, paper, scissors, they were having a lot of fun.

Chicot's head swam, a small smile on her face as she sipped a water bottle Monty had pushed into her hand. She wasn't sure how much of the night she'd remember, but in that moment, the sun long gone and the heat of the day slowly ebbing away, she hoped it would stay with her always. The last party she'd been to was for a cousin's graduation, only that had devolved into a political screaming match between her uncle and mother.

"Do you want a ride home?" Monty asked as they finished their slice. Chicot suddenly felt dizzy, but she paused.

"Wait, we've been drinking," Chicot noted. Monty chuckled, shaking her head.

"You've been drinking. I stopped several hours ago." Monty tossed their spoon and paper plate into the trash, offering Chicot her hands to help her up. Chicot's brow furrowed as she tried to recall the last time she'd seen Monty with a drink.

"You did?" she asked.

"Yeah." Monty looked around, making sure to grab her bag and then also grabbed Chicot's. "C'mon."

"Okay." Chicot couldn't think of anything better to say as she followed Monty out to her car. They were alone, no Lyza or Elvis or Elijah, and admittedly Chicot didn't think to ask where they were, even as they pulled out of the driveway.

They started down the long country road toward the faire grounds, the windows down with Fall Out Boy blasting through the speakers. It was just whatever had turned on according to Monty, but something about listening to "Young Volcanoes" while the wind whipped through her hair made the night feel so much more magical.

When they parked, Chicot hopped out, opening Monty's door for her. Monty remembered to grab their bags, laughing as Chicot practically skipped toward the dog park. It was past midnight, there were few people still awake among the RVs and trailers, and Chicot felt more awake than ever before.

"Want to come in for a night cap?" Chicot asked. They were nearing her and Elijah's RV, and she was pretty sure that Elijah would be staying at Ken's that night, so she figured this would be fine. She was not considering that they had nowhere to really sit inside besides the bed.

"I think you've had enough," Monty joked. Chicot took her hand, sticking out her bottom lip and pouting. Monty's head jerked back, her face pink in the low lights on the path around the dog park.

"I'll drink water? But we have whiskey." She took a step closer to Monty, smiling more. Monty looked up over Chicot's head, nodding slightly.

"Okay, but *only* if you promise to drink a whole glass of water." Monty followed Chicot inside as Chicot pumped her fist in the air.

"Yay!" Chicot said. She only paused when she looked at the kitchen table they'd converted into a closet space for their costumes. "Wait."

"Do you guys not have anywhere in here to sit?" Monty asked.

"We do," Chicot said quickly and then grimaced. "Okay, no, we don't."

Monty laughed, shaking her head. "Maybe you should just—"

She stopped as Duchess hopped up on the countertop, examining Monty closely. Monty stared at the cat, her mouth a perfect "O" before she held her hand up for Duchess to sniff.

"Uh, that's, she's …" Chicot had somehow forgotten entirely that she wasn't supposed to have a cat here. "A stray! That we're trying to find a shelter for!"

Monty lifted a single eyebrow at Chicot. "So, you and Elijah have a cat?"

"Yes." Chicot shivered. If she wasn't so drunk, she'd be terrified and trying to make more excuses or lie. Instead, she just watched as Monty petted Duchess's head.

"We hid a cat for a long time too," Monty admitted. "He passed last year after we moved him into our parents' because he was getting sick."

"Really?" Chicot's brow furrowed as she stepped to pick Duchess up, holding her like a baby. "I'm sorry."

"It's okay." Monty smiled at her. "What's her name?"

"Duchess," Chicot gushed. "I stole her from my family."

Monty laughed. "Weren't going to take good enough care of her?"

"I bottle fed her when she was a kitten," Chicot explained. "I couldn't let her go. She's my little baby."

"I get that." Monty stepped closer to Chicot to pet Duchess. She purred in Chicot's arms, leaning into Monty's soft hand. "C'mon, you should go to bed."

"But our night cap …" Chicot let Duchess go because she started to squirm. Monty rolled her eyes, a smile on her face.

"I don't need a night cap, I promise." Monty set her hands on Chicot's shoulders, turning her around and nudging her toward the bed. "C'mon, let's go."

Chicot didn't argue, letting Monty push her into Elijah's bed. "But this isn't mine."

"It isn't?" Monty blinked and then looked around the RV again. "Wait, there's only one bed in here. Do you and Elijah share?"

"No, I sleep up there." Chicot sat up on the edge of the mattress, her face basically in Monty's chest because she didn't realize how close she was, as she pointed at her hammock. This time at least, Monty didn't seem to notice. Instead, she followed Chicot's hand and her jaw dropped.

"How?" Monty looked at Chicot again. "Doesn't that … hurt your back?"

Chicot shrugged. "I like it up there."

"Can you get in while drunk?" Monty blinked rapidly, her arms crossing as she tilted her head. She was still looking at the hammock.

"Yeah!" Chicot grinned. "I've done it before."

She looked at Monty, sitting up straighter as Monty looked back. They were alone now, and they were close again. An idea bubbled up from the very back of her head, and because she was drunk, it came out before Chicot really gave it any thought.

"But you know …" She bit her lip. "If you wanted to stay, I'm sure Elijah wouldn't care if we shared the bed."

Monty's eyes grew wide, her whole iris visible and illuminated in the low light coming from the window. Her mouth opened and closed, her arms uncrossing as her eyes darted down Chicot's body. Chicot shivered, leaning up as she set her hands on Monty's biceps. She wanted to kiss her, but before she could, Monty took a step back.

"You're *really* drunk, Chicot." Monty shook her head. "You need to go to bed."

Chicot suddenly felt hot. Even with the AC blasting, she was overheating. She looked down at her hands briefly, one rubbing her forearm. Monty clicked her tongue.

"No, don't—" She shifted to make eye contact with Chicot. "Don't get all sad. I'm not—You didn't do anything wrong."

"I didn't?" Chicot's voice cracked because her mouth was dry. She cleared her throat, shaking her head slightly. She didn't want Monty to think she was about to cry because that was what it sounded like. "I mean, okay. Good."

"You really didn't." Monty rubbed her face. "God, you're so confusing."

"Confusing?" Chicot tilted her head to the side. A long sigh came out of her Monty.

"Don't worry about that for now." Monty crossed her arms. "Anyway, you're too drunk to have sex with anyone. Go to bed."

Chicot probably would have pushed if she were sober, but the alcohol was both making her horny and so very sleepy. "All right."

"Good," Monty said. "I'm going to go back to our RV now."

"Okaaay." Chicot shifted to pull her pants off, which seemed to stop Monty for a moment. She then stood on the bed to get into the hammock in her boxers.

"Chicot, you need to lock the door after me," Monty reminded. Chicot paused with her arms in her hammock and looked at her.

"Oh, right." She hopped down, following Monty to door, and as she stepped down onto the small path in front of their RV, Chicot smiled. For a moment, they were both pressed in the small space by the door, the two of them close enough to hug … or maybe even kiss. Chicot considered it, but then she remembered something she'd nearly buried. She'd never told Monty about the texting thing. Monty still didn't know why she wasn't getting texts back from Chicot and Elijah.

"Oh!" Chicot's voice was unhelpfully loud, enough to make Monty flinch, the frown returning to her face. Warmth spread over Chicot's chest and neck, and she rubbed her palm against her thigh for a moment. She needed to make sure that Monty knew that she wasn't just ignoring her.

"Sorry," Chicot said for startling her. "But, if you've been texting us, I don't know what's up, but Elijah hasn't gotten any texts from you."

"Elijah?" Monty's brow creased.

"Yeah, I figure maybe you have a number off or something? Elvis said you'd been trying to text us, but Elijah hasn't gotten any messages from you." Chicot stumbled over her words. "And I don't have a phone, so."

"You don't have a phone?" Monty's nose was scrunched slightly now.

Chicot shook her head. "I broke it in May and haven't been able to get a new one."

Monty's brow slowly unwrinkled, her lips parted as she took in Chicot's words. She just stared at Chicot, her face slowly relaxing into a perplexed, slack-jawed expression. Then, a twinkle came to her eye and she said, "Right, yeah. That explains a lot."

"I can look at Elijah's number for you tomorrow if you want," Chicot said. "To make sure his contact is correct."

"That would be good." Monty chuckled, but for some reason, Chicot wasn't sure what she was chuckling about. Her having the wrong number wasn't a particularly funny thing, though maybe it was funnier to Monty than it was to Chicot somehow. Either way, she was just happy to have this all cleared up.

"But, yeah, night, Monty." Chicot rubbed the back of her head. "Maybe we can have the night cap another time?"

Monty stepped toward Chicot, picking up one of her hands and kissing the back of it. Chicot stared, lips parted and eyes wide. Monty gave her a sideways smile, nodding.

"Yeah, another time." Monty winked at her.

Chicot slowly closed her mouth, pressing the back of her hand to her own lips for a moment. The thrill made her stomach turn as she reached out and shut the door after Monty, locking it. She then scrambled into her hammock and spent only a minute thinking of Monty's pretty lips before she was asleep.

CHAPTER 11

She was undoubtedly awake and unfortunately bleary with snot running down her face when Elijah turned up. Nearly everything she'd eaten the night before, starting with the ice cream cake and going in reverse from there, had come back up, and she'd spent her morning with her face in the tiny toilet of the RV. It was okay, because she remembered those blissful five minutes when she'd gotten to sit on Monty's shoulders and feel her hands holding her legs while they'd played chicken in the pool.

"Jeez, you look awful." Elijah, to his credit, came with a blue Gatorade in hand and a breakfast sandwich for her. Chicot took them eagerly, peeling back the greasy McDonald's branded paper to bite into the biscuit. It was lukewarm, but it immediately settled her stomach for whatever reason. Soaking up the alcohol or something like that.

"I'll be fine," Chicot said.

"How'd you even get back here?" Elijah was pulling a can of cat food from the cabinet for Duchess. In Chicot's hungover state, she had not thought to feed Duchess her wet food. She had dry, of course, but this was still a grave mistake. Duchess loved her wet food. This immediately made Chicot feel guilty, but Duchess had also been hiding under the bed all morning while Chicot had puked her guts out and didn't come out even after Elijah put her food down, so she would probably wait until things were quieter anyway.

"Monty ... I think?" Chicot rubbed her head.

"You *think?*" Elijah frowned. Chicot hummed around a bite of her sandwich.

"No, it was her," Chicot said. "I just don't really remember anything past being in her car."

"How much did you have?" Elijah narrowed his eyes, crossing his arms as Chicot thought.

"More than ten." Chicot shrugged. "I stopped counting."

"Ah, okay, so you did this to yourself." Elijah snorted, turning to get himself a bottle of water. "Well, c'mon, get dressed. We have to be at the gym soon."

"Fuck off." Chicot took another bite of her sandwich. "Shit, the gym."

"Shit, the gym, yes." Elijah agreed. "Now get going."

Chicot groaned, setting down her breakfast and walking to her side of the closet to dig through a basket at the bottom for something she could work out in. She settled on a pair of tight, thick shorts that were part of an old dance costume and a long-sleeved leotard that she'd used to use for cheerleading. The leotard was worn, and she didn't bother wearing a bra in it because it was tight enough to basically bind her chest. She needed new clothes.

"We should go to the thrift store." She pulled at the leotard, making sure it was sitting in the right places. Elijah hummed and tapped the jar they kept Chicot's phone fund in.

"Probably not until after this," Elijah said. Chicot groaned again, her headache making this so much worse. There was a lot more money in the jar after just a few weeks of the faire being open and Chicot filling in for Lyza. They were making good money. It just probably still wasn't enough after bills and other things, especially since they'd had to buy Elijah a few new costume pieces after the first day of the faire. It had been clear that his long, billowy bard sleeves wouldn't work long-term.

"Have you counted it recently?" Chicot asked. Elijah shook his head, nursing his water bottle, a sign that he was more hungover than he was letting on. There were a lot of singles. If they weren't actively living in an RV on faire grounds, someone would probably assume they were strippers.

Chicot checked the time and then poured the jar out onto the bed. It didn't take her long to count what was there, separating things into stacks of ten so she could total it up at the end.

"How are we doing?" Elijah stood next to her, his lips pressed together. Chicot took a deep breath.

"Better than I thought." Chicot's stomach fluttered as she bundled up the cash. "But I don't want to get too eager."

"How much is there?" Elijah asked. Chicot hesitated, frowning. It wasn't like this would actually do anything, but it felt like saying they had any amount out loud would lead to them losing it all somehow. Maybe that was just because it had been the pattern since they'd started the jar.

"Just under four hundred," Chicot informed him. "Maybe we should just get a flip phone for me."

"You wouldn't have internet access," Elijah said. "And you can't put your old sim card in it so you won't be able to recover your contacts."

Chicot deflated, her arms going around her middle as she looked at the jar of their hard work on the bed. "It wouldn't be that big of a deal."

She trailed off. Elijah frowned at her.

"For you to completely lose your siblings' numbers?" he asked.

Chicot sighed. "Okay, you're right. It is a big deal. But Juni is ten. She'll have social media soon."

"They don't even know where you are." Elijah rubbed his temple. "Listen, I respect that you don't want to talk to your parents, but Juni and Charlie only had you most of the time."

"I couldn't stay there anymore. You know that." They'd had this conversation a few times. It never devolved into a fight because Elijah respected that Chicot didn't want to see her mom, and that meant not seeing her dad, Juni, or Charlie. But he wanted her to try and maintain what relationships she could. This didn't really make

Chicot angry because secretly, she had a feeling she would one day get a call from Juni and need to go get her immediately because their mother had kicked her out. After all, that had been Chicot's experience. If she'd had the ability to leave and live with an older sibling, she probably would have taken it.

"You don't remember their numbers. And what if there's an emergency and they need you?" Elijah picked up the jar, showing Chicot the spot where they'd used painters' tape to put Chicot's old sim card into it for safe keeping. "We can't just get you a flip phone. Saving is our only option."

Chicot rubbed her forehead. It was so hard to be angry with him about this. She almost wished she could be, but it was hard when he loved her siblings as much as she did. Chicot didn't want to lose them. She hadn't wanted to lose her dad either, but he always folded to her mother.

"We shouldn't have done this before we had to practice," Chicot said. Elijah opened his mouth like he might protest, but then he looked down at his feet, pressing his lips together and causing his jaw to visibly flex.

"I'll stop before you start talking about your siblings and mom next time," he conceded. Chicot smiled, setting a hand on his shoulder and rubbing it.

"And I'll try to stop myself before I start talking about them next time," she said. "This isn't just on you."

Elijah flashed a brilliant smile, his coiled hair bouncing as a single unit as he nodded. "The bard and the jester, always a team."

"The bard and the jester, always a team," Chicot repeated, and they bumped their fists together.

Elijah then looked at his phone and rushed them out the door because they were late. They ran across the dog park, managing to take a short cut between two RVs to get to the employee lot faster. Chicot was thankful for the bit of tree cover that the path had, but it wasn't much and it didn't save them from the heat.

Lyza, Elvis, and Monty didn't even seem to notice, the three of them waving as Chicot and Elijah approached Monty's car, panting from their run. Chicot's eyes were on Monty, taking in the long, flowy skirt she wore with a tight tank top, and usually, she would then devolve into lingering on Monty's muscles, but she currently found her eyes more interesting. Mostly because they were on Chicot's legs, her lips pressed together as she raked her eyes up to Chicot's face. Chicot grinned, relishing the flush that formed on Monty's cheeks. Monty didn't look at her for the rest of the ride. Even if Chicot glanced into the rearview mirror, Monty managed to keep focused on the road.

When they arrived at the gym, there were few cars parked near the entrance. As they unloaded, Chicot offered to help carry the bags of blades they'd brought for juggling practice. Monty stood next to her, picking up a gym bag that probably contained her work-out clothes since she wasn't wearing them.

"So." Monty glanced at Chicot as Chicot hauled a bag of heavy juggling materials over one shoulder. "How much do you remember from last night?"

Chicot paused, her lips pressing into a wide line, puffing her cheeks up like a frog. Elijah called this her frog face whenever he saw it. It made Monty laugh, though, her round shoulders shaking.

"I'll take the Kermit face to mean not much?" Monty asked. Chicot's shoulders dropped, the bag slipping off and catching in her elbow.

"I remember a good amount!" Chicot laughed. "Just not how I got back to the dog park. I assume that was you though."

Monty hummed quietly. "It was."

Chicot blinked at her as Monty tapped her finger to her lips.

"Well, I guess I'll spare you the embarrassing details then," Monty said. Chicot's jaw dropped, her eyes wide.

"What did I *do*?" Chicot asked. Monty laughed, closing the trunk of the car and walking toward the gym without answering.

Chicot ran after her. "Monty! Monty, tell me!"

This only made Monty laugh harder, and when they got inside, Lyza, Elvis, and Elijah were all crowded near the door. Chicot couldn't see past them, standing on her toes to try and sort out why they'd stopped. She only realized when she heard the loud, exaggerated cackle coming from near the center of the spring floor.

"What is she even doing here?" Lyza looked up at Monty. As Lyza shifted, Chicot could see Brewhilda practicing her lines. She had a small speaker next to her, playing a recording of the music her partner usually handled live during her show. Her hand was raised, a book in the other as she pretended to add things to her "cauldron," which at the moment was just a plyometric box she was using as a stand-in.

"I don't know. It's not like she does any acro in her show." Monty frowned, shaking her head.

"Let's just try to avoid talking," Elvis suggested. Elijah quickly agreed. Then again, neither of them had heard Brewhilda say what she had about Lyza. That might have changed their opinion.

"Well, I have to change," Monty piped up. "I'll be back out here in a bit."

Lyza nodded. "Be quick."

Chicot followed Lyza, Elvis, and Elijah to an unoccupied collection of mats near the spring floor, Lyza sitting down on one of the stacks to read lines to Chicot while she stretched. Chicot made it a point to face Lyza, rather than Brewhilda, even if they were across the spring floor and pressed into a corner. Lyza had picked a spot as far away as possible, Chicot noticed. Chicot just tried to focus on getting ready for practice. Lyza would fill in for Elvis or Monty as necessary, reading the script with Chicot and giving her a chance to get better memorized.

Luckily, Brewhilda didn't seem to pay them any mind. She finished up five minutes after their scheduled gym time should have started, and then moved her box to the side, placing it with the others along the far wall. Chicot didn't see where she went after that, focused on getting into a split while she repeated her lines back to Lyza.

A resolute, "Uh-oh," was the only warning they got of anything off. It was from Elijah, his eyes trained on the women's locker room door as Monty came flying out of it. Her jaw was set, changing the whole shape of her face from round to more square as she stomped toward them. She had her bag over one shoulder, a nasty ruddy color covering her cheeks and neck. It wasn't the cute, sweet flush that Chicot had come to like a whole lot on her. Instead, it was a loud, bright burgundy that grew darker as she stared down at the floor in front of her.

"I *hate* that bitch," Monty spat. Lyza shot up out of her seat, setting her hands on Monty's arms. Monty quickly pulled away from her sister.

"What'd she do?" Lyza asked. Monty just shook her head, her nose scrunched. "If she said something about me again—"

"She didn't," Monty snapped. "I need to … I don't know, give me a minute."

Monty shook her head hard, putting her hand out to keep Lyza at a distance as she walked around the pile of mats they were on toward the pit full of foam blocks that was under the uneven bars. Lyza's chin trembled, her brows knitted together as she pulled her hands in. She just watched Monty for a moment before her face slowly hardened into stone. Spinning on her heels, Lyza began to march toward the locker room door where Brewhilda was now slowly emerging as she fought with a bag.

"Lyza. *Lyza.*" Elvis got between Lyza and Brewhilda, cutting her off before she could get very far. Chicot couldn't hear what they were saying, but she had a feeling Elvis was talking her down from literally clawing Brewhilda's face off.

"What the fuck did Brewhilda do?" Elijah mumbled. He had snuck up to Chicot's side, crouching next to her because she was still in her split. Chicot shook her head, looking toward Monty.

Monty was trying to smooth down the athletic dress she was wearing. It was a small, fluttery thing, looking particularly short on her because of her height, but as she worried her fingers over her hips and where the shorts underneath the skirt squished in her thighs, Chicot felt herself start to get sick. She frowned, her face scrunching tightly.

"Oh fuck no," Chicot said. Elijah quirked a brow at her but didn't stop her as she rolled out of her split, hopping up to go over to Monty. She ground her teeth together, a myriad of awful things that could come out of someone's mouth about someone else's body sliding through her mind. Chicot didn't hold onto any of them, all of the words taking the sounds of her fellow cheerleaders when they set their sights on destroying someone. Chicot's blood boiled, but her being angry wouldn't help Monty at the moment.

Instead, she put on a bright smile, sneaking up behind Monty and peeking around her left arm. She was close to her, looking up and just bending like she would when surprising someone in her jester costume at the faire. "Did you know, during her audition this year, Brewhilda dropped her whole bottle of glittery potion only to slip in it because she'd made it with baby oil?"

Monty gasped when Chicot appeared, her mouth slightly agape as she listened to her. It took a moment or two, but slowly, she chuckled and looked at where her fingers were trying to smooth a wrinkle out of her skirt. "Did she really?"

"Yeah." Chicot bobbed her head, stepping around Monty to look at her. "She nearly slid right off the stage, just *shwip!*"

She held out her hands, sliding one palm over the other as she made the noise. This caused Monty to crack slightly, a small curl at the edge of her lip. Chicot bounced on her toes, smiling as she decided to keep this up.

"Her hat fell off her head and into it, too." Chicot mimicked putting a hat on her head. "She slapped it back on so fast, she had a bunch of glittery baby oil in her hair after."

Monty let out a shaky giggle, her head shaking slightly. "Wait, really?"

"Yes!" Chicot bobbed her head. "I know she was a mainstay, but jeez, I was shocked she'd made it through."

"God." Monty barked a laugh, her shoulders shaking as she pressed her hands into her face. When she pulled them away, it seemed like she wiped off a few tears, likely not from the story based on how red her eyes were, but Chicot was just glad she'd cheered Monty up at all.

"I laughed too," Chicot said. "At first, I thought it was like, an intentional part of the show. Elijah hit me to let me know it was not."

Monty's eyes went wide, her mouth open as the corners quirked up at the sides. "Oh my *god*, Chicot."

"How would I have known!?" Chicot held her arms out wide. "I'd never seen her act!"

Monty was really cackling now, genuinely and belly deep. She was no longer trying to rub wrinkles out of her dress or adjust the edges. Just letting go. And Chicot was glad she could give this to her.

"I mean, we also saw Gert and Slavio that day and they intentionally drop their swords and stuff," Chicot said. "I thought it was like that."

"She's *obsessed* with being polished," Monty said. "No wonder she seems to despise you."

Chicot shrugged. "Eh, I'm just glad you guys don't hate me because of it."

Truly, Chicot stopped caring about Brewhilda's opinion entirely when she'd heard her talk badly about Lyza. And if her friends agreed with her, Chicot didn't care about them either.

Monty's smile fell, her head tilting to one side. "What do you mean?"

"Well, you know." Chicot rubbed her head. "A lot of performers are mad at us for taking the spot of someone so established."

"And you thought we might hate you for that?" Monty asked. Chicot rubbed her chin, brow wrinkled as she nodded.

"Yeah, but it wasn't like, you personally." Chicot took a step back, just sort of fidgeting. Her heartbeat was racing. She hadn't realized how much this made her anxious. "Just like, everyone generally."

"Oh." Monty's eyes searched Chicot's face for a moment. "No, we—"

Chicot didn't hear the end of what Monty said. Her foot went too far back, and she didn't realize how close to the foam pit she'd gotten with her inability to stand still. Monty grabbed for her as she fell backwards, Chicot's arms flailing so much that Monty couldn't make contact. When she hit the foam, she sank, her legs sticking straight up and her arms outstretched like she thought she could reach the sides and catch herself.

"Fuck." Chicot shifted, struggling as she tried to sit herself up more. Monty leaned over the side of the pit, looking down at Chicot, a high giggle coming out of her. At least she'd made Monty laugh.

"Do you need help?" Monty leaned down, offering Chicot her hand. "You know, you're pretty clumsy for someone so good at acro."

Chicot paused as she accepted the help, an impulse running from the top of her head to the very tips of her fingers before she really thought about it. She tugged, acting on the thought and yanking Monty into the pit right alongside her. Or it would have been alongside her if she'd thought this through at all. Instead, Monty fell basically on top of Chicot, pushing her farther down into the piles of plastic-smelling foam cubes as they both yelped.

"Jeez, did I really deserve that?" Monty struggled against the cubes, trying to drag herself out of them, but it only caused them both to sink farther. A tinkle of laughter came out of her as she tried to straighten herself, only to fall basically into Chicot's chest. Chicot had not considered that a possibility and now found herself staring at Monty's sandy hair as it stood in the air from the static electricity building.

"You did." Chicot managed to get her hand under Monty's, giving her something to brace herself on to push up. It forced Chicot back down, but they could figure that out later. Monty laughed, her head whipping around to look at Chicot. They were so close, Monty's face just a few inches from hers. Chicot hoped Monty didn't notice that she glanced at her lips on instinct, Monty still hovering above her.

That all left her mind the moment Monty moved her hand, causing several foam cubes to fall from above her onto her face. Chicot thrashed, swatting one away and causing it to bop Monty in the nose. Monty laughed harder, trying to sit herself up as Chicot wiggled under her. They were both only succeeding at getting more stuck, the foam cubes encroaching on them as they inched toward the bottom of the pit.

"Okay, no fair, you're on top!" Chicot grabbed another foam cube, using it to hit Monty on the top of her head. It squished and bounced away, and Monty rolled over, her laughter higher, bubblier as she landed in the foam next to Chicot, finally giving Chicot the chance to sit straight up. That was easier said than done as the pit continued to try to swallow her. She did manage to swing her hand, knocking several cubes into Monty's face and chest, starting to bury her. As she did, Chicot's lips curled into a content smile. Monty's expression no longer held any of those worry lines or pinched muscles from whatever Brewhilda had said. Instead, she was laughing uproariously with her hands crossed over her stomach.

God, she was cute.

It took them several minutes—and help from Elijah and Elvis— to finally escape the pit. They panted and both lay out on the mat near it for a while before they started practice. This meant they were about nearly twenty minutes late, but there was still plenty of time for them to work.

Elijah and Chicot went first this time, since they had their routine down pat already. They ran it twice, neither of them stumbling over a single line or mark before Elijah said they should work on *The Pirates Three*. In the meantime, he settled on the floor with his lute, writing up new songs. He was always doing this, and Chicot hoped that the next jar they made could be for studio time so Elijah could record some of his music. It was a ways off still, but he had supported her through running away from home, and she wanted to help him live out his dreams.

Chicot, Elvis, and Monty started their practice by running the whole show once. Since they were coming into their second weekend doing this, they wanted to be cleaner, sharper, and more precise. This meant Chicot had to bring her A-game, which was easier now that her headache from the hangover was truly waning.

"Oh no, you don't!" Chicot yelled, pointing her sword at Elvis and being as campy as she possibly could. That was the key with most Renaissance faire performances: you had to be kitschy. It was like a drag show in that way. The more over the top and exaggerated, the better.

She threw herself into a run and hopped as Monty stepped between Chicot and Elvis, Monty catching Chicot as if she weighed the same amount as a water bottle. Chicot held her sword out, easily moving into a pigeon hold with Monty looking up at her. Monty held Chicot with such ease, her strong hand settled on Chicot's hip making her feel like she was floating. Chicot flailed her sword ineffectually, looking down at Monty.

"Put me down, Middle!" Chicot shouted. "He's got the treasure."

They'd reworked the show to involve them arguing over a small, fake treasure chest instead of the ship flag. It wasn't super different from what it had been before. In this version, Wee and Middle were not sister pirates. Instead, Monty, Chicot, and Elvis put on a Three Stooges act as they fought over the chest, and they did some more acrobatics and juggling of the supposed treasure, which led to them dropping it into the "ocean." Which meant they dropped it off the front of the stage. It was pretty funny, a lot of pretending to clamber up and down each other and just missing the chest.

"Oh." Monty was putting on a fake, confused tone of voice. "But Wee, can't we just share the treasure?"

"No, get him!" Chicot yelled, and Monty quickly but carefully dropped Chicot from the pigeon hold she had her in. They then both turned their swords on Elvis, which led to a series of them doing goofy hops and leaps over each other as they bickered. However, for just a moment as Monty set Chicot down, her gaze lingered on her face. Chicot blinked up at her, only just them really noticing the closeness before she pushed that all down.

She pointed her sword, Elvis dramatically pressing his back against an invisible wall as he yelped. They then ran for him, Elvis leap-frogging over them, and they went after him again. This time, Elvis and Chicot began to juggle the swords they were holding with the treasure chest mixed in. It was cartoonish, the two of them pretending to struggle catching the blades wrong while also pretending the treasure chest was basically falling between them rather than being controlled. As this happened, Monty slipped herself between Chicot's legs, throwing her sword into the juggling mix and crawling under like she might try to grab the treasure out of the air. When that didn't work, she turned to "help" Chicot by getting her to step on Monty's shoulders while Chicot protested loudly. This usually got a few good laughs, and once Monty stood to her full height, Chicot and Elvis now juggling three swords and the treasure chest, Chicot would knock the box just right to send it flying onto the stage, where it would then tumble off usually. If it didn't, Elvis would continue juggling, slowly shuffling his way over to the box to kick it off. There was some bickering between Chicot and Monty, then they caught the swords and joked about how silly it was that they were fighting in the first place.

Lyza and Elijah clapped for them when they finished their run-through of this new iteration. They discussed all the blocking again, just to make sure it worked for them still, then they talked about what lines were working and what felt awkward. After some deliberation, they decided not to change it again. Otherwise, it might get too confusing and someone could get hurt. Instead, they ran each of the lifts another time, to make sure there was no chance that Chicot got dropped. It did, however, mean that Monty and Chicot were working on their own, since Elvis wasn't on any of the lifts now. Instead, he mostly acted as a base for their acro holds.

"Hup, hup," they said in unison. Monty held her hands out for Chicot as she stepped into her space. They moved together as a single unit, Chicot hopping so she could lift her into the air. Each time Monty did, Chicot found her breathing quickening, the moments of weightlessness leaving her mind to wander toward the feeling of Monty's hands on her ribs or waist.

"This still good? No pain?" Monty's voice drew Chicot from the racing thoughts.

"Yeah, still good," Chicot said.

"Good," Monty chirped and shifted her hold. Chicot found herself falling, which was the point of this move, but it caught her off guard this time. When she landed in Monty's arms, her hands went to her shoulders, gripping her tightly like Duchess digging in her claws if she felt like she might get dropped. Her eyes darted to Monty's face, their noses almost touching as Monty smirked.

"Sorry." Chicot wasn't even sure what she was apologizing for. Monty's eyes shifted to Chicot's lips, which normally Chicot would convince herself was happenstance, but Monty was not being subtle at all. It was like she was goading Chicot, wanting her to see the way she was looking at her.

"It's okay." Monty wet her lips, her mouth opening just as she looked at Chicot. Then she smiled, setting Chicot on her feet. "I should have warned you I was letting you go."

"It's fine." Chicot wobbled, trying to ground herself on the spring floor, but that seemed to make her vibrate from toe to head. The smell of Monty's skin lingered in her mind, eyes on the floor as she tried to right herself, but her mind was replaying the image of Monty's tongue playing over her lips like she wanted Chicot to linger on thoughts of it. Where it could go and how nice it would feel during other applications.

"Ready for the standing pit hold?" Monty's voice was normal again, cool and even like she hadn't been teasing Chicot a moment ago. Chicot bit her lip because she couldn't rightfully ask for a moment to go take a cold shower.

"Yeah," Chicot replied and got into position. Monty spared her the heated looks this time, and soon Chicot was free to go run lines. She sat on the floor for a moment first, stretching her legs out and using her it as a cover so she could press her face directly into the mat. After a few deep breaths, she sat up and asked Lyza to start reading the script to her.

"Hey." Lyza nudged Chicot's shoulder. She was doing her best not to zone out, but Chicot was tired from the hangover and her mind kept wandering right back to Monty's lidded eyes and fuchsia tongue. "By the way, thanks for whatever you did earlier."

"Huh?" Chicot turned to look at Lyza, her hands around her ankles as she sat with her legs pressed flat to the floor.

"You know, whatever you did to make Monty feel better after Brewhilda," Lyza said. "Thanks."

"Oh, that was nothing." Chicot shrugged. Lyza hummed, looking at Monty now.

"Well, still." Lyza patted her shoulder. "I'm glad you two are becoming friends again."

Chicot's gaze clouded over for a moment, her eyes loosely on Monty's form as she helped Elvis carry a staging block. She tilted her head to one side, turning to look at Lyza, but she'd stood up, so Chicot couldn't ask why Lyza had said "again". After all, her and Monty had never been friends before, and they hadn't had some sort of falling out. Not that Chicot was aware of at least.

She thought back to that first night in the car with them on the way to the restaurant, to Monty's narrowed eyes and pinched expression whenever Chicot had tried to talk to her about music. Things had changed between them, of course. They were better friends now than they had been at the beginning, but still. Something about the way Lyza had said they were becoming friends again didn't seem like just a mix-up or accidental phrasing. She seemed confident, and Chicot needed to know what she meant.

CHAPTER 12

The sun was still high when they got back to the faire grounds, Chicot offering again to help with the bags so Monty could drop Lyza and Elvis off by the dog park. She hadn't expected Elijah to leave with them, stating that he had to meet with one of the other performers for some sort of jam band. This left Chicot and Monty alone, and while things were easier between them than they had been, they certainly weren't perfect. This led to Chicot babbling nearly nonstop from the time they were left in the car to when they got to the employee parking lot. She wasn't really talking about anything in particular, just filling the dead air with anything she could. Her mind bounced around on topics from music to clothes, Monty giving short but polite answers the whole time.

That was really all Chicot could ask for at this point. Even if she'd made Monty feel better at practice, it wasn't like Monty owed her some sort of sudden friendship. Chicot knew she very much wanted to be friends with Monty. She liked the music she listened to, her cottagecore aesthetic, the way she'd drum on her steering wheel as she drove. If Chicot let herself be completely honest, she knew somewhere deep in the flutter of her stomach and the flush she got when Monty held her just right that her crush was worse than ever. She just tried to tamp that all down like grass at a campsite and pretend it wasn't there.

"... and maybe we could go to the thrift store together sometime?" Chicot didn't know where she was going with this line of rambling as they walked toward the dog park when their bags were in place. "I kind of need new workout clothes and I have a bit of money for them."

Monty's chest puffed up, her fingers no longer drumming on the strap of the bag she was holding. "You want to go shopping with me?"

"Yeah." Chicot shrugged. "I think it'll be fun. Plus, I like your style a lot."

"It's nothing like yours though." Monty chuckled. "For one thing, I wear color."

Chicot pouted. "I wear color sometimes!"

"The occasional dark blue or maroon doesn't count," Monty said. Chicot scoffed, glowering at the pebbles in the walkway because she knew Monty was right, only stopping when Monty let out a delighted giggle. Chicot's throat caught just for a moment, her hands feeling numb and light as she bounced while she walked.

"You say that as if you wear anything other than earth tones and pastels." Chicot smirked, the expression quickly turning into a wide grin when Monty laughed again.

"Okay, you've got me there," Monty admitted. "And yeah, let's go to the thrift store sometime."

They took just a few minutes to work out that the best time to go would be in the afternoon after Chicot's first lesson with Sunnie, which they'd planned for Thursday. She didn't tell Monty that was what she would be doing that morning, just said she had plans, and Monty didn't ask questions. Once they agreed and Chicot helped her get the bag of blades back into the outdoor storage on her RV, Chicot waved and went back to her own so she could immediately step into the shower. Being hungover and then working out made her skin feel like it was covered in oil.

Elijah and Chicot spent the next couple days hiding from the heat in their RV. It was hard to justify being outside when it was nearly a hundred degrees and 90% humidity, especially when they had to be outside all day for work several times a week. Then suddenly, Chicot had to meet Sunnie for her lesson, and she stopped caring about the temperature entirely.

She quickly pulled on a pair of joggers over her leotard and grabbed her water bottle. Chicot briefly contemplated her simple jester hat with the bells, the one she wore to kids' parties because the mask would sometimes scare toddlers, but she opted against it. For now, she just wanted to go as she was, nearly jogging out of the RV park past a group of performers doing yoga led by one of the *Laundry Ladies*.

Chicot briefly caught Monty's eyes as she ran past, her head following Chicot as she headed farther out into the field near the old barn stood, where people entered the parking lot on faire days. She just waved at Monty in acknowledgment.

Sunnie was waiting under the shade of the large *Albion Renaissance Faire* sign at the entrance. It was a clever choice, since most of the field wasn't shaded. He'd clearly been here long enough to know the good spots.

He happily waved at Chicot, and she quickly realized he would not be saying a word this entire lesson. That made sense. The point of pantomime was to be silent but still understood. While Chicot could do that for larger, broader things, she wasn't as good at the minutia. Those small, subtle things that Sunnie got audience members to do with just a flick of his wrist or a point of his finger. As a performer, but maybe in life as well, being understood wasn't very common for her, and she wanted to be as clear as possible.

Sunnie had a series of small props to help them: a ball, a scarf, and an old paperboy hat. He started simple: the last thing someone touched would be the first thing they thought of when given an instruction. Sunnie taught her this lesson by handing Chicot the ball and then the hat, making a gesture like he was putting something on his head. Chicot, without thinking, put the hat on—no confusion about which item Sunnie wanted her to use. When Sunnie then held one slender finger in the air, a jovial smile on his face as he twirled his it like a young girl might her hair, Chicot turned her hat around. He then did this several more times with different applications and gestures, using the ball, the scarf, or the hat as necessary.

He then set about confusing Chicot a few times by taking things out of her hands and giving them back so many times that she couldn't keep track of what she'd touched last anymore. When he gave her instructions, she didn't know what he wanted her to do, either moving the wrong thing or staring blankly at him until he started over, reducing the number of items he gave her the second time. It took a few tries, but Chicot eventually realized that this was another lesson: too much input at once meant the other person wouldn't understand.

They went on like this for a while, Sunnie eventually prompting Chicot to try giving him the objects and directing him to do things with them. Then, at the end of their session, he had her follow him through a small series of steps of what Chicot could only call a dance.

The movements were very fluid, and once Sunnie had shown her, she was able to easily follow along with him. She could tell the idea was for them to do it in sync, carefully flowing from step to step with their arms slowly rolling to evoke' the sun and natural landscape. It was beautiful and gentle. Chicot realized it was probably meant to tell a story, much like various forms of dance she'd learned in lessons as a kid. Based on the forms, she thought the story might be about the sun itself, warming the world and making plants grow.

Her chest swelled with admiration as Sunnie continued, his lines crisper, his footwork careful and steady. She didn't quite know what it was, but Sunnie was teaching her *something* deeply important to their craft. A sort of interpretive dance that must have stemmed from years of formal training of some sort, though Chicot wasn't sure if it had been in modern dance or just the results of circus school. Either way, she wanted to learn more, suddenly ravenous for an education she had cast off as a possibility years ago.

"Do you think I should go to circus school?" Chicot asked as they started back toward the dog park. The sun was now beating down on them, the shade of the sign long behind them. Sunnie hummed softly.

"That's hard to say." Sunnie seemed to take this explanation very seriously. "There are certainly things you can learn there, but I will admit nowadays with the amount one can learn online and the fact that you're already working, it may not be necessary for you."

Chicot bobbed her head. "Thank you."

Sunnie chuckled, "For a nonanswer?"

"No." Chicot picked at a hangnail on her thumb. "For a level-headed one. A lot of ... older people think school is the only way for a lot of things."

"Were you about to call me a boomer?" Sunnie asked. Chicot felt sweat drip down her forehead as she looked out at the field instead of at Sunnie.

"No," she lied. Sunnie laughed.

"I'm not *that* old," he said. "But I see what you're saying. I think maybe I have a different view because while I liked circus school, I don't use a lot of those skills in my act."

"Your talents mostly come from experience and dance then, yes?" Chicot asked. Sunnie winked at her, his cheeks rounding as he smiled.

"You're quick on the uptake." He reached out, ruffling her hair. Chicot froze up, only for a moment as warmth drifted from her belly to her chest. Sunnie reminded her of her dad, just not a cowboy and considerably weirder. In a positive way, of course. But it took everything in her not to burst into tears, wishing it were her dad treating her with kindness like that instead of Sunnie.

"Yes," Sunnie continued. Thankfully, this meant Chicot didn't have to speak. "Most of what I use in my act, I learned from dance classes. Interpretive gestures narrowed down from incredibly abstract modern dance. Honestly, I'm not even sure how I arrived there."

That made Chicot smile.

"I also started in dance," she offered. "I did it for years. I was my teacher's favorite contortionist she'd ever had."

"Maybe that's why we get along so well." Sunnie nudged Chicot with his elbow.

"Maybe," Chicot agreed. They walked in a comfortable silence. Once you spent thirty or forty minutes pantomiming at each other, the quiet becomes far less scary. For once, Chicot didn't feel the need to fill it with some sort of inane conversation. It was nice that she had someone like this, another friend like Elijah that she didn't have a sort of confusing relationship with, like Monty, or the air of needing to be co-performers, like Lyza and Elvis. She could whine to him gently about how tired she was from putting on sixteen shows a weekend without making him feel guilty. Sunnie had done that as they'd first left their lesson, complaining about sharing a backstage with the nice lady who trained cats. It was just cluttered and diffi-cult, which Chicot understood.

Before he left her to return to his own RV, Sunnie invited her to a bonfire later that week for everyone that lived at the dog park. It was something they did every year apparently, to celebrate everyone surviving the Fourth of July weekend, when the faire was open on Monday in addition to Saturday and Sunday. It also marked being halfway through the season at Albion, so it was a good time to cel-ebrate. Chicot quickly agreed. She'd already heard a few people talking about it, and she'd known they were invited, but it was nice to hear it directly as well.

The sun had already become a source of blistering heat, some-thing which Chicot was certain could cook an egg if given a cast-iron skillet and some time. She sighed as she walked into the air con-ditioning, Elijah sitting in a camp chair they'd brought in from the outside storage so they had at least two places to sit in there during the day.

"How was your lesson?" Elijah asked. He was tuning his lute again, probably out of boredom. Chicot peeled off her joggers. There was sweat pooling in her crotch, and frankly she hated that swamp ass feeling more than anything in the world.

"Really, really good." Chicot then proceeded to spend the next ten minutes recounting the whole thing to Elijah while she wolfed down her lunch. She left out a few details, but mostly gave him everything as he listened emphatically. It was at least something else to do.

When she finished, she asked him what he'd been up to, and all he did was shrug. Chicot let him have his secrets if he wanted them, opting instead to change quickly before she had to meet Monty. She looked at herself in the tiny mirror in their bathroom, pointing at her reflection and reminding herself she needed to talk to Monty about the texting thing still. She really should have done it at the party, but she'd gotten so drunk she still couldn't remember any-thing after getting into Monty's car to go home. So maybe that wouldn't have been a good idea, actually. Chicot didn't want Monty to think Chicot was ignoring her, especially since they were hanging out one-on-one now.

Elijah didn't question her as she left, but he did joke about how she was going to overheat in her outfit. He was probably right. She had pulled on some light-wash jeans that hung low on her hips and an old T-shirt for a local punk band that didn't exist anymore. Under that, she'd thrown on a shirt she'd made out of a pair of old fishnet tights from one of her dance recitals, and then several pounds of silver chains hung from her wrists, belt, and neck. She just wanted to look cool at the thrift store.

When she got to Monty's RV, she was already waiting outside, a cropped tank top on with a breezy looking quilted cotton skirt. There was just a sliver of her stomach showing, a round hill of soft skin that Chicot tried not to stare at. Around her neck was a loose, bronze-colored necklace that held shiny red beads along it, the pen-dant dipping between her breasts so Chicot couldn't see it.

"Ready?" Monty held up her car keys with a smile.

"Yeah," she said. "And thanks for going with me."

"No problem," Monty said. "I need new clothes anyway."

The thrift store was larger than any one Chicot had ever been in. It wasn't a chain she was familiar with, but Monty swore by it, so Chicot took her word. She then quickly lost Chicot for ten minutes as she tried on every vintage leather jacket they had on the rack. Monty seemed to enjoy pointing out to her that almost all of them had been tagged at over thirty dollars, causing Chicot to whine about how she knew, but she could dream.

She then followed Monty to the dresses, oohing and aahing at every checkered item of clothing she picked up. Monty seemed to like looking like a picnic blanket, which made her pause and pout when Chicot pointed it out.

"Do you ever wear skirts?" Monty had a leather one in hand that looked about Chicot's size. Chicot shook her head.

"No, I've never really liked them. I tried to wear the men's uni-form in cheerleading." Chicot was on the other side of the rack, looking at jeans. Monty set the leather skirt back without any further questions.

"Oh, you should try those on," Monty suggested to Chicot as she picked up a pair of well-worn black Levis. They weren't vintage, but someone had loved them until they were just the right amount of faded and torn. Chicot agreed, plopping them into their cart.

"I'm supposed to be getting workout clothes," Chicot lamented. Monty chuckled.

"We should probably get out of this section then."

Chicot smiled. "Or you could enable me."

"Will your dad get mad at me if I do that?" Monty asked. "And by your dad, I mean Elijah."

Chicot froze for just a second before she let out a laugh. "Maybe."

Monty narrowed her eyes, but then she walked around the rack to add a gingham skirt to their cart. She then nudged Chicot to the workout clothes as she groused about it, feigning dramatics. Chicot found a few pairs of leggings and a couple of bodysuits that could pass for leotards. There was a whole section of baby-pink ballet clothes that Monty was picking through but kept things putting down.

"Think I should become a prima ballerina?" Chicot asked when Monty picked up another pink leotard that was gathered at the front. Monty snorted, shaking her head.

"No, I don't think you'd be comfortable." She set the leotard down. "I just like that color, and I wish I had more clothes in it."

"Well, you're not wrong." Chicot shrugged. "I always liked contortion and jazz more than ballet. But we could go look at the blouses and knits for pink stuff?"

"Oh, well …" Monty's eyes drifted over to that section of the store. Chicot leaned over the cart, grinning.

"C'mon, you have like, four skirts in here. You should look for shirts to go with them." She gently picked up a couple skirts that Monty had tucked into the cart as they'd been walking around.

Monty chewed on her lip. "I'm sure if I'm getting all of those …"

"Fair." Chicot understood what it was like to be on a budget, so she just hummed, setting the skirts down. "That's gonna be a rough choice though. All of those would look really good on you."

"You think so?" Monty rearranged her finds in the cart, her fist pressed to her lip as she looked them over. One was white with rows of eyelets between the lower tiers, another was plain beige, but it was made of a nice silky material, and the last had a similar patchwork quality to the skirt Monty was wearing. It was just mostly lavender instead of red and blue.

"Yeah." Chicot pointed at a ruffly white skirt. "This one especially."

"I'll keep thinking about them." Monty smiled brightly. "Let's look at shirts."

Chicot had warmth radiating through her chest. She hoped she didn't enable Monty, but something about the soft smiles and careful consideration of Chicot's opinions made her want to do this all day. They could too, especially because they didn't have anything to do after this.

They left with more clothes than they'd meant to get, but Chicot had managed to stay in budget thanks to most of her picks having the right color tags, which meant they'd been fifty percent off that day. Monty seemed really excited about what she'd bought, and she justified her purchases with her coupon she'd gotten for making a donation before they'd started shopping.

Monty was actually the one to suggest they spend more time together. She drove them farther into town, a small city center of mostly tourist shops awaiting them, but Monty headed past those to a local coffee shop at the end of the street. It was the sort of place you found in small towns like this, run by someone obsessed with coffee and one of the few places teens could go during the summer. This meant it was busy, but Monty suggested they get theirs and walk around anyway, and Chicot was happy to oblige.

They wandered with their iced coffees around the small town square, a fountain bubbling near the middle and a small patch of grass where there was a stage set up. There was no one playing since it was late afternoon on a weekday, but it was nice to have an area to relax in. There were people with strollers taking their kids on walks, and a few teenagers were lying in the grass, making the whole thing feel oddly scenic.

Chicot and Monty chatted about music, their favorite bands, the songs they'd been listening to since their whole lives. The conversation felt so natural to Chicot that she didn't even realize when they changed subjects and started talking about growing up in rural Wisconsin for Chicot and rural Minnesota for Monty.

"We were always making weird games," Monty said. "Anything to not be bored."

"Elijah and I used to do the same thing." Chicot thought back on those times they'd been throwing around a flaming stick until one of them had gotten burnt, as if that were a perfectly normal thing to do. "Ours were always stupid though."

Monty chuckled. "So were ours. Or it was gay chicken."

"Gay chicken?" Chicot asked. "Is that what I think it is?"

"Whatever you're imagining, it's probably accurate." Monty sipped her coffee, looking down at Chicot. "It was great for me, who wanted to kiss girls anyway."

Chicot snorted, her shoulders shuddering as she started to laugh. Monty beamed, her posture straightening with pride at this accomplishment. A smirk then grew on her face as she leaned back toward Chicot, putting her lips close to her ear.

"I never lost. My guess is you wouldn't have either." Monty's voice was a low, almost sultry as her breath lingered on Chicot's ear and neck. It made Chicot's entire body feel alert, the coffee thrumming through her system suddenly making itself rather known as her heart rate picked up, nearing the level of palpitations.

She pressed her hand over her ear and neck, leaning away from Monty. She was hot all over, her eyes darting to Monty's lips. Something in her told her to do something to get Monty back, but Monty was giggling and the fight drained right out of Chicot.

"I would have lost," Chicot said quickly. "I was way too shy."

"You? Shy?" Monty asked. Chicot glowered, sipping on her coffee so she had an excuse not to look directly at Monty or acknowledge her smirk and quirked eyebrow.

"You only think I'm not because half the time you see me interacting with people while I have a mask on," Chicot said. Monty considered that a moment, looking up toward the soft, billowy clouds as she tapped her finger against her lip.

"I guess that's true," Monty agreed. "It's easier to not be shy when you're just a silly little guy ... girl?"

Chicot snorted. "Jester?"

Monty laughed. "Yeah, a silly little jester."

CHAPTER 13

Chicot still had her now watery iced coffee when she got back to the RV, along with her paper bag of clothes carefully cradled in one arm, as she pushed the door open. Elijah took one look at her when she got in and tilted his head to the side.

"Out with Monty?" Elijah asked. Chicot felt a cool drop of sweat run down her back as she set her bag by the sink. She needed to wash everything before she wore any of it anyway.

"Maybe." Chicot dumped the remains of her coffee into the sink and then put the plastic cup in their tiny recycling bin.

"A little summer romance developing?" Elijah asked. Chicot should have known better. She should have lied, even if she also knew he wouldn't have believed her.

"A summer *friendship* is developing," Chicot clarified. "Anyway, what have you been up to all day?"

"Friendship, sure, that's why you're always looking like you could die happy when she catches you in her arms during practice." Elijah sang the last several words of his sentence, emphasizing it with a few strums of his lute. Chicot's cheeks burned.

"Elijah," she said. "No more."

Elijah laughed, still strumming until he very suddenly cut it off by grabbing the neck in his hand, stifling all the strings. He then set it aside, getting up to stretch, which caused Duchess, who had been asleep on the bed behind him, to do the same.

"I got a new audiobook from the library," Elijah said. Chicot raised a brow at him.

"Something we can listen to together?" Chicot asked. Elijah laughed, nodding. They'd had an experience accidentally early into their audiobook addiction where Elijah had borrowed a mostly normal romance book about two girls in a magic school. However, there was one incredibly long, graphic sex scene that had left them both awkward, slightly horny, and uncomfortably sharing the bed in the back of the RV. They'd gotten the hammock the next day in hopes of avoiding a similar situation in the future. About five minutes after they'd turned it off, Elijah had broken the ice by saying he really hadn't known that would happen, and they'd devolved into laughter.

"It's a fantasy book, no romantic subplot. Don't worry, I checked." Elijah held up his phone, showing Chicot the cover. She didn't recognize it, but it was over twenty hours long, and frankly, they needed something to fill the time while they hid from the sun.

"Sounds great," Chicot praised. "We can start it after I shower."

Elijah agreed quickly, and Chicot gathered some clothes. She took a short, cold shower so she could rinse out her hair and only briefly let her thoughts wander to places they shouldn't. Chicot was just happy it was Monty's slick skin under her fingers in Ken's pool that distracted her, rather than anything else in the world. It was only then that Chicot remembered she'd meant to talk to Monty about the texting thing that her buzz fully died. The whole situation had completely slipped her mind while they were shopping. She'd been too busy flirting to remember important things. Granted, it seemed like Monty was also flirting with Chicot, so she didn't really stand a chance.

She turned off the shower shortly after that, reaching around the door to grab her towel. Once she was dry, she pulled her underwear before she stepped out to put her shorts on. They had to do this all the time since the bathroom was so small, so they'd gotten used to it. It was simple not to look while the other person was getting out. However, it gave Duchess access to their wet legs, and she always made her way over to lick them after they were done and trying to get their shirts on in the tiny galley kitchen that took up the majority of the RV.

They listened to the audiobook while they made dinner, and then Chicot washed her thrift haul and her many sports bras in the sink of their small kitchen. She pulled a clothing rack from under the bed, setting her damp towel from her shower under it and then hanging her bras near the back of the cab to dry. They'd have to move it to leave, but it worked for now. Usually when they were out, they'd put it on the counter.

Once she was done, she lay on the bed, her hair now dry as she listened to the story, and Elijah took his turn to do some sink laundry. He was washing his leotards. Handwashing allowed them to get much more wear out of their pieces and prevented them from needing to take the dry-clean only parts to the laundry too often.

The weekend came fast after that, and Chicot did not anticipate just how brutal the extra day would be. It did, however, mean they got an extra four shows to earn tips, and Chicot got another four from *The Pirates Three*. When she counted out the phone fund the Tuesday after, it was almost enough for an older iPhone, which meant they could probably ask Monty to drive them to an electronics store later that week. That day, they were just happy to enjoy hiding in the RV and listening to their book while their bodies recovered.

After the sun went down, they made their way to the bonfire, which was being held in the field behind all the RVs. Chicot caked herself and Elijah in DEET lotion, wondering if she should work woodsman soap into her skincare routine if they were going to keep spending time out in these fields. She was just happy it was cool enough by the time they went out for the fire to justify wearing pants, so she was able to put on a pair of old, straight-leg black jeans that gathered nicely around her waist when she belted it. Elijah convinced her to wear a tight black crop top just so she wouldn't get hot, and she tied a hoodie around her waist for later.

Elijah was in a pair of tight gray jeans and a T-shirt that hung oversized on his frame. It made him look wider than he was, eliminating the carefully cultivated "Dorito shape" he was always working toward. Chicot once asked what that meant, and he'd told her broad shoulders and a slutty little waist. She had not asked more. Now, she had to wonder if he was changing that goal. That was probably a good sign. Elijah had always obsessed over his fitness and eating habits. It worried Chicot frequently, but he assured her it was fine. She just had to believe him and watch for signs of that changing.

When they walked up to the group already gathering around several fire pits that had been dragged from the dog park into the field, it was Sunnie who greeted them first, his red bandana still around his head, making him easy for Chicot to recognize. He drew them in, keeping Chicot and Elijah close to him at first. This also meant they were introduced to a slew of performers they had briefly met, sure, but Chicot could barely remember. Even as Sunnie recited names and Chicot looked at their faces, she had a hard time remembering who was who afterwards.

Sunnie held them in his space and entertained them with stories. Long enough that it took Chicot a good while to realize that Monty, Lyza, and Elvis were not there yet. Elijah waved it off when she commented on it, stating something about them being fashionably late.

Chicot chewed on her lip, looking in the direction of the dog park over her shoulder, wondering after Monty, of course, but also Lyza. If Chicot had learned anything about pregnancy before her siblings were born, it was that a lot could happen to complicate it, and Lyza wasn't very far along. Chicot drew in a slow breath. Lyza was not her mother and she wasn't going to change drastically and suddenly if something happened to the baby. She was probably overthinking this anyway, and that was proven to her an hour into the bonfire when Monty appeared in a flowy dress with a jean jacket on over it, slowly approaching the group of performers.

She detached herself from Sunnie and Elijah, which they didn't really seem to notice since they were singing sea shanties, and made her way over. Chicot felt slightly faint as she closed the distance between them, getting to Monty before she reached the bonfire, but Monty just sort of smiled at her, a quirk to her brow.

"Hey," Monty said. "You okay?"

"Yeah." Chicot hadn't even realized how strange this probably looked. She had no reason to be so worried over Monty or Lyza or the pregnancy. Just because she knew about it, didn't mean she had to fret over it. She had enough to fret over on her own.

"You sure?" Monty tilted her head to one side, slowing her pace as they approached the group around the now raging fires. They were all contained to their pits, but they were quite large.

"Yes, yes, I'm sure." Chicot shook her head, trying not to look as nervous as she obviously was. "I just … you were really late and don't have Elvis and Lyza with you."

"Oh." Monty's expression softened, her eyes on Chicot. "They were in Milwaukee for a doctor's appointment, but it ran late so they decided not to drive back. And I had to convince myself to come."

"Convince yourself?" Chicot asked. Monty wrapped her arms around her middle, holding onto her elbows as she looked at her toes.

"I wasn't sure if you and Elijah would be here," she said. "And I didn't want to see Brewhilda again."

A slow smile crept on Chicot's lips. "Well, I am here, and if Brewhilda shows up, we can make the best of it. If you need an out, I can pretend to be sick for you."

Monty's eyes slowly rose to Chicot's face. "Yeah, okay."

"C'mon," Chicot said. "Let's get you a drink."

Monty agreed quickly, the two of them folding right into the performers. Several of them commented on Monty's outfit as they made their way to the coolers, Chicot noticed. There was a lot of, "You look so cute tonight," and, "Wow, Monty, you clean up well for such a scoundrel of a pirate," and even, "Awe, you look so cute in that dress," from some of the older ladies. This seemed to disarm Monty, absently toying with the ends of her hair as she mumbled some sort of thank you. When Monty seemed to think the commenters weren't looking, Chicot noticed that she would smile to herself, picking up her skirt and swishing it.

"Is this, um …" Chicot searched for the words as Monty paused her swishing, looking owlish, as she'd been caught in the act.

"Is this new for you?" Chicot asked. "Dressing more femme?"

She didn't have a better word for it, but the word did make Monty instantly smile. She drew back then, receding slightly from Chicot in a way that made Chicot want to chase her, even though neither of them had really moved.

"Yes." Monty nodded. "I tended to wear more masculine, baggy clothes before. I think they're trying to be encouraging. They've been like this all season."

Chicot blinked, looking down at her baggy pants. Monty's eyes grew wide.

"Not that it's—"

"Don't worry." Chicot chuckled. "I know that's not what you meant."

Monty relaxed, her palm still up as she waved her hand over Chicot's outfit. "Yes, and it looks nice on you."

"Thank you." Chicot looked Monty in the eyes, something akin to chivalry coming over her. It was a strange form of wanting to be someone who made Monty feel good about herself that she couldn't find another name for. If she had to give it a gesture, it would be the placing of the hand on the small of someone's back while guiding them along. "And your clothes look good on you too, you know. It's cute, very flowy and pretty."

"You're such a flirt for someone who doesn't answer my texts." Monty huffed in jest, her smile relaxed as she said it. Chicot flushed, heat like the afternoon sun coming to her all at once.

"I, well—" She rubbed her head, not sure what to do now that she'd been confronted directly. Monty thinking Chicot was ignoring her was what she'd been hoping to avoid with the entire conversation about texting. "Sorry, I've been meaning to say something, but I don't think you have the correct contact info for Elijah."

Monty blinked. "I didn't think about it, but I guess you don't remember that either."

"Remember what?" Chicot frowned. Monty's smile was soft and her fingers were playing with the edge of her jacket.

"You told me that you didn't have a phone while you were drunk," Monty said. "And that I probably had Elijah's number wrong."

"Oh." Chicot tried to recall the memory, when nothing came, a chuckle fell out of her. "God, I said all sorts of things that night that I don't remember, huh?"

"You did," Monty said, leaning toward Chicot. "But it was endearing, don't worry."

Chicot's eyes caught Monty's at the last second, a sudden switch in them. Behind the pupils wide from the darkness and droop of her lids, Chicot could see something hungry. It wasn't carnal, not yet, but it could be. A shiver ran down Chicot's spine as her eyes darted to Monty's soft, pink lips. She wet her own, leaning closer without thinking. They were in the middle of a whole bunch of people, they couldn't do anything, so why was Monty baiting her?

Lyza and Elvis were in Milwaukee for a doctor's appointment, but it ran late so they decided not to drive back.

The words replayed in Chicot's head as Monty looked down at her. It was almost as if Monty were hoping that Chicot would remember that, and when she did, Monty pulled away, sipping her beer. She had the RV to herself, and Chicot realized this might be Monty's way of inviting her home with her. She sipped her beer, hiding behind it for a moment in hopes that she could collect her thoughts. Her attention was still fully on Monty, even if she tried to pretend it wasn't. The rest of this bonfire was going to feel like hours.

"You know, that same night …" Monty's lips were in a catlike smirk. "You invited me into your RV for a night cap."

"Did I?" Chicot tried to act cool, her eyes on the fire instead of Monty, but her pulse thrummed in her ears and her cheeks warmed. She hoped no one else could hear their conversion. They were near the center of the group, but no one was really paying them any mind as Chicot's eyes darted around them. Most importantly, Elijah was definitely too far away to hear, which Chicot was grateful for since he was the only one who would immediately know her intentions.

"You did; tried to give me whiskey." Monty leaned toward Chicot, her smile growing. "I met Duchess."

Chicot turned from embarrassment to fear. She looked at Monty with wide eyes, trying to recall that night. She still really only remembered getting into Monty's car and the way they'd been singing along to something during the ride.

"You *really* don't remember any of that, huh?" Monty asked. Chicot shook her head, pressing her lips together.

"Please don't tell anyone about our cat." Chicot held her beer can with both hands, trembling ever so slightly. Monty twitched, holding up a palm as she shook her head quickly.

"I won't," she laughed, looking away from Chicot briefly. "I'm not trying to get you in trouble. I just didn't think it was fair that I hadn't told you what happened. And that you tried to convince me to get into bed with you."

Chicot's arms went slack, but then her jaw dropped open. She couldn't believe *she* had propositioned Monty that directly. A series of jumbled thoughts ran through her head that only got more frantic as Monty smiled.

"You don't have to be embarrassed." Monty nudged Chicot with her elbow. It was gentle, but it felt like it could knock Chicot over. Maybe Chicot had just already been off balance.

Monty leaned down toward her then, talking more softly. "I probably would have taken the offer if you hadn't been so drunk when you made it."

"I— That's good to know." Chicot's ears were on fire, and Monty's cool breath so close to her neck was not helping. However, she couldn't stop the giddy smile that spread across her face as her chest started to feel fluttery. This seemed to also amuse Monty, a chuckle coming out of her as she pulled away.

She wanted to grab Monty right there and then. To drag her away from the party and spend the rest of the night in her bed so they could lose themselves to whatever pleasure they wanted. Monty knocked back the rest of her beer and gently ran her fingers up Chicot's arm as she said she was going to get another. Chicot didn't react quickly enough, and then she was standing in the crowd of performers alone, blinking.

Her chest felt fluttery still, a lightness that wasn't matched by her limbs. They had started to feel so incredibly heavy when she wasn't paying attention, holding her can of beer at her side. Sure, her crush liked her back. They were mutually interested in each other, but after Albion closed for the season, Chicot didn't even know where she was going to go. Her thoughts spiraled. Chicot wasn't sure if she could handle a fling. She didn't know if that was what Monty wanted. Still, they both knew that they might not see each other after Albion. After all, if this didn't work out for Chicot and Elijah, they'd end up back at a gas station or doing kids' birthday parties.

Before Chicot could panic and run back to her RV, someone set their arm on her shoulder, leaning their weight on her. Chicot expected Elijah, but she startled when she saw icy blue eyes and black hair. The woman had a White Claw in hand, her teeth gleaming in the light of the fire, but Chicot couldn't immediately place her. She was bad at this. This woman was probably some performer Sunnie or Lyza had introduced her to and Chicot couldn't even keep track of her name.

"So, is that why you got so offended when I said the obvious about Lyza?" The woman's perfume smelled overly sweet as she leaned into Chicot. Her mind raced, trying to place who had said something about Lyza, and then it hit Chicot all too late when she realized that this was Brewhilda of all people holding onto her. She should have known. Chicot might struggle with faces, but Brewhilda, even out of costume, oozed mean-girl energy.

"Do you have a crush on her little sister?" Brewhilda asked. "C'mon, it's okay to tell me if you're pining after her."

Chicot didn't know how Brewhilda wanted to use this against her, but she wasn't about to let her. She pulled away from her, frowning as she took a swig of her beer.

"Lyza's my friend," Chicot said. "You don't get to say shitty things about my friends."

"I think I get to say whatever I want when they took my time slot and then you took my stage away from me entirely." Brewhilda pointed at Chicot with her White Claw, crossing her arms as she shrugged.

"We didn't take anything from you," Chicot said. "It's embarrassing that you keep blaming us for your problems."

"That's not how everyone else sees it," Brewhilda practically spat the words. Chicot's eyes scanned the crowd, looking for Elijah, Monty, Sunnie, anyone to save her from this situation. All she found was a few unfamiliar faces and the backs of many people's heads as they watched the fire. Chicot could walk away, of course, but something about that felt like letting Brewhilda win.

"It's only going to look worse," Brewhilda continued, "if you start dating my ex."

Chicot's nose scrunched. "Your ex?"

"Yeah." Brewhilda smirked, her eyebrows flicking as she licked her lips. "You know, Monty. Who has suddenly decided she needs to be some sort of pastel cottagecore poser."

Brewhilda stuck her tongue out, making a "bleh" noise as she rolled her eyes. Chicot crushed her can without realizing she'd been squeezing it. Brewhilda squeaked as beer splattered on her, the rest running down Chicot's hand.

"What is your *goal* here?" Chicot asked. "Because all you're succeeding in is making sure that I take every. Single. Stage and time slot you have at every Renaissance faire in the country."

"As if you *could*," Brewhilda hissed, shaking her arm off to try and get the beer off it. "You and your stupid little clown act is a dime a dozen. They just didn't have one this year because the last jester retired."

"Elijah and I *can*." Chicot leaned toward her, dripping, broken can at her side as Brewhilda balled her hand into a fist. "Where are you going next? Pennsylvania? Georgia? Whichever it is, we'll take *your* spot."

At this rate, more people were looking at them, some of them mumbling. She could just barely see Sunnie's bandana over Brewhilda's shoulder, and he was pushing his way through the crowd toward them. Chicot didn't move. She set her jaw and straightened her shoulders, goading her to do something. Brewhilda's hand opened back up, and for a moment, Chicot thought she might have her eyes clawed out by Brewhilda's matte black, coffin-shaped nails. Sunnie had his hand on her shoulder before she could thankfully.

"Brewhilda! I didn't realize you were here." Sunnie grinned, putting himself between them. "Nathan is looking for you."

Brewhilda narrowed her eyes, chewing on her lip as she tapped a nail on her can. She lifted her chin, looking toward the crowd.

"I'll go find him," Brewhilda said and turned on her heel. Once she disappeared into the crowd, Sunnie whistled, looking down at Chicot.

"What'd she say?" He carefully extracted the crushed, dribbling can from her hand. "You looked ready to kill her."

"It doesn't matter." Chicot sighed. She glanced around the crowd again, and Elijah was making his way over, but she still didn't see Monty. That was probably for the best.

"If you almost killed her over it, it does." Sunnie raised an eyebrow at her. Chicot pressed her lips together. She knew he was right, but she didn't want to admit it. She scratched her neck as Elijah joined them.

"What's going on?" Elijah looked between Chicot and Sunnie rapidly.

"Nothing, just—" Chicot jerked her head in the direction Brewhilda went. "I may have told Brewhilda we'd steal her time slots and stages at every ren faire in the country."

Elijah blinked at Chicot slowly and then snorted, clapping a hand on her shoulder. Chicot nearly fell over, bending slightly when he grabbed onto her and shook her. Sunnie snorted, a bark of laughter escaping him.

"And we will." Elijah wrapped an arm around Chicot now, squeezing her in a half hug. "Look at you, standing up for yourself."

"Is that what I did?" Chicot asked. Sunnie ruffled her hair quickly.

"Sure sounds like it," he said. "You certain didn't say anything uncouth?"

"I don't think I did." Chicot's chest collapsed, her smile growing as Elijah shook her more and Sunnie grabbed her other shoulder, joining in on it.

Her eyes caught Monty's as she stepped between the people in the crowd, a beer in her hand as her skirt fluttered behind her. Chicot's breath left her, Elijah still shaking her as a smile spread across Monty's face, her head tilting to one side. She chuckled as she approached them, her hand rising to her lips to wipe away a drop of her drink, the cuff of her jacket covering the very bottom of her hand.

"Why are you treating Chicot like a hacky sack?" Monty asked. Elijah and Sunnie stilled, Sunnie setting an arm on Chicot's shoulder as he shrugged.

"She deserved it," Elijah said. Monty snorted, shaking her head as she grew closer.

"Did you?" she asked Chicot. Her lips were pursed, cheeks rounded in amusement as she stepped close to Chicot again.

"Probably." Chicot leaned closer Monty in return. Elijah let go of Chicot then, turning so he could pat her shoulder one more time and then making some quick excuse so he could vacate. Sunnie seemed to take this as some sort of cue, promptly doing the same so that Monty and Chicot were alone again.

"Hey, uh—" Chicot looked around, her eyes lingering on Brewhilda for just a moment. "Would you still be interested in that night cap? Maybe a chance to have more privacy?"

Monty's voice went up in pitch. "I'd like that."

Chicot licked her lips as she stepped around Monty, looking back at her. "Shall we then?"

Monty bobbed her head, quickly turning to follow Chicot away from the group, back to the RV park.

Monty led her back to the RV she shared with Elvis and Lyza. A few others had trickled away from the bonfire, seeking quiet or a place to chat. Chicot settled under the small awning on a camp bench outside, waiting for Monty to get a bottle of something while she listened to mosquitoes get zapped by a small light hanging at the corner of the overhang. Their camper was larger than Chicot and Elijah's. By Chicot's guess, it probably had a real bedroom inside, unlike theirs.

"Ice?" Monty's head poked out of the door, and Chicot just nodded at her. She came back shortly, pressing a cool glass to the back of Chicot's neck and chuckling when she shivered. The drink was bitter and sweet, some cherry flavor too, but mostly she tasted the bourbon. A hum came out of her as she licked the cool liquor from her lips, Monty's eyes lingering on her as she did.

"Old-fashioned?" Chicot asked. Monty smirked, her head bobbing once.

"Elvis and Lyza got real into them, and now Lyza can't drink." Monty sat beside Chicot, her weight naturally causing Chicot to sink toward her. Not that either of them really minded as they relaxed among the buzz of AC units and looked at the dark sky while they talked.

"It's good," Chicot said. "You make them well."

"Thanks," Monty said. They talked about drinks for a while longer, discussing cocktails they liked, Chicot sharing the ridiculous beer-mosas her and Elijah sometimes made, Monty laughing as she made dramatic retching noises. They sipped their concoctions, Monty's arm slowly drifting around Chicot's shoulders as it started to finally, truly cool off, the two of them scooting close to each other for warmth.

"Hey, uh," Monty said after a while. "Can I talk to you about something?"

Chicot perked up, turning to face Monty better. It meant she had to pull away, holding her now empty glass. "Of course."

"So." Monty rubbed her neck. "Could we ... maybe keep this to ourselves for now? As best we can."

Chicot bounced her leg, sipping the sweetened water from the bottom of her glass as she looked straight ahead. She was having flashbacks to the cheerleader she'd slept with a few times in high school, who'd always wanted to hide that they were seeing each other and had strung Chicot along for months. But this probably was nothing like that, and when she looked at Monty, she seemed as nervous as Chicot felt.

"I just," Monty continued. "I'm worried that if we tell Lyza, she'll get very ... Well, she'll ..."

Chicot's muscles relaxed. She didn't even realize how tight her body had been. The camp bench shifted under her as she turned to Monty, her lips quirking up.

"Meddle?" Chicot asked. Monty groaned and pressed her hands to her face.

"Yes." Monty pressed her lips together when Chicot barked out a laugh.

"She can't help herself, can she?" Chicot asked. Monty glowered, shaking her head.

"She cannot." Monty sighed and set her head in her hand, looking at Chicot.

"Yeah, we can keep it to ourselves," Chicot said. She tapped her finger on the rim of her glass, meeting Monty's eyes as she thought about Brewhilda's comment at the bonfire. It might be good to keep it out of the public eye as much as they could, lest they want to deal with faire-wide gossip.

"Can I ask you something?" Chicot tapped her nail against the edge of her glass, looking at the ice as it rattled.

"Yeah, of course." Monty smiled, her head tilting to one side.

"Um, Brewhilda said that she was your ex." Chicot paused, watching as Monty's eyes grew wide. She shifted, her shoulders pulling tight for a moment, and she nodded. They stared at each other, Monty's mouth hanging open as she took another look at Chicot.

"Sorry, that wasn't what I was expecting you to ask." Monty chuckled awkwardly. "But yeah, she and I dated a few years ago while we were at Albion and Georgia. It fell apart, and then I'd stupidly go back to sleep with her sometimes. I decided at the end of last year, no more of that, though."

Chicot bobbed her head and bit her lip. "Was she the one who told you that you didn't look good in feminine clothes?"

"Sort of?" Monty twirled a lock of her hair in her fingers. "I mean, yes, she did. She had this thing about only dating butches when she dates women and always made comments if I so much as wore a skirt. But I was a tomboy as a kid so I . . . I already had things about it."

"I had a feeling, based on something she said," Chicot explained. "And well, I know it's not worth much, but I do really think she's wrong."

Monty snorted, smiling. "Thanks."

They met each other's eyes, Chicot's heart racing slightly. Her fingers trembled so she squeezed her glass, Monty's hand drifting to her jaw. She leaned forward slightly, carefully pulling Chicot so their lips could brush against each other's. Shivers ran from the very tips of Chicot's fingers to where Monty's tongue now slid against her bottom lip, fire lighting in her belly. Monty's fingers felt cool against the skin of her jaw, slowly moving to her shoulder as Chicot scooted closer.

Chicot lost track of time, her whole world narrowing down to Monty's lips and tongue, the way her hand drifted to Chicot's knee, shifting under to pull her closer. It was awkward on the camp bench, the two of them desperately trying to explore each other without enough space to do so.

"Want to go inside?" Monty asked after a while. Chicot's mouth went dry, and she nodded as Monty took her hand. She had no idea where her cocktail glass was, her feet moving her along and into the RV without much thought. But Monty had both of them, carefully setting them in the sink before she took Chicot's hand again, pulling her past a ladder that led to a bed above the driving cab, through the kitchen, and into the bedroom at the back of the RV.

Monty's bedroom had a bed that took up most of it, plush sheets and a quilt in lavender and white spread across it. In one corner, there was an acoustic guitar on a stand, an Ibanez which, according to Elijah, was the best brand out there. There were some built-in shelves across from it and a single star-shaped lamp that bathed the room in warm light bright enough to read in, but not obnoxiously so like LEDs could sometimes be.

"One sec," Monty said and slipped out of the room again. Chicot just nodded, looking around while she was gone.

Chicot's eyes lingered on one photo of Monty standing with Lyza in full ren faire garb as her body vibrated with anticipation. They weren't in their performance costumes, but something that looked like they'd been guests. They were both soaked through, their matching linen chemises clinging to their skin and nearly see-through, corsets darkened from rain, and their hair stuck to their wet skin around their faces. She stared at Monty, the bright smile on her pretty, round face and light eyelashes nearly hiding her eyes from view. Something about the photo looked familiar, but Chicot couldn't place it exactly. It felt like she had seen it before, but she didn't know where. Maybe it was one they had in the backstage area?

That left her mind entirely when Monty came back. She set one hand on Chicot's jaw, drawing her in as Chicot wrapped her arms around her neck. Monty's strong hands slipped to the small of Chicot's back, her world narrowing again as Monty easily scooped her up, sitting her on the edge of the bed as she started to press Chicot back. She had brought in a harness, and as soon as Chicot's mind registered it, it blurred, the only image remaining that of Monty wearing a strap.

Chicot nearly jumped out of her skin when there was insistent banging. Monty furrowed her brow, glancing back at her closed bedroom door before she looked at Chicot.

"Chicot!" Elijah's voice was raised, and he sounded drunk and excited. "Please come out here!"

"Are we hiding this from Elijah too?" Chicot asked. Monty sighed, tossing the harness somewhere into the mess of sheets on her bed.

"We don't have to." Monty straightened up, opening the door as Chicot followed, trying to get her shirt on again. Monty, to her credit, looked more amused than anything. Chicot, on the other hand, was annoyed.

Elijah was jumping and waving as Chicot opened the door. He was plastered, slurring his words and almost calling Chicot by her given name. Chicot squeaked as he caught her by the waist when she hit the bottom of the stairs, picking her up and twirling her around. Behind her, Monty laughed, and Chicot started to laugh too, trying to figure out what on earth Elijah was trying to tell her.

"Wait! What?" Chicot laughed as Elijah spun her again. Some people were looking their way, largely seeming annoyed at how loud they were being this late at night. Elijah settled Chicot on the ground, taking her hand and pulling her.

"Actually, we should go to our RV." Elijah then looked at Monty. "Sorry, I need to take her."

Monty chuckled. "It's okay. You kind of seem like you'll need help getting into bed."

Chicot looked up at Monty, frowning. She slumped as she looked back at Elijah, tempted to tell him they could talk in the morning. As she watched Elijah sway on his feet, Chicot groaned. Monty was right. Elijah probably needed to be taken care of, so Chicot rolled her eyes and nodded, "Sorry. Rain check?"

"Yeah." Monty waved at her slightly. Elijah had already started to pull Monty along, heading home. She basically had to run to keep up with him as he tugged on her arm. Once they were a good distance away, Chicot grumbled, "You *better* have a really good reason for this."

"Trust me, you'll understand soon." Elijah wagged a finger like he was lecturing her. Chicot rolled her eyes. She could only be so mad at him for interrupting her and Monty if this was really important. She followed Elijah back, where a very confused and shirtless man was sitting up in the bed. Chicot was 90% sure it was Ken, only because it was the most logical option. Without any clothes, he just sort of looked like a man to her. He furrowed his brow, waving at Chicot as Elijah stopped her in the kitchen.

"Hi?" Chicot started. Elijah grabbed both her shoulders, turning her to face him instead of Ken now. She felt like this was a repeat of when Elijah and Sunnie had been shaking her earlier that night. "Oh god, what is going on?"

"We got an audition at Pennsylvania!" Elijah said it like it was all one word, so quickly that Chicot almost didn't fully process it at first. She shook her head, squeezing her eyes shut.

"What? How? I thought we didn't get a callback?" Chicot asked. Elijah grinned, setting his hands on her shoulders again.

"Someone dropped out." Elijah's fingers pressed into Chicot's skin, not hard enough to hurt, but enough to make her feel very awake. "They need to fill the spot, so they called us back."

All at once, Chicot started to tremble, rising to her toes and hopping with Elijah as they both started to scream together. It sent Duchess directly under the bed, her eyes the only thing visible in the black void underneath it. They did this for a solid minute, and Ken just sighed once they finished, throwing the blanket off him to stand up, conceding to the fact that he wasn't going to sleep any time soon.

"We got an audition!" Chicot threw her arms around Elijah, the two of them spinning in place slightly as Elijah hugged her back. He suddenly seemed far more sober, and Chicot wondered how much of that had been an act to get away with dragging her off.

"Congratulations." Ken had an easy smile on his face, his eyes quickly moving from Chicot to Elijah and his expression growing soft.

"Sorry." Elijah laughed as he tipped his head back. "I just can't believe we did it."

"Now we just have to get in," Chicot added. "When is it? Do we send a video, or do we have to go there?"

"Uh." Elijah paused, pulling his phone from his pocket to read the email. "They want us there in person, and it's at the end of the month. On a Thursday so we won't miss any faire days."

"Okay." Chicot nodded slowly. "Okay."

"How are you getting from Wisconsin to Pennsylvania?" Ken asked. Chicot's muscles stiffened, and she felt Elijah's do the same thing as Ken finished his question. Their RV was at the very center of the dog park. They couldn't just move it, and even then because the audition was on a Thursday, they couldn't risk breaking down on the almost thirteen-hour drive.

"We'll have to fly," Elijah resolved. "And rent a car."

"How much is in our savings?" Chicot asked.

Elijah's face traveled as far as they would need to for this audition. It started at thoughtful then rapidly went to unsure and landed on deflated.

"Not … enough for everything," he said. Chicot took a deep breath, her chest numb as she slowly turned toward the phone fund jar. Ken stepped out of her way as she reached for it, holding it in both her hands.

"Oh, Chicot. I'm sorry," Elijah said. Chicot shook her head.

"I care so much more about us getting to continue to do all of this"—Chicot gestured around the RV—"than having a phone."

Elijah's eyes fell on the jar, growing more vacant as he took it from Chicot. "Then we have to get this right."

"We do." Chicot pressed her lips together, meeting Elijah's eyes. They nodded at each other, the RV getting quiet around them. Then Ken piped up.

"I can drive you and pick you up from the airport." He held up a hand like he was trying to politely ask a question in class. Chicot chuckled, endeared because honestly, Ken was sweet. She liked him for Elijah. Elijah smiled, stepping over to cup Ken's cheek as he kissed the other.

"Oh my god," Chicot squealed. "I need to tell Monty. And Sunnie!"

She spun on her heels, Elijah laughing as she bolted out the door. Chicot paused, turning around entirely and going right back inside to look at Elijah.

"You okay?" Elijah stepped toward her.

"I'm not sure ..." Chicot rubbed her cheek. "I shouldn't tell Monty until we know for sure."

She didn't really know what Monty wanted from her. Whether she wanted to be Monty's girlfriend or if this was just a fling during Albion. Chicot didn't know what she wanted either. Her heart hammered in her chest, fingers numb as she tapped them against her lips.

Ken excused himself to the bed again. Which frankly, Chicot did not blame him for. She was surprised he had stayed after all the yelling. Then again, it was late and he probably couldn't drive home if he'd been drinking.

"Why don't you think you should tell her?" Elijah asked. "Are they going to Georgia or something next?"

Chicot shook her head. "No, no. They're going to Pennsylvania. It's just ..."

She fidgeted with the hem of her crop top, pressing her lips together. Elijah just folded his arms, giving her the space to think.

"I *really* like her," Chicot confessed. "And what if she ... What if she only wants this to be a summer thing?"

Chicot rubbed her arm, trying to shake off the tingling feeling on her skin. She wasn't sure she wanted to find out that Monty only wanted a summer fling right before an audition that could change the course of their careers. She chewed on her lip as Elijah tilted his head.

"You can always talk to her about this after." Elijah's voice was gentle. "If it's too much stress right now."

"That might be for the best." Chicot sighed. "Oh, and don't mention her and me to Elvis and Lyza just yet."

Elijah took a deep breath. "Yeah, okay."

His eyes slid toward Ken now curled up in a ball under the blankets. Chicot nodded slowly, biting her lip.

"I should tell Sunnie," she said. "But I'm going to tell Monty after. And I should think about if I want to keep helping Monty, Lyza, and Elvis there in case they ask."

"Oh, I didn't even think about that." Elijah took a deep breath, releasing it slowly. "Do you think you can handle another sixteen shows a weekend for another eight weeks?"

"I think so," Chicot said. "But I don't want you to think I'm neglecting our show."

"I don't," Elijah shook his head, "I know you're not. And if we go to Pennsylvania, Trevor and Adrian said I could play with their bard band for some extra money since they lost their lute player."

Chicot nodded, offering Elijah her hand. He took it and squeezed.

"We're in this together?" Elijah asked. Chicot nodded.

"Yeah, 'til the end."

CHAPTER 15

The weeks started to feel like a marathon as they counted down to their audition. Between practicing, faire days, and the extra lessons Sunnie was giving her, Chicot felt like her head was constantly spinning. Her and Elijah also reworked their blocking, which might have given them away to Lyza, Elvis, and Monty. However, the three of them didn't say anything about it as they watched Elijah and Chicot practice during their usual time at the gym. They swapped their bit with the tack for simply having Chicot not tie off the balloon, reducing the failure rate of the trick. Plus, it was almost more humorous when Chicot simply let the balloon go and it flew around as it lost air.

Chicot took apart her mask, refining the mechanism that allowed her to blow up the balloons, making it easier for her to get it out of the way so she could also use a slide whistle during the show. The first time they did this in practice, Monty and Lyza laughed so hard that they were both crying. Elijah took this as encouragement to push it further, making the jokes sharper, having Chicot pantomime more, and even toying with the idea of Chicot stealing Elijah's lute at one point. Chicot nixed that idea, since she couldn't play it at all with gloves on. They renamed their act for Pennsylvania, going from *The Jester and The Bard, Forever at Odds* to *Court Jester Chicot's House Rules*. This had been born from new lines they had added to the introduction where Elijah implied he was a new court bard learning the rules from a jester who didn't speak. Elijah also said it was snappier and more marketable, and Chicot simply went along with it. He knew better than her on this sort of thing anyway.

When she wasn't working with Elijah, Chicot was either at the faire or with Monty. She thought it would be difficult not to tell Monty about the audition. But to Chicot's surprise, Monty made it easy. She did it by finding times to set Chicot ablaze whenever she could. Monty had gotten good at targeting the small things that sent Chicot into a feverish series of daydreams about Monty's hands or tongue or teeth. The worst part was that she backed it up with moments when they were alone, taking Chicot apart whenever they found the time.

Chicot welcomed the distraction. When she wasn't practicing or working, she was thinking about the audition, and her mind found infinite ways she could mess up the whole show. If she lingered on this too long, she started to panic, and Monty was an incredibly good at getting Chicot out of her head. Monty seemed to pick up on this, checking in on Chicot when she could without necessarily asking what was going on. Other times, Monty simply provided a diversion. Like when Monty squeezed Chicot's thigh just right while they were on their meal break before she left to go back to advertising *The Pirates Three*. Chicot was at least able to linger on the way Monty was going to press Chicot into the mattress later instead of her audition stress.

They were managing to mostly fly under Lyza and Elvis's radar, even as they got bolder about finding places to tuck away and make out. On off days, they'd go into the town center together for coffee and it often devolved into them finding a secluded spot to park Monty's car so they could be alone. That was the only time it was hard not to mention the audition, because Chicot wanted so badly to see how excited Monty got when she found out she might get to be at Pennsylvania with her. The only thing that stopped Chicot was the fear that Monty wouldn't be excited about it, and if that was the case, Chicot would be better off finding out after their audition. For now, she needed to focus.

"Hey." Monty ran her fingers through Chicot's hair and then grabbed her chin, tipping it up to get her to look at her. It made Chicot shiver. They were in the back of Monty's car, the sun slowly fading behind them as they chatted about books they'd read.

"Yeah?" Chicot tilted her head forward, kissing Monty's fingers since they were there.

"Do you know if you'll be getting a phone before the end of the season here at Albion?" Monty asked. Chicot froze, her fingers ghosting over the fabric of the back seat, trying to find something to hold onto.

"Um, I'm not really sure," Chicot said. "Why?"

Monty shrugged. "I was just thinking about it."

Chicot raised an eyebrow at her, but Monty smiled, tipping Chicot's chin up again and kissing her, all thoughts leaving Chicot's head. When Monty pulled away, she grinned at Chicot, her fingers trailing over Chicot's jawbone, something she did quite often. It was small, subtle, the tilt of her fingers until they reached Chicot's ear, but it was comforting. Like Monty wrapping Chicot in a blanket or putting an arm around her.

"Brewhilda really fumbled the ball." Chicot's brain hadn't caught up with her mouth, her words spilling out without a real thought behind them. Monty's eyebrow arched at her, one corner of her mouth tilting up.

"Because you're going to steal her spot at every ren faire east of the Mississippi?" Monty asked. Chicot's cheeks burnt. She hadn't realized people had been talking about that comment.

"N-No," Chicot said. "I meant with you. Sorry, that was probably weird."

Monty blinked at her, face slowly growing rosy as she stared at Chicot. Then she laughed, her hand covering her mouth as she bent into Chicot's space, her hair brushing Chicot's chin as she snaked an arm around Chicot's middle. Chicot laughed with her, meeting the kiss that followed as she let Monty press her back into the seat of her car.

"I hope you really do take every single one of Tegan's spots," Monty whispered. "You and Elijah work so much harder, and you deserve it so much more."

Chicot blinked. "Who is Tegan?"

Monty blinked at Chicot. "That's Brewhilda's real name."

"Oh!" Chicot laughed. "Fuck. I mean, I barely recognized her out of costume, so you can't expect me to know that."

Monty tilted her head to the side, her mouth opening and closing as she got one of those narrow-eyed looks that Chicot had become so used to. Her fingers ran absently over Chicot's arm.

"She doesn't wear a mask or anything though." Monty's voice lilted up at the end like she was asking a question, but she'd definitely only made a statement. "Just heavy makeup."

Chicot let out an awkward chuckle. It was probably better if Monty knew about this anyway. "It's a little embarrassing, but I'm not very good with faces. I usually recognize people by their hair or how they dress. Save for people I've spent a lot of time with. I'm getting there with you and Lyza and Elvis ... but if I saw you in a crowd or far away ..."

Monty considered that for a moment, her eyes distant.

"Is that why you always seem to look at my clothes first?" Monty asked. Chicot rubbed the back of her head and nodded.

"Yeah," Chicot admitted. "But also, you dress cute and you almost always have that lil plush bunny charm from your car keys hanging out of your pocket. It makes it easier."

"Well." Monty's speech was slow, like she was thinking as she spoke. "Then I'll make sure you can see it. If I'm approaching you from far away."

Chicot's thoughts scattered, racing as she smiled wide at Monty. Besides Elijah, no one had ever been so quick to make this easy for Chicot. They usually expected her to get better on her own, to stop being confused that they were yelling at her from across the playground or football field. But Monty wanted to help her. She wanted to make sure Chicot could always pick her out of a crowd. That made

Chicot's belly flip, a shiver running from the very pit of her stomach all the way up to the top of her head as she processed that Monty wanted Chicot to be able to always see her.

"Is that okay?" Monty asked, drawing Chicot out of her thoughts. She hadn't realized how long she'd been quiet, her grin now splitting her face as she leaned up to pull Monty into another kiss, the two of them devolving into the heat, the windows of the car fogging as Chicot found herself enveloped in Monty's warmth and soft skin.

"It's more than okay," Chicot told her, licking her lips and thinking of the bonfire. "You know, we never did get to finish that night cap."

Monty's brow raised, her arms bracketing Chicot in on either side. "I wasn't sure if I should mention that Elvis and Lyza are going to be staying in Milwaukee tonight …"

"Maybe we should head back then?" Chicot's eyes raised, lidded as they lingered on Monty's lips. Her legs shifted, falling farther open for her. "It'll be dark, so no one else will probably notice us."

"What, like we're teens hiding from our parents?" Monty giggled, leaning toward Chicot as she caught her lips in a sweet kiss. Chicot chuckled.

"No, from nosy neighbors," Chicot quipped. Monty grinned.

"Then let's give the sun a few more minutes to go down." Monty kissed Chicot's collarbone. "And then we'll leave."

Chicot grinned, tipping her head back to give Monty more space. They couldn't really do anything here, so she just had to be patient. It was harder than Chicot expected to keep her hands from sliding somewhere they shouldn't just yet or trying to get between Monty's legs right there.

They were both rumpled by the time they moved back into the front, Monty in the driver's seat as they sped back to the dog park. She had her hand on Chicot's thigh the whole way, a shiver going through her whenever Monty squeezed.

Chicot didn't see much of Monty, Lyza, and Elvis's RV. The lights were dim, and Monty had Chicot by the hand, pulling her through the small kitchen to Monty's bedroom at the back. The only light was that lamp in the corner again, but it was dimmed low so that it mostly provided ambience, which in this case was probably for the better, as Monty pulled Chicot close to her.

Their lips crashed together, Monty kicking the door shut and grabbing at the blinds in the small window next to the bed. She managed to get them down without breaking away, one hand spread wide on the small of Chicot's back as she did it. Chicot didn't really have time to be impressed, her stomach fluttering as Monty nudged her backwards onto the bed. She hadn't realized how much she'd wanted Monty's hands on her like this. They'd been on Chicot so many times of course, eight shows a weekend, practice each week, but they were warm and soft right now in a way they weren't when Monty was lifting her. She buried her fingers into Monty's hair, tugging on Monty's dress for her so she could crawl on top of Chicot without it being in the way.

Monty's mouth tasted sweet, a hint of the chocolatey coffee she'd been drinking still lingering on her tongue as she ran her hands up Chicot's sides. She held her so firmly, Chicot squirmed slightly when something tickled, but she couldn't really get away. It made her skin tingle, her head tipping back as Monty's mouth moved from Chicot's lips to her jawline. Chicot's fingers found their way to Monty's jacket, helping her shrug it off and tossing it next to the bed, a rush of shivers running down her spine as Monty smiled at her when she did it. She sat up, leaning forward to kiss Monty's jaw, a satisfied moan coming out of Monty when Chicot ran the tip of her tongue along her neck.

"Can I go down on you?" The words came out of Chicot so naturally, her fingers gently sliding up the fronts of Monty's thighs. She had never quite been this bold in bed, her nerves usually fraying and tugging so tight she could never get any words out. But Monty, for whatever reason, seemed to put her at ease. "Please?"

"Yes," Monty murmured. Her fingers fidgeted with the sheets at Chicot's sides.

Chicot was already rolling them over, Monty a willing participant because Chicot was certainly not strong enough to somehow overpower her. She paused once she was sitting between Monty's legs, her eyes finding her face in the low light of Monty's bedroom. God, she was *in* Monty's bed. Chicot licked her lips. Monty's face already had a pretty pink flush all over it, mostly on her cheeks, which made her jaw look softer and even cuter. Chicot wanted to plant kisses all over them, but she was focused on other things at the moment.

Monty's fingers shifted to Chicot's face, eyes trained on her lips as she traced Chicot's features. Chicot leaned forward, giving her a chaste kiss and a smile before she was helping Monty get her dress off so it could join her jacket. Monty protested slightly about being the only one losing clothes, so Chicot stopped to ditch her crop top. She hadn't been wearing a bra, but at this point, she didn't think it mattered. It did earn a nice, quiet noise of surprise from Monty.

Chicot buried herself in Monty's skin then, her tongue finding the spots that made Monty twitch with anticipation and her teeth nipping places that made her moan. Her soft, lacy bra cupped her breasts so nicely, but Chicot had imagined this moment more than a few times alone in the shower and it hadn't been there. It didn't take much time to get it off, her hands gently squeezing as she took turns lapping at Monty's nipples. Monty responded with low, breathy noises, her fingers gripping Chicot's shoulders tightly, eventually having to ask Chicot to move on because Chicot could have stayed right there for the rest of the night. Of course, there were other things she wanted to do, other noises she wanted Monty to make.

Her fingers dragged over Monty's sides, Monty's tummy twitching ever so slightly as she laughed. Chicot apologized, the two of them smiling at each other for a moment as they reveled in the touch of each other's skin, even if they were tickling each other by mistake. When her palm grazed Monty's strong thigh, Chicot knew she was going to be lost to this for a very long time. Monty, who was so kind and sweet and guarded, was opening up to her, and Chicot wanted to see every part of it.

Monty's panties had ribbons on them, and while they had lace at the edges, they weren't the same shade of pink as the bra. Chicot couldn't help the way she stopped to admire them for a moment. However, they prevented her from getting to exactly what she wanted, which meant they had to go, and quickly joined the pile slowly amassing.

When she kissed Monty's inner thigh, Monty groaned and her head fell back against the pillows behind her, one hand now loosely holding onto Chicot's hair. Chicot went slowly at first, giving Monty the chance to say no, to back out, to tell her to stop, but it never came. Her lips found soft pubic hair, her tongue peeking out as she teased Monty's inner lips. Monty's grip tightened, a gasp escaping her, and she met Chicot's eyes. Hers were lidded, lips parted as she ran a gentle finger over Chicot's cheek and nodded at Chicot. Chicot just shot her a grin before she buried her face between Monty's legs.

Monty wasn't particularly loud, but Chicot found quickly that she could read her. Every swipe of her tongue or change in pattern made Monty's hips twitch slightly. Chicot planted one of her thumbs just above Monty's clit, holding the soft skin of her hood out of the way so she could relish in the way she gasped and rolled her hips as Chicot teased her tongue over it.

"Fuck, it's been so long." Monty's voice came out cracked and a shiver ran down the leg that Chicot was currently holding onto for dear life because she was fairly certain Monty could crush her between her thighs. "Chicot, *please.*"

Chicot got the memo, her eyes fluttering shut as she settled in to focus on Monty's clit. She wrapped her lips around it, sucking gently as Monty's voice jumped an octave, her fingers pulling Chicot's hair hard enough to moan. Chicot pressed her hips down on the bed, trying to get some sort of friction, but it was a largely fruitless effort. It didn't matter, because when Monty's voice broke off, her muscles tensing around Chicot's shoulders and chest as she came was all that Chicot needed. It left her wet and twitching, Chicot's lips hanging parted as she pulled away. When Chicot picked her head up, her eyes swam slightly, air reaching her lungs for what felt like the first time in a while as Monty tugged her up for a kiss. Chicot barely had a chance to wipe her mouth off before she met Monty's lips, still dazed and wanting.

"I have a strap." Monty's lips were pressed against Chicot's ear. It made Chicot shiver. "Or I can use my fingers."

An ache formed in Chicot's belly, her hands on Monty's shoulders as she tried to ground herself. She didn't really think it was going to work, so she gave up quickly. Chicot could stay on this cloud for the rest of her life if it meant Monty would whisper against her ear like that again.

"Fingers," Chicot answered. She wanted the connection, the skin on skin, the control of a curled pointer finger, and most of all, she wanted to feel Monty's strong hands on her. Monty nodded, a snicker coming out of her as she pressed Chicot onto her back. She then made quick work of getting Chicot's baggy jeans off, mostly struggling with her belt before she had Chicot down to her underwear.

Monty took her time just like Chicot had, and it made Chicot want to beg and plead because she was already so worked up, but something in her told her that wouldn't work. She stopped caring entirely when Monty's tongue slid over one of Chicot's nipples, her thumb toying with the other as Chicot squirmed.

"Your tits are so cute." Monty's warm breath slid over Chicot's skin, her chest tingling as she rocked her hips against the bed again. Chicot didn't have time to think about it before she whimpered, her fingers finding Monty's hair as she continued to toy with Chicot's boobs.

"Oh, that was adorable." Monty smiled at Chicot, sitting up to look at her face more directly. Chicot's skin felt like it was on fire. She had never experienced anything like this. Maybe it was because she was used to being the top or because the last few people she'd hooked up with were men, but something about the gentle timber of Monty's voice, the way she knew just where to touch Chicot, it had her on edge already.

"I—" Before Chicot could find a response, Monty slipped her fingers under the band of Chicot's boxers, her thumb gently teasing her lips open, brushing her clit ever so slightly. Any words that were going to come out of Chicot were replaced with a moan, her back arching off the bed as Monty dipped her thumb between her lips again.

"God, you're so wet," Monty mumbled. She didn't seem to want a response this time. It was more of a revelation than anything. One that made her pupils blow wide like a predator ready to strike. Chicot lifted her hips so Monty could get her underwear off, a squeak of surprise coming out of her as Monty grabbed one of Chicot's legs and pulled her closer. Monty chuckled softly, a single finger now sliding up Chicot's pussy, just barely opening her lips.

"*Monty*," Chicot gasped. Her eyes focused on the ceiling because if she looked at Monty, she would fall apart. She was sure of it. Monty seemed to take this as a sort of challenge, though, on her knees with one leg between Chicot's as she slipped a finger inside of her. She leaned over Chicot, her hand planted next to Chicot's head as she looked down at her. Whenever Chicot's eyes fluttered open for a moment, she saw Monty watching her, watching every tiny reaction she had as she added another finger or curled them in just the right way.

Chicot was loud. She couldn't help it. She just hoped no one outside of the RV heard them, and if they did, they had the decency not to say anything. Monty didn't even seem to care, bracing her knee against the back of her hand for leverage so she could fuck Chicot a little harder, her fingers deep and large enough that Chicot moaned with every thrust, her head tilted back.

"Are you close?" Monty's voice was a whisper against her ear again, Chicot clinging to her shoulders. Chicot nodded, her eyes lidded and bleary as she looked up at Monty, shivering when she chuckled softly. "Come for me."

"Fuck." Chicot's eyes widened, a moan coming out of her as her hips rose to meet Monty's hand. She gasped when Monty curled her fingers again, her thumb now pressing against her clit instead of taking the occasional teasing swipe. Monty rolled the soft pad against Chicot's clit and it was over, her eyes rolling back as she'd lost herself for a second, Monty's name the only word she could form. Her eyes stuck on Monty's cool gray ones as she watched every second of Chicot's orgasm cross her face.

It took a few minutes for Chicot to truly come back to Earth. When she did feel herself hit the ground, it was on the soft bed next to Monty, the two of them panting. Monty's fingers were in her hair, nails gently running over her scalp as Chicot's eyes lulled closed. She didn't want to fall asleep yet, so she shifted, gently pulling away from Monty's hand to sit up.

"I feel like we should have done that sooner." Chicot leaned down to plant a soft kiss on Monty's lips, a grin spreading across her face when Monty giggled.

"Maybe." Monty's fingers lingered on Chicot's warm skin, Chicot's entire body hot even with the AC blasting. They watched each other for a while, their eyes mostly on each other's face but drifting away here and there. Eventually, Chicot shivered, and Monty got up to find her something to put on. Once Chicot was in a shirt that would have been big on Monty—which meant she was borderline swimming in it—and she had her underwear back on, she slipped into the bathroom.

She splashed warm water on her face, shaking it out of the ends of her hair. When she joined Monty in her room again, Monty was in her bed with the blankets over her legs. A soft salmon-colored shirt hung off her shoulders with a large logo of some restaurant that Chicot didn't recognize on the front. In her hand was a vape that was shaped like an old pipe. The only difference was that the well where tobacco would go had an LED screen in it. Monty held it up and took a slow drag from it.

"It helps me sleep," Monty said. Chicot crawled into the bed next to her, smiling.

"Can I have a hit?" Chicot asked. Monty smiled, offering her the pipe. Chicot carefully slipped it from her fingers, their skin brushing and sending a warm shock through her. She had a feeling practice was going to be much difficult now that they knew what their bare skin felt like when it touched.

Chicot gently pressed the lip of the pipe against her mouth, taking a slow breath so she didn't overdo it. She carefully handed the pipe back off as she held the vapor in her lungs, letting it burn slightly before she exhaled.

"Where'd you even get that?" Chicot asked. Monty chuckled softly, tucking the pipe into a safe spot in the built-in shelves next to her bed.

"One of the pipe shops at the faire in Ohio had them," she said. "They were too funny to pass up."

Chicot chuckled. "Wanted to feel like Rosie Cotton stealing Sam's pipe, huh?"

"I did." Monty slid closer to Chicot to wrap her arms around her middle. Chicot pressed into her shoulder, inhaling softly. Monty's skin still smelled like oak moss and sugar, something that Chicot guessed came from her lotion or a perfume; she wasn't really sure. She liked it, and as she sunk into the buzzing feeling of being high and Monty's warmth, Chicot couldn't help but wonder why she had thought this was a bad idea at any point.

CHAPTER 16

Chicot spotted him from atop her box during their third perfor-mance of the day the Sunday before their audition. They were leaving at five a.m. in just two days and there he was, a stupid cowboy hat he'd had all her life with an Easter bunny charm that Chicot had tied onto the rope around the brim as a little kid still sitting on it. There were two familiar little people next to him, their faces excited and their grins wide. He looked toward the stage, his eyes narrowed slightly, his head tilted as she tried to keep up with their act.

It was dizzying. The man with a face she had been told over and over was so similar to her own was watching her dance around on stage as Elijah played the lute next to her. They were testing their new version on the audiences, and everyone had been loving every second of their melodies and dances and jokes.

Her father simply had his lips pressed together hard as he watched. Chicot did her best to look at any other patron until they were finished. Then she turned her back, picking up their table as quickly as she could, and practically running backstage regardless of whether Elijah followed.

"Are you okay?" Elijah set an arm on her upper back as she set the table down and ripped her mask off. They'd finished, but Chicot had made mistakes, small ones, unnoticeable to the audience but definitely noticeable to Elijah.

"M-My dad was out there." Chicot swallowed hard, pressing a hand to her chest as she leaned on the wall. "He had to know that was me."

Elijah's expression pinched and he looked toward the curtain that led to the stage. "Are you sure?"

"Yes." Chicot tried to control her breathing. "He was wearing his hat. It was him."

They had to be out there to advertise the final show of the day, and Chicot's dad was still wandering about in his cowboy hat that identified him to her. The man who had always wrapped her up in hugs and told her everything would be okay, who would let her hide with him among the cows when her mother had sent her to her room.

But he had never called after she'd left. He'd been raised in the church in the depths of the deep woods of Wisconsin, so there was no way he was ever going either, even if she had a phone.

Worst of all, he had to have Juni and Charlie with him. There was no other explanation for why they were here. Juni must have asked to come. She loved it at the faire as much as Chicot had as a kid. Chicot should have realized and she was kicking herself for letting herself be blindsided. Her siblings were here, seeing her show and not even knowing that it was their big sister up there. At least, they wouldn't until they saw *The Pirate's Three*.

"Chicot, maybe you should go to the break area." Elijah knelt by her side. As he did, Elvis opened the backstage door to get his stilts and sign. He took one look at them and his brow wrinkled with worry.

"Everything okay?" Elvis asked. Chicot nodded quickly, putting her mask back on. If her dad couldn't see her face, he'd be just as oblivious to her as she would to him if he didn't have his hat on.

"Yeah, fine." Chicot grinned under the mask, squared her shoulders, and pushed herself to move past it. "I'll be okay, Elijah. I'm just a little warm."

"Okay …" Elijah dipped his head, watching as Chicot grabbed her balloons for making balloon animals and stepped out into the masses. She then turned back to Elijah, lunging out with one leg and gesturing wide with her arm, beckoning him without a word. They had a show to promote, money to make, and they couldn't dwell on her dad being at the faire. After all, he had brought her there in the first place. It was because of him that Genevieve had become Chicot, a silly jester who could make people laugh and laugh and laugh. So that was what she'd do. She'd perform.

Balloon animals were easy, and with pantomime and sleight of hand, Chicot could make little kids giggle until they were either screaming from excitement or no longer upset. She focused on kids who were crying, doing jigs to get up to them, offering them silly hats or dogs or swords. It worked almost every time, and each time their parents looked relieved when they calmed down.

She jingled the bells on her head, played games with the performers dressed as forest fey, trying to look ethereal as they snuck around the faire. See, Chicot could be normal as she found an open space to do cartwheels with her balloon swords, handing them off to kids. She produced cards seemingly out of thin air with their show information, beckoning people to come with laughter and magic. It was during one of Brewhilda's shows near the back of the faire, the loud punk music blaring as she spoke nonsense rhymes she pretended were spells, that Chicot spotted the hat again.

He was standing with Juni and Charlie at his side, loosely watching Brewhilda's set with a disinterested look on his face. Her dad had been the one to introduce her to The Ramones, The Clash, Dropkick Murphys—old punk. She wasn't surprised he didn't seem to care for whatever Brewhilda had written for her show. It was pretty soulless, not that Chicot would have called it out prior to Brewhilda being a total jerk to her.

Chicot took a deep breath, doing a jig as she tried to pass by her siblings and father, but Juni in her princess dress with her long, flowing brown hair pointed in her direction. She grinned.

"The jester!" she shouted. "It's the jester, up close!"

Chicot turned, waving as she stepped over her feet awkwardly. She didn't want to approach or get too close, not with her dad there, but she wanted to hug Juni and Charlie so bad. Now ten and six, her younger siblings were so much bigger than the last time Chicot had seen them. Charlie's eyes were big, blue-green, and smiling without a smile on his face yet. He had a mop of sandy brown curls, a giggle coming out of him as he pointed toward Chicot, agreeing with Juni.

It wasn't Chicot or the jester that broke—it was the person under the mask, Genevieve.

She stepped toward them, her hand out as she wiggled her fingers, getting Juni to put out her hand and close her eyes. Chicot then pulled something special from her pocket, producing a pot of body glitter she saved for special interactions. It was from the booth that sold elf ears, so it was safe for her to rub a little into Juni's small palm, her precious sister. Chicot took more, poking each of her chubby cheeks, rubbing in just the right way to leave heart shaped marks on her. By now, her dad was looking down at her, leaning toward Chicot slightly.

When Juni opened her eyes, she tapped her feet, squealing in glee as she thanked Chicot loudly for her gift. Chicot bowed to her, dramatic and large as Juni did a curtsy. She then quickly made a sword for Charlie out of balloons, taking the time to even add a shield as Juni showed him the glitter.

"Genevieve?" Her father's voice was low. He had been waiting patiently for a moment when the kids were distracted. Chicot swallowed hard, tilting her head side to side to act as if she were confused.

"That's you, isn't it?" her father asked. "You were up there with E.J."

Chicot tensed. She hadn't really expected her dad to recognize Elijah. He had been afflicted with similar issues to Chicot. It was something her mother had complained about endlessly. He could never pick her out of a crowd, and she refused to do anything to make it easier for him.

She handed the sword to Charlie after knighting him with it, offering the shield next. Charlie beamed, shouting an overly loud thank you at her like he was trying to be heard over music that wasn't there. Chicot then turned to her dad, shimmied her shoulders and skipping away like a good jester should.

When she looked back, Juni was waving wildly at her, and her dad's posture had completely collapsed in on itself. His head turned to fully face Chicot, his mouth hanging open slightly. Chicot turned, trying to put it out of her mind. The last thing she needed before their audition was to let her dad get into her head.

She told Elijah as much when they were in their trailer later, so he dropped it.

Chicot kept to herself the next few days, really only leaving the RV to work with Sunnie. When she saw Monty, she obviously sensed something was up, but didn't seem to know what. She would frown when Chicot wanted to go back to her bed and sleep, trying to rest up as much as possible before the audition. Monty never stopped her.

The night before they left, Monty did pull Chicot close after Monty had come to Chicot's trailer to ask her about going to dinner. Chicot had declined, and Monty hadn't been upset, but she kissed her cheek and mumbled against her skin.

"Whatever's going on, you'll be okay." Monty ran her fingers over Chicot's jaw, a gesture of comfort that Chicot struggled to lean into. Her stress had gotten so high, and seeing her dad and siblings had only made it worse. They were tucked between RVs, Chicot's back against the cab of hers and Elijah's. The grass had grown tall between all of the motorhomes, tickling Chicot's legs as she tried to focus on Monty.

"Thanks." Chicot's voice was monotone. She couldn't help it.

"And I'll be here if you need me," Monty said. Chicot nodded, her lips pressing into a line, and she leaned into Monty again, her arms going around her middle. They were usually not like this in the dog park, more careful about starting gossip, but Chicot didn't really care that someone might see them. When Monty's arms were around Chicot, she instantly started to feel better.

"You give good hugs," Chicot mumbled against the soft fabric of her sundress. Monty chuckled, squeezing Chicot harder.

"Only to people I care about," she said. Chicot's lips curved, crooking up into a smile as she buried herself in Monty's smell for a moment.

Monty kissed her on the lips before they parted, waving as she walked away. Chicot only then noticed that she had the bunny charm sticking out of the pocket of her dress, a smile growing on Chicot's face. She waved at Monty and then turned back into the RV.

When she walked back inside, Duchess was sitting on the bed inside the suitcase they were packing their costumes into. Chicot just walked by and set their lint roller in alongside her. They would need it if this was the form of protest she was choosing.

"Ken is going to stay with her," Elijah reminded Chicot, trying to assuage Chicot's worry about Duchess. She felt bad leaving her all alone. Even if it was just for a few days.

"I know." Chicot took a deep breath. "To be honest, I'm still rattled."

Elijah crossed his arms. "I had a feeling. Considering the audition and your dad …"

Chicot shrugged. "I'm feeling better though."

"Monty helped?" Elijah asked. Chicot's face warmed, but she nodded.

"Good." Elijah set a hand on Chicot's shoulder, squeezing. "We're going to be amazing. If you could perform that well while you were worried about your dad being around, then we will be fine."

Chicot hadn't considered it that way. She let a smile creep onto her face, rocking back and forth on her feet.

"You're right." She stood straighter and offered Elijah her hand. He clasped it in both his, the two of them grinning as they shook rapidly.

Their excitement didn't abate as they got back to it, playing music while they finished making sure they had everything they needed. All the props, the mask, the costumes. Once they had it all, they forced themselves to get into bed. It was hard to sleep, the two of them talking on and off about their plans, where they would eat, the god-awful early hour Ken was picking them up at the morning, and what time their flight was at.

Chicot didn't even remember falling asleep, but when her alarm woke her up, she remembered the awful dream she'd had about her father yelling for her. She had been lost in the corn fields beyond their pasture and had been hiding from him. Chicot did her best to shake it off as she carefully nudged Duchess out of the hammock. Duchess was decidedly annoyed, but she hopped onto the bed, sniffing at where Elijah had been lying.

Ken turned up about fifteen minutes after that, early because he seemed nervous to be late. Chicot couldn't complain about that. He got their single suitcase into his car while they finished eating the breakfast Elijah had made. It was just peanut butter and banana sandwiches, but they tasted amazing when the sun was barely up and Chicot was in need of coffee.

"Uh, before we leave." Ken had popped back into the trailer after getting the luggage put away. "I have something for you, Chicot."

"Oh?" Chicot finished her glass of water, setting it in the sink. Ken produced a phone from his pocket, a little older, but it was still in good condition. It was a Pixel, different from what she'd had before, but he held it out to her. There was a pink case on it, well-worn but still intact, with a pit of a checkered pattern on the back. It looked like a dress Monty would wear.

"Are you serious?" Chicot touched the phone, turning it over in her hands. It had been so long, but this was a big gift. She felt bad taking it. She looked at Elijah, who seemed equally surprised.

"It was my mom's," Ken explained. "She got a new one a few months ago, and we already have an extra emergency phone, so I asked her if I could give it away since we weren't going to use it."

"Thank you." Chicot held the phone to her chest for a moment and then stepped to give Ken a side hug. A grin grew on his face.

"Honestly, the thought of you being on a plane with no music kind of made my skin crawl, so I wanted to help," Ken joked. Chicot knew it was more than that. Ken cared about Elijah, and by extension, he cared about Chicot. Her mind drifted to something Sunnie had said to her when he'd first offered to help her work on her pantomime.

So you've got the most important part of being a performer down already then. Community.

Tears started to form at the corners of her eyes, burning slightly as a laugh came out of her. "Thank you, Ken. This means a lot."

Ken and Elijah looked startled, both of them panicking, and then Elijah turned to get Chicot a tissue. Elijah took time to make her laugh, to get her to stop crying even if they were happy tears because he was worried about her getting dehydrated. Meanwhile, Ken switched out the sim cards, getting the new cell turned on and downloading all her old apps for her.

When he handed it to her again, Chicot smiled at the photo of her, Juni, and Charlie that was still on the lock screen. She didn't really look at much else, logging back into her Spotify account as she sat in the back of Ken's chic sedan, relaxing as she thought about what she might say to Juni once she was done with the audition.

Chicot stood in the overly air-conditioned theater, her hand just above her brow to block the stage lights as she watched a group of swordsmen perform on stage. She sipped her water, her leotard tugging awkwardly on the top of her head as it always did, and listened to the performers exchange glancing blows while they shouted at each other. They were great, and Chicot couldn't really pick out any obvious mistakes in their show. In fact, everyone they had watched had been clean and polished, prepared to immediately start. She did her best to put it out of her mind, sweat pooling in her spandex body suit despite the cool room around her. Now, this process felt familiar. This was not her first time doing this, it was one of many, and she was beyond ready for it.

"*Court Jester Chicot's House Rules* on stage please." The voice was firm and inattentive, like they had been at this for hours—which they had. Elijah took her hand, the two of them walking out in front of the casting directors sitting halfway up the rows of seats. They were surrounded by other potential performers, some already auditioned, others still waiting nervously to be brought backstage.

Chicot had her mask off for now, as it had been requested. The directors had them each spin around for them so their full costumes could be seen, Chicot doing it carefully and only adding a shimmy at the end so they could take her in. The movement earned her a smile, something that she'd been hoping for. Sunnie had mentioned how much the directors liked to see personality.

"Please introduce yourselves," the casting director said. Elijah went first, bowing with his lute at his side. When it was Chicot's turn, she stepped up and crossed her legs, bowing deeply.

"My name is Chicot," she started. "And I play the part of the Court Jester Chicot, a pantomiming jester."

When she finished her statement, she did a flourish and clipped her mask onto her face, placing her hands under her chin and striking a cute pose as she wiggled her fingers. The directors laughed, one of them leaning over to whisper to another, amusement on their face.

"Thank you." The main director that had been conducting the auditions now seemed less bored, his eyebrows raised as he gestured with an open palm. "The stage is yours. We would love to see your performance in full. Please use the tape line as a curtain if you'd like."

They grabbed their small prop table and the crate they were provided, walking out on stage to place each on the tape marks they had requested before their audition. Once they had their things in place, Elijah thanked the directors and Chicot bowed in sync with him. The two of them then went to their starting marks, nodding to each other. Then, they began.

Chicot tumbled across the stage, easily hopping up onto the box. She didn't look at the directors, focused on striking her first pose as she waited for Elijah to come in. From there, it was like this was what they'd always been meant to do.

Elijah played his lute, sang songs, bickered with Chicot, and Chicot contorted herself, teased Elijah, and pantomimed to explain her house rules. Occasionally, she stopped him as he did something "wrong" and exaggeratedly pantomimed to show him what he was supposed to do instead. The directors laughed at the right moments, their voices the only thing that Chicot picked up on.

"I have no idea what she means! Do you all know what she's trying to get me to do?" Elijah asked the audience, who weren't paying them much mind. Thankfully, one person was actively watching them, and they shouted out exactly what Chicot and Elijah needed.

"Stand on the box while you sing!" the performer yelled. Their voice carried, and it made everyone else in the crowd laugh as Chicot pointed to the speaker. She gestured with open palms as she looked back at Elijah, effectively conveying, *See!? See!? It was not that hard!?*

Elijah rolled his eyes dramatically, stepping up on the box. "There, are you happy?"

Chicot set her hands on her hips, nodding in just the right way so her bells wouldn't ring loudly. Elijah then scoffed and flicked one of them on her jester hat, and Chicot stumbled away from him, overreacting with severe offense as she covered the points as if he had just touched her butt or something.

"Oh, what?" Elijah asked. "Are the bells sensitive?"

He shook his head and rolled his eyes, one hand on his hip and his lute in the other. Chicot responded by sliding her hands down her head around her chest, crossing her legs as she swished back and forth. There was a peal of laughter from the crowd as she pretended to be shy and awkward about him touching her bells. Elijah pressed his hand to his heart then.

"All right, I'm sorry!" Elijah said. "What do you want me to do next?"

They then launched into a silly series of pantomime, in which Chicot tried to get Elijah to play the right song for the mood, switching from a lute version of "Careless Whisper" to one of his original tunes that Chicot would do a cute dance to, ending with her contorting herself while she was standing on her hands.

"Oh, now we've got a show going!" Elijah shouted, and he started to play faster, hopping off the box. Chicot got out of her contorted position, tumbling back and standing with her arms in the air. "One more big trick from Court Jester Chicot, everybody. Clap please."

He started a chorus of applause before he went back to playing his lute, Chicot looking confused for a moment before she acted fake shy, waving her hand as if he were pumping her up unnecessarily. She then hopped onto the box again, pretending to be unbalanced for a moment as the music started to get even faster. The clapping kept up, the crowd managing to keep on beat and in unison, which was impressive. When she looked out at the crowd, the main director was even joining along.

Chicot got on her elbows, shifting into an elbow stand with her legs bent over her head. She then wrapped her lips around the mechanism in her mask, blowing up a balloon as Elijah's playing got faster and faster. When the balloon was at full size, Elijah abruptly stopped as he whipped out a blow gun, shooting a dart at Chicot and popping the balloon.

There was another peal of cheers from the small crowd they were in front of before Chicot hopped down and met Elijah in the middle, taking his hand again so he could do their outro. They thanked the crowd, deeply bowing with their arms linked and then standing, panting in front of the directors.

"Thank you very much, *Court Jester Chicot's House Rules*. You can leave the stage." The director's voice was lighter now, warm even. They thanked them again as Chicot got her mask off, and then they exited to the hallway where a gaggle of people dressed like halflings smiled nervously at them, waiting for their turn.

Elijah picked Chicot up in a hug, then they ran together to the changing rooms. They hadn't bounced like this since they had gotten the news about the callback, and now all Chicot could think about was telling Monty that they would also be at the Pennsylvania Renaissance Faire. Of course, she didn't know yet. But after that performance? She was certain that they would absolutely be making it into the cast. Maybe they'd even get to share a stage with *The Pirates Three* again.

They stayed for the rest of the auditions, showing their support to the other acts and calling out if they seemed to request it. Chicot didn't see anyone she knew, at least she didn't think. It seemed like maybe this was just for new acts they were considering.

When the auditions were completely over, Chicot followed Elijah out of the mansion they used for auditions. She was smiling, bouncing as she walked, and she held her phone in her hands, wanting to text Monty or Sunnie, but she didn't have their numbers yet. She'd get there. Right now, she could just celebrate with Elijah, and celebrate they did, ordering a heap of Chinese food and getting drinks for back in their hotel room.

"To the best jester and bard duo in all of Wisconsin!" Elijah held up his beer can for Chicot. Chicot clinked hers against his, a mouth full of rice and sesame chicken.

"To the best jester and bard duo in all of the USA!" she yelled, and Elijah threw his head back and laughed.

Elijah showed her updates about Duchess from Ken, the two of them cooing over their cat as they ate and drank. Eventually, they settled back into the single bed they were sharing, full of good food and bloated from beer as they stretched out among the flimsy pillows.

"Ken got a job with the blacksmith at Pennsylvania," Elijah said. Chicot perked up, turning to face him.

"Really? That's great." Chicot patted Elijah on the shoulder, sluggish from the feast they'd had and mentally exhausted from finally being done with the audition.

"Yeah." Elijah crossed his arms over his chest. "I really like him."

Chicot smiled, grabbing onto the pillow and hugging it as she laid her head on it. "He's a good guy."

"Monty's a real good lady, too," Elijah returned. Chicot's heart skipped, her face pressing into the pillow to hide, but she was grinning. She couldn't take it.

"She is." Chicot looked at Elijah. Elijah nudged her gently.

"Look at us," he said. "Falling in love at our first faire."

Chicot laughed, rolling onto her back, "God. We're pathetic, aren't we?"

"Hopeless romantics might be a better way to say it." Elijah rolled his eyes. Chicot snorted.

"Yeah, maybe." Chicot looked at the popcorn ceiling and wondered if she could count them all in one night.

"I know you left home because of your mom." Elijah's voice was quiet, barely a whisper above the AC unit, which they'd cranked to the maximum. "But I'm really glad that you came with me."

Chicot turned to him, her hand reaching out for his to squeeze. "We both needed to leave."

"We did." Elijah nodded. "That town wasn't good to us, was it?"

Chicot shook her head. "It wasn't."

"But now we have all of this." Elijah turned onto his elbow, facing her. "We have all these people, so many of them queer and so many of them willing to love us."

Chicot's mind drifted to Sunnie, the way he'd taken her in without a second thought. The way he'd teased her about her crush on Monty during a couple of lessons. She had always wanted to talk to her dad about girls that way. Instead of him, she got it from Sunnie, a man she'd only known for a little while.

"Yeah." Chicot sighed lightly. "And they'll keep loving us, no matter what."

"It's so much better than home." Elijah turned onto his back now, his arm flopping off the bed.

"No, Albion *is* home." Chicot smiled.

Elijah's teeth flashed in the low light of the motel room, a grin so wide that it made his cheeks look like two perfectly domed cupcakes. "Yeah, we have a home now."

When they got to their airport the next day, it was pouring rain. Chicot was soaked through, the raincoat she had brought wrapped around their luggage with their costumes in it instead. She didn't really mind. It was a nice contrast to all the summer heat of Wisconsin, but it did mean she had to spend the first fifteen minutes once they'd gotten through security trying to dry her clothes at least somewhat so she wasn't soggy on the plane. Elijah had to do the same thing, so they were in their respective bathrooms.

She had not paid the phone much mind since she'd gotten it, though she did appreciate finally having her playlists back. Her eyes were on it on the counter, looking over the text message she'd written out for Juni to explain why she'd left and how sorry she was. She wanted to be sure that Juni knew Chicot cared about her and the only reason Chicot had stopped responding was because she'd broken her cell. So, Chicot transferred the text into her notes app, so she could tweak it until she got it right.

Her shirt was nearly dry from the hand drier when a notification popped up. She hadn't seen it in a long time, the dating app she'd been using on and off since she'd left home. It had never really worked out for her, since most of the people on it weren't nearby, but it was just for women who wanted to date women, which meant sometimes she'd connect with someone who lived a state away because the radius was so large.

CallieLily: Hey, long time since we've talked. How are you doing?

Chicot stared at the message, trying to remember which girl this had even been. She clicked on the notification, realizing quickly it was the one she'd been chatting with from Chicago. They had never been particularly romantic, but Chicot realized she probably needed to tell her about Monty and that she was off the market. She worked as an engineer somewhere, her life so ... normal compared to Chicot's.

JesterJump: Good, sorry it's been so long. I've been working at the Albion Renaissance Faire and broke my phone. I only just got a new one. I want to be honest though. I kind of started seeing a girl there.

CallieLily: Oh, that's awesome, congratulations! I remember you hadn't heard back when we last talked. That's so cool. Also, what's the girl like? Is she cute? Congrats on that too :)

Chicot bit her lip, thinking of Monty for a moment. She remembered Callie being really nice, so this wasn't really a surprise. Maybe she should make it a point to go hang out with her in sometime as friends. She could even bring Monty.

JesterJump: Thank you! She's super sweet. Into cottagecore, really strong, and she gives amazing hugs.

CallieLily: Oh my, you sound a little in love. ;) She your girlfriend yet? Or are you falling intoWLW stereotypes over there?

JesterJump: Not my girlfriend, but I want to ask her. I was waiting to hear back about this big audition I just did for the Pennsylvania Renaissance Faire.

CallieLily: Girl, you have to ask if you're smitten! Don't wait!

JesterJump: lol, I promise I will! I'm not a useless bisexual, I swear.

CallieLily: >:(you better not be or I'll come to the faire and make sure you ask.

JesterJump: hahaha, I will not let it come to that, I promise.

CallieLily: Good! Now, how are you feeling about the new Rune Factory announcement Nintendo made?

They chatted a while longer about video games. Chicot had to look up the announcement she was talking about, but she was decidedly disappointed since the new game looked so different from the rest of the series. She'd barely thought about video games in months, but she chewed on her lip and thought about the pretty knight in the fourth *Rune Factory* game. The one she'd romanced and loved without even realizing that maybe there was a reason she liked her so much more than the male options.

She smiled to herself. Her 3DS was in the RV. She should start a new game and romance that character all over again. Chicot nodded to herself as she made this plan, clicking out of her chat with Callie once they'd exchanged Discord usernames since Chicot planned to get rid of the app. She wasn't looking to date around anymore, not when she had Monty waiting for her back home at Albion.

Her thumb stopped over the gear icon as she looked at the list of girls she'd been talking to. Callie's messages were at the top, followed by a girl who had messaged Chicot sometime in June, but Chicot hadn't had a phone to respond. Under that was a tiny profile picture next to the name *FalseCake*. It was a girl, sandy blonde hair with a round face, a grin from ear to ear, and her hair sticking to her skin. Chicot had seen this photo before in Monty's bedroom and she smashed the profile picture to see it larger without thinking. There it was, a photo of Monty and Lyza, rained on and clinging to each other with smiles on their faces.

Chicot clicked back to her messages, bile rising in her throat. Her finger hovered over the unopened messages Monty had sent her, the most recent one dated shortly before Chicot had told her that she didn't have a phone. She couldn't open them, and suddenly a flood of women entered the bathroom, tired and ornery from just getting off a flight.

She shoved her phone into her pocket, gathering her things as she escaped the throng of people, trying to get out of their way. When she found Elijah, he looked panicked, grabbing her hand and pulling her as he explained he'd been in the middle of texting her that their gate had changed and now they were in the complete wrong place. She hurried after him, her fingers twitching. Chicot wanted to look at the messages from Monty, but as they searched for their new gate, it became clear they were going to miss their flight if they didn't figure things out quick.

The messages left Chicot's mind, asking gate agents questions since Elijah was too panicked to talk. He didn't do well with sudden changes, so Chicot had to take over and take care of him. It was fine. They made it onto the plane before the door closed, the two of them sitting in different rows, shoved into unwanted middle seats.

Chicot closed her eyes, dropping her head against the back of the seat as the flight attendants asked them to put their phones on airplane mode. Her stomach dropped, her hand touching her phone, but she just did as the flight attendants said, her fingers trembling. Her headphones were in their suitcase, which meant Chicot had nothing to listen to for the rest of the flight. She was alone with her thoughts, going over all the reasons Monty hadn't told her that they had talked on the dating app.

CHAPTER 18

They touched down, and Chicot had all but chewed through her lip. Elijah noticed immediately, his brow furrowing as he gave her his lip balm. He didn't pry when Chicot asked him not to, each of them slipping into their respective bathrooms again for a post-flight pee and handwashing session. She understood now why the people that had flooded the bathroom she'd been in at the previous airport were so ornery. Being on a plane just did that to you.

She had her phone out as she waited by a kiosk in O'Hare Airport. They'd decided to land in a larger city so they could have a direct flight each way, but this meant Ken had to drive them about an hour and a half back to the faire. Worse off, it was Friday and they needed to be ready to perform in the morning. Chicot took a few deep breaths, scrolling through the dating app inbox for a while before she closed it again. She didn't want to read the messages from Monty yet.

Elijah joined her, his eyes tired and sagging, but he smiled at Chicot. "We did it. We made it."

"Not completely yet." Chicot smiled. "Don't jinx us."

"You're right." Elijah said. They didn't say anything else until they had their checked bag. When they were standing in the vestibule, the summer heat and humidity encroaching on them, Elijah nudged Chicot.

"You okay?" he asked. Chicot didn't know where to start. Elijah was so protective of Chicot at times, she didn't to tarnish Monty's image in his head before she knew what happened. She just didn't understand why Monty wouldn't have just said something about it. It felt like she was waiting to see how long it would take Chicot to realize who she was, which Chicot hated. So, she just nodded.

"Yeah, just tired and ready to be home."

Elijah accepted that answer, squeezing her shoulder and waving Ken down when he arrived from the cell phone lot. He asked them a million questions once they were in the car, and even if Chicot was still feeling bad, it did help to be excited about the audition. She answered with Elijah, slowly coming around until she was deep in the conversation, pushing down all the thoughts of the person she'd been distracting herself with for weeks.

When they got back to the faire, they set their luggage in the RV since Ken offered to take them to The Final Frontier for dinner. Chicot was tired all the way down to her bones, the marrow assuredly screaming for sleep just like the rest of her was, but she agreed. She wanted fried cheese curds and good beer.

It was Friday, so the bar was loud and a band played on one side of the room, but Chicot relaxed the moment she could smell the stale beer and heard a country cover of "Pink Pony Club" by Chappell Roan playing. This place was an extension of Albion, it felt like it was part of their home, and she had never been so happy to be pressed into a booth alongside Elijah, half asleep and drinking beer at nine at night.

Chicot got herself up to order more drinks somewhere around ten. She, Ken, and Elijah had been joined by some of the other workers from the food stalls, a few of which Chicot could sort of recognize from Ken's party. Most of them, she wasn't able to place and now she found herself thinking about Monty again. She had been so sweet about Chicot not being able to recognize people easily. Chicot felt her stomach flutter as she remembered the feeling she'd had in the back of Monty's car, and it quickly turned to roiling.

Her hands hit the bar and she steadied herself, trying to straighten up so she could ask for another round, but her stomach hurt thinking about Monty secretly laughing that Chicot hadn't realized she was from the dating app. Though, maybe she wasn't. Chicot knew it was possible that she was just being unreasonable. But after years of people mocking her for this exact thing, it was hard for her to think otherwise. At least she had an explanation now for how annoyed Monty had been with her at first. Chicot looked at her feet. This wasn't even Monty's fault. If she could just recognize people when she saw them, then maybe she wouldn't have put her and Monty in this situation.

She huffed, her face pinched as she tried to force herself to make eye contact with the bartender. She came to her quickly, taking Chicot's order and handing over the beers in quick succession after she popped the pull tabs open. Chicot thanked her, handing over cash and telling her to keep the change as she gathered everything up. She spun around, expecting the crowd to clear slightly so she could get away from the bar.

Instead, there was a woman with black hair and sharp blue eyes staring directly at her, a White Claw in hand. She frowned at Chicot immediately, shaking her head.

"God, why do you always look at me like you have no idea who I am?" Brewhilda's voice was sharp, but some of her words came out slurred. She was drunk, more so than Chicot had ever seen her.

"I just wasn't paying attention," Chicot said. It wasn't a lie. She had been zoned out, thinking about something else.

"You're not better than me, bitch." Brewhilda scoffed. "Quit acting like it."

Chicot rolled her eyes. "Whatever."

"Anyway, where's my sloppy seconds? She's not with you?" Brewhilda asked. Chicot bristled, a bolt of anger running down her ribs and making her skin crawl. "You two have been out together every Friday for the past few weeks, so what? Trouble in paradise over there?"

"Shut up," Chicot snapped. "And leave me the fuck alone. I never did anything to you."

Brewhilda snorted. "Like fuck you haven't. Took my spot on stage then locked down my usual fuck buddy in a relationship that's gonna fall apart the moment y'all leave Albion."

"We didn't take your spot!" Chicot's voice was loud enough that people were looking now. "For fuck's sake, I *saw* your audition. You're lucky you have a job at all."

Brewhilda's eyes narrowed, her teeth bared at Chicot as her hand rose. She took a single swipe, her coffin-shaped nails scraping Chicot's skin painfully. Chicot stumbled backwards, her legs giving out from the shock as she hit the sticky dive-bar floor. Beer cans dropped around her, froth and foam flowing all over her clothes and the tile.

"Don't ever say anything like that again, you shitty little clown." Brewhilda raised her hand like she might hit Chicot once more, but someone caught her arm. Brewhilda's eyes were blown wide, black lipstick smudged as she tried to pull away from whoever had grabbed her. Chicot just touched the marks on her cheek, looking up at her as she tried to figure out what had happened. Before she could, some burly, bald man wearing a Harley Davidson jacket picked her up, setting her on her feet. He was asking her questions, though Chicot couldn't really hear them.

She wanted Monty to wrap her up in a hug. The thought quickly soured worse than the beer would on the floor as she remembered the dating app profile, her smiling face and wet hair laughing at Chicot in her thoughts. Chicot curled in on herself as Brewhilda was pulled away into the crowd, but the large biker man was leaning down to Chicot, trying to speak more gently to her. The bartender was right beside her across the bar, asking the biker questions as Chicot's eyes swam over the people in the room.

Her gaze met a jean jacket, basic and unfamiliar until she saw a bunny charm hanging out of the pocket. Chicot felt something coming up, turning on her heel and dipping under the biker's arm. He tried to yell for her, the bartender doing the same, but Chicot pushed through the crowd to the bathroom. She knelt on the dirty tile when the girls waiting let her pass, losing all the fried cheese curds and beer she'd been drinking that night. Her ears rang when she finished throwing up, keeping her on the floor for another minute while she wondered if Monty had followed her or if that had even been Monty in the first place. Chicot wouldn't be able to tell the difference, and that left her shivering.

When she got out of the bathroom stall, there were three drunk women fawning over her, telling her that she'd be okay and just to rinse her mouth out. No sign of a plush bunny charm or jean jacket. If that had been Monty in the bar, she hadn't followed. One girl handed her one of those toothbrushes that was basically just a wipe that went over your finger. She took it, the minty flavor washing out some of the sour beer that still lingered in her mouth.

"You okay, sugar?" The woman's voice was low and soft, the muffled sound of the bar outside making it seem even quieter. Chicot recognized her leopard print vest, a trans pride flag pin on the pocket next to a pin that proudly stated "Trans Women are Women" with an angry cat on it. She was one of the bartenders, her arm gently going around Chicot's shoulders as tears started to stream down Chicot's face. Chicot wanted the comfort she knew Monty would have brought before Chicot had seen those text messages. Now, she wasn't sure if it would even make her feel better to have Monty there.

"I'm having a bad night," Chicot sobbed. The woman rubbed her arm, hugging her tightly against her chest as the gaggle of drunk girls all tried to make Chicot laugh. It didn't really work, but the woman holding her squeezed Chicot tightly and let her cry.

"When you're ready," the bartender said. "I have your friend Elijah outside. He's going to take you home. He came running for you."

"Aww, see, you have such a good friend waiting for you!" one of the drunk girls cooed, still trying to cheer Chicot up. Chicot swallowed.

"Elijah's the best friend," Chicot explained.

"Want me to take you to him?" The woman still had her arm around Chicot, holding onto her tightly. Chicot's mouth wobbled as another sob came out of her, nodding as she cried. The bartender gently ushering the drunk, worried girls away so she could bring Chicot out to Elijah, who opened his arms up for her quickly. She pressed in close to him, and Elijah half-carried her back to Ken's car.

"I'm reporting her. I don't fucking care if it wasn't on faire grounds. She *hit* Chicot!" Ken was loud as Chicot lay in the back seat.

"I know, I know." Elijah was much calmer in this situation somehow. "But we need to be careful about this. I don't want her to lash out at Chicot again."

"She'll be fired before she does if I have anything to do with it," Ken grumbled. "I hate that asshole. I hate her so fucking much."

"You're preaching to the choir," Elijah commiserated. His eyes drifted back to Chicot, finding hers and holding. "But we have to follow Chicot's lead on this."

"It's whatever," Chicot dismissed. "I provoked her."

"You did *not* deserve to be hit. That was *not* your fault." Ken tried to turn around in his seat, but Elijah promptly directed him to focus on driving.

"Ken's right." Elijah's voice was much more level, but at the very back of it, where it first left his throat, Chicot could hear the seething anger slipping past his tongue. "You didn't do anything to deserve this, okay?"

"Okay." Chicot sighed. "Either way, I'll tell management. If she's acting like this with me, she's probably done it before."

"That is *exactly* my point," Ken said, and then launched into another tirade about Brewhilda's actions. Chicot just closed her eyes. If it hadn't happened to her in that very moment, she would probably be just as outraged as Ken. For now, she was still in shock, and being in the car was making her motion sick. She just wanted to be home.

When they got to the dog park, very few people were out. With tomorrow being a faire day, most people went to bed early, but a few hung out by fires or sat chatting as they smoked on lawn chairs. Chicot saw Sunnie's signature red bandana around his head. She didn't want to worry him, so she walked into her trailer, leaving Ken and Elijah outside.

Duchess came running to her, meowing loudly as Chicot walked into the bathroom. She looked in the warped mirror, frowning at the sight of the three scratches that Brewhilda had left on her cheek. They were pretty angry and red, but they'd probably heal fine.

She washed her face with Duchess sitting on her foot, then threw a few treats for her. Elijah and Ken were still outside, so she stripped off her clothes, which were now gross from falling in the bar, and then climbed into her hammock in just her underwear and the tank top she'd been wearing as an undershirt. Her arm curled under her as she lay on her side, and Duchess meowed from below, eventually just hopping into the hammock with her.

Chicot rubbed her ears slowly, thinking of the bunny charm and wondering if that had been Monty at the bar or someone else entirely. She hadn't even tried to look at their face before she'd run away to puke, so she couldn't really say. All she knew was that if it was Monty, she had probably hurt her feelings. Chicot wondered if that was bad, all things considered. She shook the thought away quickly because it wasn't fair to Monty. Chicot was probably just feeling residuals from years of her mother mocking Chicot for not recognizing relatives in photos.

Chicot didn't know anything, really. Just that she wanted Monty to be her girlfriend and that she didn't know why Monty hadn't said anything about the dating app.

Duchess jumped out of the hammock when Elijah joined them. The two of them almost immediately went to sleep, though Chicot was up a while thinking far too hard about everything.

When they got up, they started doing their normal faire day routine. Chicot was sluggish, so Elijah compensated, already in costume and double-checking that they had everything she needed, even carrying her mask and collar for her. Chicot appreciated it.

The faire was quiet as they entered, carrying Chicot's costume back to the backstage area since they'd taken it with them to the audition. Chicot was glad to find they were alone for now, carefully hanging her collar, pants, and vest that went over her leotard for performances. She then stretched before she started to put them on, getting ready to advertise their show as they always did.

When she stepped out, mask in hand, Elvis and Monty were just arriving, Lyza trailing behind them as she spoke with another performer that Chicot couldn't place. Monty's eyes got huge the moment she saw Chicot, stepping toward her with such speed that Chicot didn't really have time to react.

"Oh my god, what happened to your face? Are you okay?" Monty reached to take Chicot's chin in her hand, but Chicot recoiled slightly. There was a twitch in Monty's brow, her eyes narrowing at Chicot as she frowned. Chicot tried to act normal, stepping back as she looked anywhere but at Monty.

"Uh, there was an incident at The Last Frontier," she said. "You ... weren't there?"

Monty shook her head. "No, I drove Lyza and Elvis to Milwaukee. We didn't get home until past midnight because of an accident on the highway."

Chicot relaxed slightly. Even if she needed to talk to Monty still, at least she hadn't made everything worse by running away from her in the bar. Elijah appeared at Chicot's side then, Elvis wandering up with his brows raised.

"Brewhilda hit her," Elijah told them. Monty's jaw clenched, the muscles in her forearm tensing so hard that Chicot could see her veins popping out.

"Not super hard." Chicot held up her palms. "And it was really more of a slap."

"Still, though," Elvis said. "Have you told management? What happened?"

Chicot recounted the story, leaving out some of the insults and details about Monty, like the sloppy second comment. Lyza wandered up halfway through, her face going from pleasant to hardened in an instant.

"Come on." Monty grabbed Chicot's hand when she finished. "We're going to make a report."

Chicot shook her head. "N-No, I will. I want to do it after today, okay?"

"Why in hell would we wait? Her performances should be canceled," Monty snapped. She then let go of Chicot quickly when Chicot twitched, looking at her feet as she apologized.

"I just …I want to get through today and then tell them." Chicot rubbed her head. "I want to put it out of my mind and focus. There's too much other stuff happening."

"What other stuff?" Lyza asked. Chicot clammed up, her mouth hanging open, and she just sort of looked at Elijah.

"Well, we went to Pennsylvania for a callback and now we're waiting on a response." Chicot held up her hands, waving them and doing spirit fingers, weakly adding, "Surprise."

She hoped this would at least seem like enough so she didn't have to explain to all of them about the dating app. Chicot didn't even know how she wanted to approach that yet, and it seemed to work. Lyza and Elvis squeed with excitement as Monty's eyes got big. She looked at Chicot, staring at her directly like she wanted to do something more, hug her, say something, but she couldn't in front of Lyza and Elvis. Chicot's lips twitched into a small smile when she saw Monty's shining skin and the grin that now sat on her round face. Monty didn't look concerned, or anxious, or distressed—she seemed elated.

Chicot's face split into a smile, her posture curling as she nodded at Monty. She should have known better. Monty wasn't going to break her heart before her audition. She probably wasn't going to break it at all. Still, the dating app ran through her mind and Chicot's happiness faltered.

Then, trumpets sounded through the park. Opening ceremonies had started and they all had to scramble to get their signs, heading toward the doors where people would soon be streaming inside. They took their usual places, and Chicot quickly started to interact with kids and parents, adults and teens; people she could make laugh. It was easier behind the mask. No one could look at her closely, and she could put everything out of her mind.

She skipped and handed out balloons and cards, making her way slowly back to the stage so she could switch into her pirate gear before their first show. Elvis showed up first, thankfully, meaning Chicot and Monty weren't alone to talk because Chicot had a feeling if they were, she would spill everything out all at once, and in the middle of the workday was probably not a good time for that.

Their performance went off without a hitch, Monty catching and holding her like a dream. They even hit their third hold with the three of them easily with no wobbling, something they'd been struggling with before.

The marks from Brewhilda's nails were easily covered with a little makeup, so it seemed to go largely unnoticed by audience and cast members alike when Chicot didn't have her mask on. Overall, the day felt normal even if she was making it a point not to be alone with Monty. If Monty so much as touched her right, Chicot would probably melt back into her arms and forget all about the dating app, which she knew wasn't fair to herself. She needed to talk to her about it, but as they started their third show of the day and Monty lifted Chicot above her head, it was hard to remember why it mattered at all. Chicot hadn't even opened the messages yet, too afraid they'd hurt her feelings, but Monty's kind, gentle hands on her made her forget that worry. Why was she so afraid Monty was being mean to her in the first place? She decided she could blame that boy who'd pretended he wanted to date Chicot so he and all his friends could laugh at their text messages and call Chicot nasty things behind her back.

As Chicot rose above the crowd for the last time during their second show of the day, striking the pose as they carefully balanced in a human stack that didn't make much sense to the eye, but was perfectly balanced, she caught a flash of something in the crowd, an old cowboy hat with an Easter bunny on it. Monty grabbed her, carefully lowering her as Chicot started to fall out of the hold. It wasn't a true fall, just a slow release so they could get down, but Chicot didn't quite do it right. This meant Monty had to lower her faster than expected, Chicot's feet hitting the stage harder than normal. The crowd didn't seem to notice, but her ankle certainly did.

Chicot still held her hands up, smiling as the crowd cheered and ignoring her dad entirely. She took the basket she used to collect tips from Monty, walking around the crowd and ignoring the pain in her ankle for the moment. Her dad didn't approach her, and she wondered if Juni and Charlie were there somewhere. She had been texting Juni on and off, and Chicot hoped this wasn't about that.

When they got backstage, Chicot took a deep breath, leaning against the wall as they consolidated the tips. Elvis was excitedly chattering, but Chicot only tuned in as she massaged her ankle. Monty was looking at her with her lips drawn and brow furrowed rather than at Elvis.

"Some dude came up and put two hundreds in my basket," Elvis was saying. "He didn't say a word, just did it."

"Really?" Monty's attention seemed mostly on Chicot, but she was responding to Elvis. She'd probably noticed Chicot nearly fall out of the hold, so Chicot just hoped it didn't become a whole thing. She avoided looking directly at Monty, hoping that would keep her from asking any questions. Chicot just wanted this weekend to be over already.

"Yeah, a guy in a cowboy hat, didn't even look like the ren faire type," Elvis continued. Chicot's brain clicked on suddenly, her eyes turning to him.

"Was there an Easter bunny on the hat?" she asked. Which was stupid. There had only been one man in a cowboy hat in that crowd..

"Yeah, you know him?" Elvis asked. Chicot shrugged, but her heart was going to break through her rib cage and run a marathon if it beat any faster. That was weird. Why had her dad given them so much money?

"Seen him before," Chicot said. Monty crossed her arms, looking down at her, but Chicot said she had to get ready for her show with Elijah. She pulled her hood up, slipping off her pirate gear to reveal her leotard for the jester costume.

Elvis just shrugged, dividing up the tips and tucking Chicot's into her bag for her. He then walked out before Elijah could get there, leaving Monty standing next to Chicot. Chicot had miscalculated this plan. She had no excuse to leave now.

"Are you okay?" Monty asked. Chicot was sitting on a box as she struggled to pull on her pointy jester shoes.

"Yeah, of course," Chicot answered. Monty knelt in front of her, taking the jester shoe from her and sliding it on herself since Chicot had trouble reaching if her hood was already up. Chicot shivered as Monty touched her calf, her gentle hand holding Chicot still despite her want to fidget.

"Your feet and ankles are okay?" Monty asked. "You really fell, right? Was it because of that man?"

Chicot bit her lip, shrugging. Monty pressed her lips together, a sigh coming out of her.

"Are we okay?" Monty leaned forward, her brow knitted as she fidgeted slightly with Chicot's shoe.

"Y-Yeah." Chicot couldn't look at her. "What makes you ask?"

"You just—" Monty frowned. "Why didn't you tell me about Brewhilda right away?"

"We didn't get back until late. You were probably asleep, and I didn't want to worry you," Chicot explained. It hadn't even crossed her mind to tell Monty the night before. She had wanted nothing more than to go to bed with Duchess on her and Elijah sleeping beneath her hammock.

Monty pressed her lips together, slipping Chicot's second shoe on with gentle hands. She then stood up, cupping Chicot's cheek, running her fingers along her jaw. Chicot's lips parted, her eyes swimming over Monty, taking in her pirate jacket and the linen clothes she wore underneath.

"I want you to worry me, okay?" Monty squeezed Chicot's jaw. It made Chicot want to squirm, she didn't know if it was to get closer or farther away from Monty. Monty let her go, stepping back as she looked at Chicot. "Break a leg."

The bells on her head rang as she nodded. Monty smiled but it never reached her eyes, stepping toward the door.

"Monty!" Chicot said abruptly, too loud for the small space. Monty stopped, looking back at her with her hand on the knob. Chicot had wanted to ask about the dating app, but all the confidence drained out of her like a canteen with a hole at the bottom, and instead she shook her head slightly.

"The cowboy hat guy," Chicot said. "It's my dad."

Monty frowned. "Do you need me to tell security?"

Chicot shook her head quickly. "No, I think he's harmless. It's just—I thought I should tell you."

Monty stared at Chicot for a long moment. She always seemed to see right through Chicot when she wasn't telling the truth. They stood looking at each other, and then Monty nodded.

"Okay," Monty said. "If I need to tell someone, just say the word."

Chicot confirmed that she would, and then Monty slipped out of the backstage space with her stilts in hand. Her back hit the wall behind her, squishing the collar she was wearing slightly as she looked at the ceiling. She pressed her hands to her face, feeling disembodied for a moment or two before she took a deep breath. Elijah would be there soon, and she needed to get it together.

Of course, the moment they stepped on stage, the first thing that Chicot saw in the front row was a man in a cowboy hat, an Easter bunny ring attached to the rope around the brim. She couldn't catch a break.

CHAPTER 19

Chicot ignored the crowd for the entire performance. Thanks to all of the practice, she was able to easily make her way through without a single issue. Save for one moment where she moved wrong and her already sore ankle gained a newer, sharper pain. It had largely faded by the time they took their bows, walking the crowd to collect tips afterwards as they always did. Chicot swapped the jigs she did for people when they tipped her with a cute waggle of her head. It looked cartoonish, and people seemed to understand it was a thank you.

The crowd had mostly cleared and Chicot hadn't seen her dad, so she hoped that maybe he had just been there to confirm and now he was gone. Guess he needed to know for sure his daughter had grown up to be a clown.

It was as she was leaving to do crowd work and promote their show that she saw him again. He was waiting by a large tree, his hands in his pockets. His eyes were green, face no more wrinkled than it had been the last time she'd seen him, but he'd grown his mustache back out to the thick, fuzzy brown caterpillar that he'd had when Chicot had been in elementary school. Chicot tried to walk by him like she hadn't really noticed him, but he sighed and followed her.

"Listen—" He was jogging to keep up. "Gen—Ah, Chicot, was it? Is that what you're goin' by now?"

His footsteps were loud, but his voice was low enough that no one really looked their way. Chicot stopped when he called her chosen name, her thoughts completely scrambling to the point that she felt like she couldn't walk. She nodded once, blinking at him. She had never expected to hear him say that name. She'd thought he'd keep calling her Genevieve even if hearing that made her want to crawl out of her skin. But here he was, calling her Chicot and staring back at her.

He seemed to gather that he had a chance, pushing his hat up as he took a breath. He wasn't out of shape necessarily, but he had a beer belly and he didn't exactly run much on the farm.

"I just wanted—Wait, I wrote this down." He stopped and held up a finger, as if asking her to humor him. Then he pulled a note card from his pocket, his voice changing slightly as he started to read aloud. "I don't know what your mom said to you, and I'm sorry I didn't call sooner, but I don't care if you want to date girls. You're my kid and I love you no matter what."

Chicot's mouth dropped open, but now with him reading like this, people were looking. In particular, some of the performers were signaling at Chicot to see if she needed help. She made the hand sign to let them know she was okay, then grabbed her dad's wrist, yanking him along so they weren't in the very middle of the faire. He went with no fight, just following, and let Chicot push him basically into the bushes along one of the fences.

"What?" Chicot was ninety percent sure she had hallucinated some part of what he had just read to her. Or maybe all of it. Her dad looked at the note card he was still clutching and then he frowned.

"Did I not phrase that well? I got it online from one of those Reddit forums," he admitted. Chicot pulled her mask off now, her brow furrowed. What had her dad been doing? It sounded like he'd been on the parenting forums or something, which was weird because he'd always said parenting books were useless. It seemed to Chicot like that would apply to Reddit forums as well.

"You know what Reddit is?" Chicot asked, her mouth hanging open slightly. It seemed to have been open since he'd started reading from the notecard. Her dad huffed, his mustache wiggling.

"Yeah, where do you think I look when I need to fix our thirty-year-old tractor?" He crossed his arms. "Listen, focus. I'm trying to tell you something important."

Actually, that was a fair point. Chicot looked up at him again, his face and jaw so much like hers, but with a mustache under a nose much larger than her own. His shoulders were stiff, his palms turned up, one hand still holding the notecard. This was genuine, but Chicot still had a nagging little voice in the back of her head telling her that this road could lead right back to her mom. She didn't want to believe it. She wanted her dad to mean the things he'd read.

"What did Mom tell you?" Chicot hugged herself tight around the middle. Her dad sighed and kind of spun his hands in a circle as he tried to come up with words.

"The details aren't important," he said. "But she said you were gay."

"I'm not gay. I'm bi," Chicot clarified on instinct. Mostly because it was something she normally had to correct people on. She did like men. She found herself attracted to them. Still, it was probably best to be honest and straightforward.

"Well, that's fine too." Her dad rubbed his neck, shuffling on his feet. "I know you left because of it either way, so when I saw you here, I just wanted to tell you that I'm not like your mom. I don't care."

Chicot looked down at her feet, chewing on her lip. When she looked up at him again, he was still staring right at her, his posture rounded as he leaned toward her slightly. She didn't really understand. If he didn't care, then she should have heard from him. It had been almost a year before her phone had broken. He'd had plenty of time.

"But you didn't call?" The corners of Chicot's eyes started to sting. Her dad fumbled for a second and then he shook his head.

"Your mom told me you didn't want to hear from us." His jaw was set now, his hands balling into fists, crushing the notecard. "That you said not to call until you called us."

Chicot's breath caught in her throat, a sob threatening to escape. Her dad hadn't taken her mom's side. He hadn't decided his wife was more important than she was.

"No." She shook her head. "Mom told me you'd never want to see me again. She told me to get out and never come back."

"God, I—" Her dad rubbed his temple. "I'm sorry, Chicot. I didn't know. I thought that maybe you just wanted some independence."

Chicot had assumed her whole family was gone. That at most, she'd get to be with her siblings again once they were old enough to get out from under her parents' thumbs, but that hadn't been the case at all. She hiccupped, wiping at her face as her vision swam.

"No!" Chicot wrapped her arms around her middle, clutching her mask tightly as she shook her head. A sob slipped past her lips. "No, I went to Elijah's. I didn't have anywhere else to go."

"I owe that boy and his parents so much." Her dad sighed. "I'm so sorry, Chicot. I should have called. I—Here."

Her dad stepped forward, pulling her into a tight hug. Chicot settled herself against his chest, the bells on her head jingling slightly. He held her there, and the world felt less like it was going to slip right out from under her. She pressed her face into his shoulder, the off-putting scent of his sweat oddly comforting. It felt like every hug he'd given her at the farm, when he'd come in from tending the cows, stinking slightly but still very much wanted.

When they separated, her dad kept his hands on her shoulders, making sure she was steady as she wiped the tears from her face. She slipped a hand under her hood, adjusting her hair so it laid smoother and swallowing a lump in her throat. Chicot needed water.

"Listen, I know you're at work, but one more thing." He pulled out his wallet, starting to rifle through it. Eventually, he produced a debit card, offering it to Chicot. *Genevieve Laurens* written out in sharp letters on it, but it wasn't for a bank she had an account with. He handed her the notecard he'd been reading from too.

"I wanted to give you this," he said. "It's the college fund we set up for you when you were just a baby. The rest of the info is on the back of the notecard. I figured it could do you some good now."

Chicot stared, her mind blank as she held them in her hands, flipping them over to see the information on the backs. Even if it was just a few hundred dollars, it would probably help so much.

"I know it's not a real apology for everything, but it's something, I hope," her dad hedged.

She looked up at him again, her eyes glistening with tears, so much that she couldn't really see straight. Chicot flipped the note-card back over, reading at his scratchy handwriting with the words of acceptance he had read to her. They were more important to her than the money. Before Chicot could move to hug her dad again, a presence appeared at her side, the jangle of tiny bells on Sunnie's belt alerting her to who he was as he set a hand down on her shoulder.

"Chicot, is everything okay here?" Sunnie didn't look at her, instead locking his eyes on her dad. She lifted her fingers to her face, trying to get rid of the rest of the tears.

"Ah, I'm sorry." Her dad held up his palms. "I just wanted to give her some money. I didn't want to get her in trouble or anything."

"No, it's—" Chicot squeezed her eyes shut. Her dad probably didn't even realize that Sunnie was worried he had cornered a young female performer or how what he'd just said sounded. Not that Chicot was slacking off at work. "It's fine, Sunnie. This is my dad. He was just giving me my college fund since, well, I'm not going to college."

Sunnie relaxed slightly, looking down at Chicot, and he nodded. "Oh, I see. Sorry I misunderstood. It's nice to meet you."

He shook her dad's hand, and for a moment, Chicot felt very strange about the two of them meeting. Sunnie and her dad were alike in many ways, and so different in others.

"Have you been, um, mentoring her?" her dad asked. "You're the other clown, right? That does the silent talking?"

Sunnie blinked at her father. "Yeah, Sunnie the Spectacular."

"Oh, that's really cool. I always liked your show," her dad complimented. "Thank you for taking her under your wing, I'm sure there aren't many places to learn this sort of thing, and you know, if she wants to do it ..."

"Yeah." A smile crept across Sunnie's face as he looked at Chicot. "Yeah, she's amazing, I've really enjoyed getting to teach her more. She's a real good kid."

"She is." Her dad nodded and then looked at her. "You are."

"Thanks, Dad." Chicot smiled, mouth closed because this had gone from strange to flustering quickly.

"Uh, anyway." Her dad shuffled on his feet again. "I'll leave you be. I didn't mean to bother you at work. And, uh, I'll call."

"Yeah." Chicot said. "That would be good."

Her dad waved at her before walking away. He occasionally looked back toward them until he was out of sight.

"You okay, kid?" Sunnie asked, nudging her. Chicot nodded, tucking the card and note away carefully so she didn't lose it.

"Yes." Chicot rubbed her eyes and took a deep breath. "Anyway, the show must go on."

Sunnie pressed his lips together. "If you need to take a breather ..."

Chicot withered. "That's maybe a good idea."

Sunnie walked her back to the break area, waiting until they were safely inside before he asked about the scratches on her face. She explained the whole thing with Brewhilda, which frankly felt like a million years ago now. He listened carefully and then just hummed when she said she'd tell management after the day was over.

"Is anything else bothering you?" he asked. Chicot folded onto the picnic table they were sitting at, sighing.

"Yeah, it's stuff with Monty," she said. Sunnie pursed his lips, setting his elbow on the table and leaning over to look at her more directly.

"Tell me about it," he said. "If you'd like to."

Chicot opened her mouth to say it was okay, but then she realized that Sunnie was completely separate from this conversation. Elijah was too, to an extent, but Monty had become his friend, and so had Elvis and Lyza. Sunnie was the only one truly disconnected because he knew Monty, Elvis, and Lyza as coworkers more than anything.

So, she unloaded on him, explaining all the things about her struggles to recognize people and how nice it had felt for Monty to be so kind about it. How she was insecure now because of the dating app since Monty had known it was her from the start. That Monty was probably laughing at her behind her back, even though Chicot had no real evidence for that outside of experiences she'd had in school with someone being mean to her. She laid it all out, and when she finished, she took a deep breath.

"I just don't know what to do," Chicot said. Sunnie chuckled softly, shaking his head.

"You know, I don't date," he said. "But if I did, I think I'd just talk to her."

"Well, obviously I should talk to her." Chicot pressed her hands to her head. "I just don't know how to do that without accidentally coming across like I'm accusing her of something."

Sunnie shrugged. "If she breaks up with you because you accidentally accused her of something, she's probably not worth dating."

Chicot blinked at him. He blinked back.

"I told you before I started giving advice that I don't date," he reminded. Chicot laughed and set her head in her hands.

"No, you're probably right." Chicot watched the bubbles in the water cooler rise to the top as someone walked away with a glass. "I guess if we fight, we fight. Fighting is normal, right?"

"I think a little fighting is normal," Sunnie corrected. "Especially with two people who are young and care about each other."

"Yeah," Chicot agreed. "I guess when I think of fighting, I just imagine my parents, and get scared to confront anyone I'm dating."

Sunnie hummed. "I don't have advice for that."

"I didn't expect you to." Chicot smiled at him. "Thank you for listening though. That helped."

"Glad I could," Sunnie said. "Also, I know that was your dad, but please never be alone like that in a blind spot. I barely saw the two of you. I only knew you were there because one of the roaming fey performers told me where to look."

"Don't worry." Chicot shook her head. "That won't happen again. And I only did because it was my dad."

Sunnie ruffled Chicot's hair. "Okay. I just worry."

"I know," Chicot said.

Sunnie then made her drink a full glass of water before he'd let her leave the break area. She took a few detours on her way back, walking through the crowd and doing silly dances for kids, clearing her head slightly. Chicot wanted to talk to Monty, immediately if she could, but she also knew they had more shows to do that day. It would be better not to throw them both off.

"One of the fey mentioned your dad was here again." Elijah was pacing in the very small back room when Chicot slipped inside, still waving at a little boy she'd given a balloon sword to.

"Uh, yeah." Chicot rubbed her arm, taking her mask off for the moment. "He read from a notecard to tell me he doesn't care if I'm gay."

Elijah stopped, his jaw slack for a moment. "Okay, he's a little misguided, but he's got the spirit."

Chicot snorted, shaking her head as she sat on one of the boxes. They had about fifteen minutes before they needed to be on stage and not much to do. If she was being completely honest, this was also taking her mind off things with Monty.

"He gave me access to my college fund too." Chicot produced the debit card, sliding her fingers over the raised letters of her name. She then set it on the box so it wouldn't fall out of her mildly precarious hidden pocket.

"Oh." Elijah rubbed his jaw, brow furrowed. "So, he was really trying to make amends, huh?"

Chicot nodded. "Yeah. It's weird. I always thought he'd take my mom's side no matter what."

"Well." Elijah sat next to her, his hands planted on either side of his hips like he needed to hold himself in. "I wish he'd made that clear sooner."

Her head tilted to the side, and she looked down at her feet as she remembered Monty putting her shoes on for her earlier. Chicot took a deep breath, her eyes closing as she thought about Monty's gentle hands and caring words.

"I don't even know why he's with that woman." The words slipped from Chicot's lips before she'd really processed them. She had never said anything like that before, and she didn't know what about her dad showing up had changed things. However, in light of seeing her dad for the bumbling, well-intentioned person he really was, her mother's intentional slights and jabs seemed even more obvious.

Elijah seemed shocked by this revelation as well. He set a hand on Chicot's shoulders, hugging her against his chest even as her collar folded awkwardly between them.

"I've been waiting for you to say something like that for years," Elijah admitted. "It didn't feel as nice as I'd hoped it would."

"It didn't for me either," Chicot said. Elijah pressed his lips into a hard smile and then he let Chicot go, holding out a fist to her. Chicot smiled, placing her hand over it instead of bumping it like she was supposed to. An in-joke they'd done since middle school.

"Scene partners still?" Elijah asked.

"Always." Chicot shook their hands like they were greeting, and Elijah snorted, throwing his head back. She watched him flash a smile brighter than the sun, one that proved he'd been born to be a bard.

After that, they started to warm up for their show as usual, saying tongue twisters in unison as Chicot stretched just to be safe. They were in the middle of "Betty Botter" when Monty burst into the backstage area with Lyza close behind her, the two of them panting slightly.

"Some dude cornered you after your show?" Monty's voice carried, filling the space with anxiety all over again.

"Are you okay?" Lyza ducked under Monty's arm to get inside, still carrying their show promotion sign. She set it aside quickly, gesturing for Monty to close the door behind her.

"No, no." Chicot shook her head quickly, bells jingling loudly as she did. "It was my dad. I brought him over there."

Lyza and Monty both visibly relaxed, Lyza muttering something unintelligible under her breath. She then squatted down next to Chicot, setting a hand on her shoulder.

"Still, though, you okay?" Lyza mumbled.

"Yeah," Chicot said, smiling. Lyza let her go then, standing up and gathering her sign back up. Even as she left, Monty lingered. Elijah raised a brow at Chicot but didn't leave her alone. Bless Elijah, he always knew when Chicot really needed him to stay close.

"I'm glad you're okay." Monty wrung her hands together slightly and leaned against the door. "I've had some … experiences."

Chicot took a deep breath. "Sorry, I didn't mean to worry you."

"It's okay." Monty pressed her lips together, her eyes lingering on Chicot. Her voice was quieter than usual, and she wet her lips before she looked at Elijah again. "Anyway, I'll leave you guys to it. Break a leg."

"Yeah." Elijah said. "Thanks."

Elijah's head whipped around the moment Monty had closed the door. His eyes bored holes in Chicot as she tried to look only at her foot as she stretched her leg out.

"What was that weird energy?" Elijah asked. Chicot shrugged.

"Oh no." Elijah shook his head. "No, you don't get to just shrug that off!"

Chicot groaned, shifting out of her stretch and simply pressing her hands to her face. She had been trying to avoid this conversation as much as she wanted to have one with Monty about it.

"It's not something I can explain until I talk to Monty about it directly," Chicot offered. Elijah crossed his arms.

"And when are you planning on doing that?" Elijah knew just how to call her out when she was being avoidant. As much as she did want to talk to Monty about the dating app, she wasn't sure when the right time to bring it up was. This wasn't going to be as easy as the thing about her phone or the audition. Though, now that she thought about it, that mix-up was probably because of the dating profile. How long had Monty known who Chicot was? She had been hiding this from her the whole time. Chicot was miffed all over again.

"I don't know." Chicot's posture crumbled. "Not during the day when we have two more shows to do together?"

Elijah opened his mouth to speak and then sighed.

"Okay, that's fair." He set a hand on his hip. "Just don't put it off too long, Chicot."

"I know, I know," Chicot dismissed. Elijah frowned at her, gently bopping her on the head.

"Do you?" he asked. "Because I've never seen you happier than when you're with Monty. Whatever it is, just talk to her!"

Chicot groaned, her ears hot as her face assuredly started to turn all shades of pink. She didn't realize Elijah had been paying that much attention. She had noticed that Elijah was similar with Ken.

"I will." Chicot threw her hands up. "But if we don't get into Pennsylvania, it's not like it's going to matter anyway."

"Wait, what?" Elijah paused. Chicot pressed her lips together.

"How could we keep this up if we are thousands of miles apart doing faires all the time?" Chicot looked up at Elijah. "Especially if we part basically right after we start … seeing each other."

She realized she had no idea what to even call her relationship with Monty. Suddenly, it occurred to Chicot so plainly that Monty could be laughing at her behind her back and *also* see her as a casual fling. Chicot had to immediately stomp that thought out. If she let it linger, she would be a mess on stage.

"Well …" Elijah sighed. "Okay, I don't have an answer either, but I could also say the same with Ken and me. Do you think we shouldn't try?"

Chicot grumbled an answer, which Elijah quickly asked her to repeat properly.

"Yes, I think you should try." Chicot sighed. "And I should try with Monty too. And I will. I just need to talk to her about this first."

"And then you'll explain to me what it was?" Elijah asked. Chicot groaned again, nodding.

"Yes, I will explain after," Chicot conceded.

"Good, then do it tonight." Elijah picked up his lute and started to tune it.

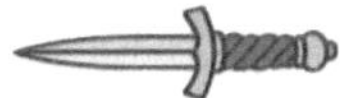

Chicot pushed herself through the last four shows of the day, managing to not have any major issues. Her ankle was certainly sore by the end, and she would have to do something to rest it after the next day, when she had eight more shows to do. She couldn't let it fall apart before then.

Monty had seemed to notice the injury, lowering Chicot more carefully, not letting her fall but rather placing her back down when she needed to. Usually, they let gravity help, as it meant Monty wasn't straining as much trying to control Chicot's weight on the way down. Now Monty was glistening with sweat after the final per-formance, the late July heat and extra exertion getting to her. Still, when she swept her sticky bangs back and tipped her water so it ran down her neck, Chicot couldn't help but let her eyes linger on her throat.

They needed to talk, of course, but when Chicot heard Elvis saying he was leaving the faire before closing ceremonies to take Lyza to a nice dinner, Chicot couldn't help but wonder if maybe just spending the night in Monty's arms would fix everything. Was it the healthiest option? Probably not, but it would be easier. Elijah's chid-ing voice in her head made her put that thought out of mind.

When the day finished, Chicot found Elijah and Ken, the two of them flanking her as they went to the main office. The directors listened to her carefully, standing alongside the one of the owners of the faire and someone who acted as human resources. Chicot wasn't sure what they could do since Brewhilda hadn't hit her on faire grounds, but they did seem genuinely concerned. The owner assured Chicot that they would do their best to keep safe. That was all Chicot really wanted at this point, to avoid Brewhilda if she could. The walk back to the RV felt long after that, her bodice already off and Elijah carrying her mask for her.

CHAPTER 20

A shiver ran down Chicot's spine as she stepped out of the RV despite the heat. She had a brace on her ankle, one with gel inside it that she had stuck in the fridge before putting it on. It wasn't the cause of her chill, but it did make it worse as she closed the door behind her. She stood by it for a moment, listening to Elijah talk to Duchess. The words weren't clear, but he was certainly talking to the cat. After all, who else would he be talking to?

She walked the long way around the trailers toward Monty, Lyza, and Elvis's RV, her hands trembling slightly. People looked at her and waved, poking at their fires or carrying instruments from one RV to another so they could sing camp songs together as the world cooled around them. Chicot waved back, wondering how many of them would be at the next faire they went to or if she would ever see them again. Nothing was guaranteed in this kind of job, so she thought about this often. The same as Monty not being with her wherever they went next. She caught Brewhilda's eyes briefly as she passed her trailer. She scowled at Chicot, sweeping up a rug she'd placed under her sunshade and picking up a shelf she'd had plants on. Brewhilda was packing her trailer to move it, and Chicot found herself apathetic at the thought of Brewhilda losing the rest of her performances. In fact, she couldn't help but think so long as Brewhilda wasn't at her next faire, everything would be fine.

Chicot knocked on Monty's RV door and folded her hands behind her back, then in front of her, then shoved both into the pockets of her cargo pants instead, all before Monty even opened the door. When Monty did appear, Chicot didn't even know what to say. She was wearing a pretty dress with little peaches all over it, one of the ones that Chicot had helped her pick at the thrift store a few weeks ago. Over that was a tan apron with frills at the shoulders that cinched the waist of the loose dress in slightly.

"I was about to go over and get you," Monty said. Chicot blinked at her, mind still blank from whatever this was to say much more than, "Oh," as she stood there.

"Do you want to come in?" Monty stepped back so she was out of Chicot's way, and Chicot simply nodded.

She followed Monty inside to find most of the lights low. There was a lamp on the counter, and the winking fairy lights above the cabinets and kitchen table were on. It gave everything a nice, warm glow as Monty swished through the kitchen. She didn't have shoes or socks on, her hair had a bow clip in it to hold some of her bangs back on each side, and she briefly rounded her shoulders, looking sheepish.

"I knew we'd have some time on our own, so I thought I'd make you dinner," Monty reasoned. Chicot's pulse raced and she wet her lips as she tried to remember she was there for a reason, but as Monty smiled at her, what it was simply left her head entirely.

"I missed you." Chicot walked over to press herself into Monty's arms. She smelled like lavender and lemongrass, a body spray that Chicot had seen in her room on one of the shelves the last time she was here.

Monty hugged her back, squeezing Chicot tightly as she chuckled. "How was the audition, by the way?"

"I think it went really well," Chicot said. "The directors laughed at our jokes, and the other performers auditioning even got into it."

Monty grinned. "I'm so glad."

She leaned down to kiss Chicot's cheek, complimenting Chicot and Elijah before she turned to get two glasses and a bottle of wine from the counter. Chicot melted into her easily, Monty's soft touches and smiles, her excitement as she explained that she made them some sort of Italian chicken and hadn't even overdone the pasta. They sipped wine and talked over dinner, and for a while, Chicot forgot entirely about her new phone in her pocket and the dating profile that had put her so on edge.

They ate gnocchi and chicken breast that had been doused in a salty wine sauce that Chicot couldn't identify, their glasses filled with the remains of the same bottle. Chicot didn't know Monty could cook like this, a shy smile growing on Monty's face as Chicot praised her.

"Thanks, I had to cut the chicken really thin since I didn't have an oven to finish it in," Monty said. "But I'm glad it worked."

Chicot swallowed another bite, her eyes on Monty's coral lips. "You made it work better than if you had an oven."

Monty chuckled, the two of them eating and talking about a new band they'd both started listening to. Chicot found herself completely lost to Monty's thoughts on the little Seattle punk band, laughing as Monty explained why she liked certain songs or found them relatable. Things were easy, soft, and Chicot wanted them to stay like this.

"You know, I was a little worried something went wrong with the audition," Monty revealed. They were both mostly finished with their food, the bottle of wine already at half as Monty added more to both their glasses.

"Why?" Chicot asked. Monty tilted her head, her brow furrowed.

"You were acting a little strange about it," Monty mumbled. "And then I heard about the fight with Brewhilda. I know how she is, I thought she maybe said something to make you feel less confident."

Chicot's shoulders relaxed, her eyes going to the window next to the table. The curtains were drawn.

"Oh, um." Chicot sipped her wine. "No, she didn't say anything about the audition."

Monty blinked. "Really?"

Chicot looked at her, creases forming in Monty's forehead as her face scrunched with worry. She drummed her fingers on the table, waiting for Chicot to elaborate. She had half a mind to lie, to just let all of this die out.

"Chicot, if something's changed …" Monty seemed to brace herself. Chicot twitched, shaking her head quickly because it was true. That was the worst part: *nothing* had changed about how she felt about Monty. She still liked her, still felt fluttery when Monty touched her, still thought about kissing her throat, still wanted her strong hands to catch her. Chicot wanted all of Monty. She was just terrified that maybe the Monty she knew wasn't who Chicot thought she was.

"No, it's not like that." Chicot pressed a hand over her eyes, taking a deep breath. "Sorry."

"It's okay." Monty's voice was low, and even without seeing her face, Chicot could tell she was nervous, defensive even. "But please tell me what it is."

"Why didn't you tell me we knew each other from a dating app?" Chicot asked quickly. "And why didn't you bring it up when I told you I didn't have a phone? I just don't get why I found out while I was on my way home from an audition that apparently you've known who I am this whole time, while I didn't recognize you—"

Monty put her palms up, "Stop, stop. I'm sorry."

"About which part?" Chicot's voice cracked. "Did you think it was funny that I couldn't recognize you?"

"No!" Monty twitched at the sound of her own voice and shook her head. "Well, at first I did."

"What?" Chicot limbs felt light, like she was filled with helium, ready to float up to the top of the RV and get stuck. Monty shook her head.

"Not like that." Monty pressed her hands to her face and groaned. "I knew I should have said something. I'm sorry."

"I think I need to go." Chicot's stomach turned as she slid out of the booth. Monty jumped up grabbing her hand as she fumbled over her words. She sounded like an adult from a Peanuts cartoon for a moment, until Chicot's brain caught up.

"… I am sorry," Monty said. Chicot stared at her, trying to process whatever she'd said before she apologized again.

"Chicot?" Monty asked. Chicot took a deep breath and carefully pulled her hand from Monty's.

"I think I need some air," Chicot said. Monty pressed her lips together, but let Chicot go.

"Will you come back?" Monty asked. "I can explain. I promise. I just … my words are failing me."

Chicot opened and closed her mouth, then she nodded. If she changed her mind, she could just text her through the dating app. So she glided through the kitchen, Monty close on her heels, and stepped down into the grass outside their RV. As soon as she did, Chicot turned and started for the large field that surrounded the dog park, walking slowly at first and then running as fast as she could with her ankle how it was.

CHAPTER 21

Chicot didn't stop until she got to the bench on the far side of the faire grounds. She panted, looking behind her to see if anyone was there, but Monty hadn't followed and no one else had either. Her ankle pulsed, her blood rushing in her ears as she sat down, pressing her hands over her face as mosquitoes bit into her legs. She wouldn't be able to spend much time out there without bug spray, but she didn't move regardless.

The sound of frogs screaming slowed her thoughts, her attention fully on them as she let the bugs sip on her blood without so much as trying to swat them away. After a full minute of slow breathing, Chicot sat back, letting her hands slide to her lap as she replayed the conversation she'd had with Monty in her head. She probably should have let Monty have more time to speak, to think, but it was too late for that. She tried to remind herself, there was probably some logical explanation for all of this.

She wasn't sure how much time passed while she sat there, but her ankle stopped pulsing and her butt started to feel sore. Chicot didn't really want to move, pulling her legs up to keep them from being in the grass, hoping it would help keep the bites at bay. But her arms were already covered, which meant it probably wouldn't help much.

"Chicot!" The voice startled Chicot from her thoughts, and for a moment she thought it was Monty, but realized quickly it was actually Lyza. She held up a spray bottle in her hand, her purse still hanging over one shoulder like she had only just gotten back.

"I brought you bug spray," Lyza said when she got close enough to sit on the bench. Chicot stared at it, taking the bottle from her.

"Thank you," Chicot said. "When did you ... How did you know?"

"Just a bit ago." Lyza smoothed her skirt as she settled next to Chicot. "Monty was crying, but she said it was her own fault, then insisted I bring you that. Elvis said you might be here."

"Oh ..." Chicot started to spray her feet and legs. "I should probably go talk to her."

Lyza shrugged. "That's up to you."

Chicot stood to spray her arms and chest, frowning as she did. Lyza didn't seem happy with her, but she didn't seem totally angry either.

"Do you want to know what's going on?" Chicot asked. She squeezed the bottle in her hands, feeling the plastic on her palms. Lyza sighed, crossing her arms as she worried her lip.

"Monty made me promise I wouldn't meddle." Lyza met Chicot's eyes. Chicot looked at her hands and thought for a few moments.

"Then we should probably respect that request," Chicot concluded. Lyza frowned deeply. "Yeah."

"Umm ..." Chicot looked back to the dog park. "We should maybe get back."

"Yeah." Lyza huffed, her eyes narrowed at Chicot as she stood. Chicot offered her the bottle of bug repellent back, but she didn't take it.

"You know, my sister doesn't let on, but Tegan—Brewhilda— really hurt her." Lyza was walking just a few steps ahead of Chicot now. "Made her feel less than for the things that she liked and the way that she dressed."

"Monty told me a little." Chicot's voice lilted with uncertainty. She didn't know why Lyza was bringing this up now.

"And you have never done that to her," Lyza continued. "You've always been so good about making her feel confident when she's insecure."

Chicot furrowed her brow, pursing her lips. Lyza just went on, even though Chicot hadn't responded.

"If I know one thing about Monty, it's that she's going to try to do the same for someone who's made her feel so good about herself." Lyza looked back at Chicot, eyes still narrow. "She wouldn't make them feel bad if they were insecure about something."

"Y-Yeah, of course not." Chicot's words were thin, weak. She couldn't bring herself to admit to Lyza that she'd thought the worst when Monty had said she'd thought it was funny that Chicot hadn't recognized her.

"Of course not." Lyza turned on her heels again.

Chicot looked at her feet, her hand rubbing up one arm, feeling the greasy bug spray still lingering there. She started to jog before she thought, her body moving on its own again as she passed Lyza, her pace quickly increasing.

"I'll fix it!" she called to Lyza. As she glanced back, she was surprised to find a soft smile on Lyza's face.

"Good luck!" Lyza shouted back and continued to mosey through the grass.

Chicot's ankle was pulsing when she got to the RV door, knocking on it rapidly. Elvis appeared in it, eyes wide and worried.

"Oh, Chicot," he said.

"Is Monty still here?" Chicot blurted. Elvis shook his head.

"No, she said she was taking a walk to her car." Elvis pointed behind him to where the employee parking was.

"Thanks!" Chicot scrambled away from the door, her ankle now actively hurting with each step she took. She told herself she probably just needed to stretch it, running through the bursts of pain as she made her way to the path that wound toward the small row of parked vehicles.

She wasn't sure where Monty's was parked at the moment, eyes scanning over the trees surrounding the path. Monty was tall, so Chicot would spot her, but when she got to the end of the path and the field opened up around her, she didn't see Monty. She started looking for cars, hoping that Monty hadn't decided to take a drive. Chicot limped, her ankle sorer than it had been. She kept moving anyway, her eyes sharp as she scouted for Monty's silver Subaru.

"What are you doing?" Monty's voice was thick and throaty as she stepped around the back of the black Jeep that was parked in front of her car. Her face was wet when Chicot spun around to look at her. "You're limping, Chicot. What were you thinking?"

"I'm sorry!" Chicot took a step toward her and immediately regretted it. Her ankle screamed and she had to take her weight off it. She was not sure she'd be able to perform the next day if she kept this up.

"No, Chicot, you're not the one that needs to apologize." Monty stepped into Chicot's space, slipping an arm around her to support her ankle. "*I'm* sorry. This is *my* fault."

"But I assumed you were mocking me or something." Chicot's voice cracked as she spoke, tears starting to stream down her face, both from the pain in her ankle and because of how stupid she'd been.

"Yeah, but I can see exactly why you thought I was." A laugh came out of Monty, broken and soft.

"Yeah, but—" A laugh forced its way out of Chicot's chest, her tears still dripping. "But I should have known better. You wouldn't treat me like that. I'm sorry."

"It's okay." Monty looked at her and then carefully shifted to scoop Chicot up like a princess. Chicot squeaked, but she wrapped her arms around Monty's neck and let it happen. After all, she probably shouldn't be walking.

"I really did think it was endearing, by the way," Monty added.

"Endearing?" Chicot asked. Monty started walking up the path toward the dog park again.

"I mean." Monty sighed. "It's sort of cute and funny, right? We met on a dating app, and you didn't recognize me right away. I thought it was endearing once I realized you were being genuine and not just ignoring me."

"And that's why you were so surly at first?" Chicot asked. Something in her needed to confirm it. She needed all of the details or she was going to find something to overthink later. Chicot had done nothing but that over the past several days, and she knew it wouldn't stop if she didn't have clarity.

"Yeah," Monty chuckled. Relief didn't wash over Chicot like she'd hoped. Instead, there was a new level of shame seeping into her stomach, making her fingers numb.

"I'm so sorry," Chicot said. Monty shook her head.

"No, no, like I said, I thought it was endearing." Monty tightened her grip on Chicot as she stepped off the gravel and onto a path that had been worn through the grass. Chicot's lip quivered, a new round of tears stinging her eyes.

"Most people don't," Chicot confessed, voice tight. Monty glanced at Chicot, sighing as the wrinkle came back to her brow.

"When you told me about having trouble recognizing people, I felt like a jerk," Monty said. "And I didn't want to make you feel bad since I'm sure people have before, so I thought I should just try to take this secret to my grave."

Chicot looked at Monty, taking in her soft jaw and the way her eyes were totally focused on the path, probably so she didn't trip and drop Chicot or maybe because she was afraid she'd make Chicot more upset. But Chicot's stomach fluttered, her teeth sinking into her lower lip. She'd never had someone try to make things easier for her or go so far to make sure she didn't feel ashamed. Monty really wasn't messing with her at all. She was even carrying Chicot because Monty would rather be tired than let Chicot mess up her ankle more. Chicot moved her hand to Monty's jawbone, following it with the very tips of her fingers the way Monty had done to her. Trying to provide at least that comfort in return.

"Monty," she said softly. "Can you put me down for a second?"

Monty looked at her and stopped, her head leaning into Chicot's hand slightly. She settled Chicot on her feet, still holding her arm so that Chicot didn't have to put as much weight onto her hurt ankle.

Grass brushed at her bare legs, still tall despite being beaten down by cars over the summer. Chicot got on her toes, gently pulling Monty down into a kiss. Monty reacted slowly, surprise tinging her movements as she set a hand on Chicot's waist.

"I'm sorry I ever doubted you," Chicot offered. "I should have known you were just trying not to hurt my feelings."

A breeze kicked up around them, a mix of cool night air and dust hitting them. Chicot didn't care that it was going to get into her eyes or make her feel scratchy later. There really wasn't anywhere she'd rather be.

Monty's lips wobbled for a moment, tears starting well in her eyes. "I'm sorry too."

Chicot smiled, leaning up to wipe Monty's tears away, kissing her and making jokes until she felt better. When she did, Monty scooped Chicot up again, this time having Chicot get on her back since it was easier. Monty carried her the rest of the way down the small path, the two of them in comfortable silence for the moment. The only sound was the quiet hum of RVs' air conditioners and frogs croaking loudly across the faire grounds.

Monty didn't put Chicot down until they were back in her RV. Lyza and Elvis were already tucked into the loft, the two of them mumbling greetings. Though, Chicot briefly caught Lyza's eye, her nose turned up slightly and her smirk a bit smug.

She let go of Monty's shoulders when she set her on the bed, Monty turning around to face Chicot quickly. Monty delicately touched the ankle brace, her eyes sliding up to Chicot's face.

"You might need to take tomorrow off," Monty warned. Chicot shook her head slightly.

"I'll probably be fine in the morning." Chicot reached out to Monty, taking her hand and pulling her in for another kiss. Monty, despite rolling her eyes slightly, fell into it easily, the two of them slowly lying back on her bed as they indulged in each other's lips. Chicot's fingers grazed Monty's neck and shoulders, holding onto her for dear life because she never wanted to lose Monty over something so stupid as a misunderstanding or some distance while they were at two different faires.

"Hey, are we … ?" Chicot's words died on her tongue as Monty looked down at her, her lips wet and parted, eyes lidded, her hair mussed from sweat that Chicot brushed out of her face. "You look so pretty."

Monty's cheeks flushed. "What were you going to ask, Chicot?"

Chicot grinned. "Are we girlfriends?"

Monty's eyes grew wider, her brows rising, but it all quickly settled as a smile curled at the edges of her lips. She bobbed her head once.

"We are," she confirmed. Chicot shifted, kissing Monty again and again and again.

CHAPTER 22

Chicot's ankle was mostly better when she woke. It helped that Monty had thought to stick a pillow under it and give her an ibuprofen before they'd gone to sleep. She'd even remembered to text Elijah where she was, confirming that she had, in fact, talked to Monty and that everything had worked out.

In the light of the early morning sun, Chicot played with Monty's hair while she snored softly on Chicot's chest. She had woken early by accident and couldn't sleep anymore, which meant Chicot got to play on her phone while Monty kept her pinned to the bed. Chicot certainly wasn't complaining. Or at least, she wouldn't until she had to go to the bathroom.

She cleaned up some of her old apps, deleting first Hinge and then Tinder, finally lingering on the dating app just for women who wanted to date other women. She looked at Monty, confirming that she was completely asleep before she opened it again. Her finger lingered for a moment over the conversation between them. After a moment, she clicked on it, watching several messages pop up from Monty, all from the past few months. First, there was a normal greeting, then after they'd had that first dinner to talk about backstage, more messages had been sent.

FalseCake: Hey, I understand if you haven't said anything because you don't want things to be awkward, but I really don't care if you're not interested in me. I just want us to have a good faire season.

FalseCake: Listen, I'm not sure why you don't want to respond, but I wanted to give you an out. I know my sister asked you for help, but if it's too awkward for you to work with me, I understand. I wouldn't blame you for backing out.

FalseCake: Thanks for today. I know Brewhilda is a lot to deal with. I try not to let her get to me like that, but she really did. So, thanks.

Chicot blinked as she reread the messages. They stopped after that, probably because Chicot had informed her that she didn't have a phone to read them on, but they were so … mundane. She then scrolled up to find a conversation they'd had about music. One where Chicot had suggested PUP to Monty after learning she liked Fall Out Boy. Laughter started to bubble up inside her, her stomach and chest twitching enough that Monty grumbled and rolled off her. Chicot followed her, wrapping an arm around Monty, spooning her against her chest and kissing her shoulder.

"Chicot, it's *so* early," Monty grumbled. Chicot kissed her neck, a spot she knew Monty had a hard time ignoring.

"Yeah, but some early morning exercise is always good for the body," Chicot said. Monty's eyes cracked open, soft and gray as she frowned at Chicot.

"You better mean sex and not actual exercise," Monty groused. Chicot laughed, locking her phone and tossing it aside.

"Yes, that is what I mean." She carefully took Monty's shoulder, getting her to turn so she could kiss her again. Monty slid an arm under her waist as she did it, pulling her closer as they lost themselves to each other for a while.

It was nearly an hour later when the pounding on the door started. Chicot briefly wondered if something was horribly wrong, but she pulled her boxers back on and found her shirt as Monty did the same.

They stepped out into the hallway right as Elvis let Elijah inside. He barreled toward Chicot, scooping her up in his arms and spinning awkwardly so he didn't knock her against the walls of the narrow RV hallway. Chicot braced her hands on his shoulders, preparing to land on one foot if he put her down suddenly, Monty ineffectually waving her hands next to them like they should stop.

"We got in!" Elijah yelled as soon as he stopped spinning.

"We did?" Chicot's eyes blew huge, her fingers gripping Elijah's shirt tightly. "We got in?"

They yelled at each other a few more times, much to the chagrin of Elvis, who covered his ears. He was still smiling and Lyza was bouncing in excitement.

"You got in!?" Lyza asked. Chicot's eyes darted to Monty quickly, Chicot just beamed at her.

A look of shock crossed Monty's face, her jaw slackened for a moment before an open-mouthed smile crept onto her face as Elijah finally lowered Chicot to the floor. Monty reached for Chicot, pulling her close as she hopped on one foot to try and save her ankle strength for the day.

"Really?" Monty's voice was low, the two of them tuning out Elvis, Lyza, and Elijah all cheering together behind them. Chicot grinned, her arms going around Monty's neck as she pressed a kiss on her lips.

Chicot confirmed, "You're stuck with me for another twelve weeks."

Monty laughed, cupping Chicot's face and kissing her again. "I want to be stuck with you for a lot longer than that."

Chicot grinned, the two of them exchanging little kisses before they joined in the other three's celebration. Lyza had procured a bottle of non-alcoholic Champagne from somewhere, saying she'd bought it for exactly an occasion like this. She poured them each a glass, the five of them clashing the coffee mugs they'd used together. As Chicot took a sip, Monty's hand on the small of her back holding her close as she leaned on the counter, she grinned to herself. Just a little jester, happy to be with her new family.

THE END.

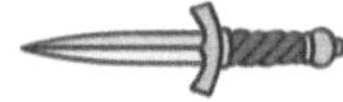

AUTHOR | GAME MASTER |CONTENT CREATOR

Hi there! My name is Jess Galaxie and I write books, create videos, and all around enjoy being a nerd. During the day, I work as a content marketing manager for a large enterprise, and by night I write, play Dungeons & Dragons, make costumes, and much more. You may have seen me on either my Tik Tok or my YouTube channel, where I tend to talk about my passions and create movie-length video essays about characters I love.

Beyond my hobbies, I am a member of the LGBTQIA+ community, and care deeply about advocating for, and representing my community in my writing.

www.ingramcontent.com/pod-product-compliance
Lightning Source LLC
Chambersburg PA
CBHW032253310726
48973CB00008B/2395